JAN _ 2016

Residue

LAURY FALTER

Text copyright ©2012 by Laury Falter

First Edition: April 2012

Falter, Laury, 1972-
Residue: a novel / by Laury Falter – 1st ed.

Summary: When sixteen-year-old Jocelyn Weatherford is whisked
away from a preparatory academy in upstate New York to live with her
extended family in New Orleans, she is unprepared to encounter the
dangers awaiting her. Yet even as she is thrust into an unfamiliar world
of witches and voodoo magic, the greatest threat of all may be the boy
she has fallen for. While handsome and charming, he is also a
Caldwell...a member of the family the Weatherford's have been feuding
with for centuries. As their forbidden love grows it becomes the volatile
spark that forever changes their world and everyone in it.

ISBN-10: 0985511001
ISBN-13: 978-0-9855110-0-5

For my mom.
Thank you for teaching me when innocence fails
strength sets in.

CONTENTS

ψ

1. *S C A R*

It was on the eve of my sixteenth birthday when I learned that I came from a long bloodline of distinguished witches and that my particular lineage just happened to be cursed. This life-altering realization began abruptly, painfully, and while I was surrounded by other students in my English Literature class.

Only a few minutes remained before the end of the lackluster hour on 18th century novelists as I sat impatiently waiting for Professor Clements to dismiss us. Then I felt it…a slight pinch at the base of my right wrist.

At first I'd thought a spider had scrambled unacknowledged across my desk to leave me a small memento with its tiny fangs. But the feeling didn't remain at my wrist. Slowly, progressively, it moved up the length of my limb toward the elbow. By the time it reached midway, I'd twisted the soft underside of my arm toward me.

My breath caught then, after realizing it wasn't a spider bite. The thing causing my discomfort, which resembled what I imagined a third-degree burn might feel like, was actually something far worse.

There, on the fleshy part of my arm, which only seconds ago I knew to be smooth and flawless, was the distinct, taut undulation of a scar.

This was no normal scar, however. There was something unmistakably odd about the mark, something I had never seen or read of before. A moment ago, I didn't have a single scar on my body. And one this large would have been caused by significant injury of which I'd never encountered.

It remained in motion, growing slowly, steadily searing its path, and only ending when it reached the fold of my elbow.

Despite its blistering heat I remained stationary, amazed at what I was witnessing, trying to make sense of it. Then, by instinct alone, I glanced at my other arm expecting to see another injury growing there too. Covering that limb was a stretch of milky-white skin and a white metal bracelet wrapped around my wrist, a gift my mother had given me which, by her instructions, I have never removed. The clear white, crystal quartz stone embedded in it caught my attention for only a moment and then I returned to the far more serious issue on my right arm.

Even as my mouth hung open, I couldn't seem to control my breathing. My lungs were stuck in place, immovable. In fact, the only things moving were my heart, which was beating much harder now, and my fingers, curling in to a clenched fist that looked ready to hit something. Then, the scar stopped but the pain remained.

I felt as if it were almost screaming at me to notice it.

Sandra Kitrick, who'd been ignoring Professor Clements in favor of feverishly writing a note to her friend for most of class and one prone toward dramatics, looked up and gasped, jarring me from my focus.

She'd now seen it, too.

"Are you…" she began, never getting the chance to finish.

Chairs were now scrapping across the tiled floor, gasps were being emitted from those closest to me, and heads were suddenly bent over me for a closer look at my arm.

Great, not only was I in pain, I was now a spectacle. I wanted to turn and give Sandra a sarcastic thanks but realized this may not be the best time for it.

Professor Clements weaved her way between the students to reach my desk, her curt tone a sign of irritation at the class's disruption. "Jocelyn Weatherford, what are you up to now? If I have…"

I looked up to find her ashen, her mouth ajar, her eyes wide and locked on my arm - the scar on my arm to be precise.

Professor Clements' eyebrows furrowed then. "Is that…Have you had that all along?" she asked in a way that confirmed she already knew the answer.

"No," I said, proud to find my voice steady.

The scar was now a long, purplish disfigurement, an inch wide and reaching from my wrist to my elbow. It would have been hard to miss today or any day since I'd arrived at this school.

My answer spurred her to action, her commonly cynical expression transforming to one of panic. "Move," she commanded the class, making a path through to the door. "Move! Back to your seats and finish Chapter Three. Move!"

The class shuffled quickly back where they'd been moments ago and I was following Professor Clements, having enough sense to sling my book bag over my shoulder. It was clumsy, not wanting to move my uninjured arm too much, but looking like a fool was the least of my worries at that point.

I was ushered, or more precisely yanked, out of the classroom and into the hallway, where our walk to the nurse's office was quick and silent.

I'd lived at Wentworth Preparatory Academy in upstate New York my entire life, having been deposited here by my mother when I turned old enough to be admitted at the ripe age of five. I didn't remember much prior to that date, but my memories were vivid from that point on. I had celebrated my birthdays, my first straight-A report card, my first crush (on Dylan from the boy's academy down the road). This was my home and yet, for the first time, I realized I'd never been to the nurse's office.

I was healthy, never having come down with a single cold or suffered an injury greater than a paper cut. Unlike everyone else I knew, my skin had never seen a single blemish, my knees had never been scraped. I had no freckles, birthmarks, not even a pimple. As of only a few minutes ago, I didn't have a scar anywhere on my body.

In fact, as I passed the darkened glass wall lining the dining room's entrance, my instinct was to perform a quick inspection to see if anything else had transpired. Maybe my hair had fallen out or my ear had ballooned up. What I saw instead was a briskly moving girl just as tall and lanky as she'd been when I saw her in the mirror this morning. My hair was still there, straight and black as a starless night sky with its permanent curls at the ends bouncing as they always did off the middle of my back. My hazel eyes were their average size, my nose and overly plump lips were unchanged. Everything appeared to be normal, to my relief. Everything except the scar on my right arm.

Professor Clements guided me through the hallways and down a flight of stairs to the academy's first floor, shoving open a door at the second turn on the left. A single word was etched in the frosted glass, NURSE. Inside, it was bright, white, and quiet, like a sanctuary, or a morgue depending on your perspective.

Professor Clements was a rather robust woman with powerful lungs so that when she barked "Nurse Carol!" I jumped and temporarily forgot the searing pain the scar was causing.

She shouted it twice more before a calm voice came from the next room.

The words reached me just as she emerged from around the corner. "Well, well...At long last."

It was an odd response given the urgency Professor Clements had shown, I noted. In fact, the woman seemed more curious than hurried. Dressed in a standard white nurse's uniform with the same padded-soled shoes a nurse would wear, she smiled warmly while crossing the room toward me.

I had seen Nurse Carol before but we'd never spoken until now. On the grounds of an all-girls school that required students to wear a white button down shirt and plaid skirt with matching blazer at all times, a nurse's stark white uniform stood out. While she never approached me, I couldn't help noticing when she'd scan the dining room or the hallways until her eyes landed on me, as if she were checking in to confirm I was all right.

Professor Clements snorted in annoyance at the delay before launching into a tense discourse. "I have a student here needing immediate medical-"

Nurse Carol didn't allow her to finish. "That will be all, Professor."

Professor Clement's head snapped back. "Well, I..." She released an exasperated sigh. "I wasn't done speaking."

"I'm sure Jocelyn thanks you for your assistance. I can handle it from here."

While that response didn't seem to sit well with my teacher, she must have figured there was no sense in

5

delaying the inevitable. She would need to return to her classroom eventually and let Nurse Carol do her job. She gave me a curt nod and Nurse Carol a glare before leaving the room.

The door closed before either of us spoke.

"I understand you have an injury," she said, her voice free from nerves.

This was good because mine were in chaos.

Without waiting for me to respond, or even to tell her what had happened, she assessed me. Finding me favoring my arm, she took it and turned it for a closer inspection.

Her gaze was unperturbed as she took only a second to perform a cursory evaluation of it.

Then she did something that truly set my nerves on edge.

She released me, marched toward the phone, dialed, and after a brief pause, she announced, "It's me. And it's begun."

Begun, I thought. What's begun?

Remaining silent and listening for clues, I was disappointed when she didn't speak again until after she set the receiver back in its cradle. Then she looked at me, her easygoing demeanor gone. "You're going to need to pack your bags. You leave for New Orleans in fifteen minutes." She gave me these instructions offhandedly, as if it were a foregone conclusion, as if I had some hand in making them.

"What?" I demanded the searing pain down my arm forgotten. "You have no right to make that decision. Who do you think you are?"

I was hoping my words would instill some sense of apprehension in her but she easily ignored them. Then she countered by delivering the news that would change my life forever.

"Jocelyn," she said her tone steady and calculated. "You are in danger."

6

2. FATE

"Danger?" I repeated, staring at Nurse Carol in astonishment.

The only danger I was in was the possibility of losing my lunch after all that had transpired within the last few minutes.

She answered vaguely with more of a prompt than an explanation. "Yes, you'll need to pack and you don't have much time."

I released a sigh that had become lodged in my throat. "What kind of danger exactly?" As an afterthought, I added, "And I'm not going anywhere." I was starting to wonder if Nurse Carol needed a little help herself, by way of a psychologist.

She stopped shuffling through the numerous jars she had stored in a cabinet and turned to me. Then she reached out and took hold of my arm to lift it into my view.

"You are in this kind of danger, one that you cannot prevent and will not be able to foresee." She released my arm before delivering the bluntest part of her message. "This, Jocelyn, is just the beginning."

"Of what?" I said, startling myself at my ferocity. "I don't understand."

"I will leave that for your family to explain."

Her head was tucked back in the cabinet again so her voice was slightly muffled.

"What family?" I asked, bewildered.

My family consisted of my mother and she had never visited unless it was a school-sanctioned holiday. When she did, it was only for that allotted amount of time in which she would have airline tickets ready for travel to various locales. Those were the happiest, most memorable days of my life, and if I were really forced to pack for a move to New Orleans the only real possessions of value I'd bring were the photographs taken during our trips together. I'd never been introduced to any other member of my family, my free time having been carefully constructed by my mother to avoid such interactions.

"Your aunt will be meeting you at the airport. She's flying in as we speak."

Only then did I get a sense of just how serious this scar had become. Since it materialized, I was going to leave the only home I'd ever known to live with relatives I'd never met.

"How do you know my mother will approve of this?" I inquired, still defiant.

Nurse Carol swung around toward a row of file cabinets, withdrew a piece of paper and handed it to me before returning to the medicine cabinet. In far fewer words than those written on the piece of paper by my mother Nurse Carol explained, "Under very detailed instructions, at the first sign of an unexplainable ailment, you are to be released and sent to live with your family in New Orleans."

Stunned, I stood there, holding the evidence of her proclamation and yet I couldn't seem to speak, to affirm that I believed her. It made no sense. My mother had gracefully evaded any attempts I'd ever made to ask questions about them, much less meet them.

Then the paper was gone from my fingers and the jar Nurse Carol had been searching for was placed in my palm.

"Use this every hour covering every part of the scar until it diminishes." Her head dipped then, peering at me from beneath her lashes. She must have noticed my surreal state because she urged, "Do you understand?"

I nodded, my expression still frozen in disagreement.

"Good, I've secured the campus for you. Now go. You have less than ten minutes to pack. Meet me at the front entrance. I'll drive you."

While I didn't understand what she meant by "secured the campus," or bother to leave her office as quickly as I knew she'd like, I wasn't concerned with either of those realizations. My feet gradually carried me through the few students trickling toward their next class. I knew each of them by name, but I didn't know them well enough to say goodbye. Even if I did, I'm not sure I could have conjured the words. The rest of the students were already seated, including my best friends, so when I reached my dormitory room it was expectedly empty.

In the five minutes I had left, I wrote a note to reassure them I'd call, grabbed my cherished photo album from beneath my pillow, and then stopped at the door for one final look around.

I did a scan of Alisa's science posters and Elizabeth's beloved row of plants on the windowsill. Then, still bewildered as to why I needed to leave this life I'd created here so quickly, I mindlessly took a keepsake from my bedpost-a black top hat worn during one of the academy's pageants in which we'd taken first place.

Then I was out the door and buckled in next to Nurse Carol as she sped down the tree-lined road and through the academy's main gate. In the rearview mirror, I watched the massive red and white brick building shrink until we turned onto the main roadway, my heart sinking as quickly as the distance between us grew.

I knew that most of the faculty and some of the students would be overjoyed at my departure. I'd caused enough havoc within those walls to stir up controversy regularly. If it hadn't been for my family's money, I'd have been sent to public school years ago. But I'd stayed in place and it had become my home…and I would miss it.

Nurse Carol's simple two-door sedan expertly carved its way through the traffic, or maybe she just knew how to drive it, so that we reached the airport in record time.

She'd dodged every question I asked so that when I stepped out of her car, I had given up. At some point, you begin to feel foolish pestering someone for information when they have repeatedly refused to offer any. She did, however, guide me to the ticket counter where I thought she'd leave me on my own. I was wrong.

Instead, she stopped in front of a petite woman with frizzy red hair, a wide smile, and a smattering of freckles across the bridge of her nose.

"Lizzy," said Nurse Carol wrapping her arms around the woman's shoulders as one does with a very old friend.

Then the name triggered my memory. Lizzy was my mother's sister-which made her my aunt. I took a closer look at her and could see the resemblance. My mother was taller, the same gene I'd been given, but the two shared the same upturned nose and bright eyes.

Nurse Carol and Lizzy were still hugging when something occurred to me. How could a nurse at my school know my aunt before I did?

The recognition of it caused me to suck in a quick breath, drawing their attention.

They turned to me and caught sight of my bewilderment.

While Nurse Carol seemed poised to perform a proper introduction, Aunt Lizzy ended that possibility with a squeal of delight and a swing of her arms around my shoulders. Then my body was flopping back and forth as Aunt Lizzy swung me from side to side, her tiny frame somehow effortlessly summoning the strength.

She was laughing heartily when my feet finally found the floor again.

"You have no idea how much I've anticipated this day," she said.

I smiled back, though I'm sure it was a shaky one. "I've wanted to meet you, too."

She giggled at me and leaned in to whisper. "I meant you coming to live with us, dear."

Again, I was taken aback. It was the second time today that someone seemed to have known I would be shipped off to live with my family in New Orleans well before I had any clue of it. Giving my reaction no notice, she threw down a wad of cash in front of the airline ticket representative and said, "Two tickets to New Orleans on the next flight out."

"Two?" I asked, perplexed. "But how did you get here?" I'd assumed she'd simply disembarked to meet me before re-boarding.

After a brief, knowing glance in Nurse Carol's direction, she replied to me in an offhanded manner before hurrying to change the subject.

"I have my own form of transportation, dear. I just couldn't bear the wait. Your cousins will be thrilled too. Just thrilled. I haven't told them yet. They're still at camp." She paused briefly and lowered her voice to a whisper. "That's code for the sabbat festival, Mabon. But, of course, you know nothing of that." She patted my cheek as one would to soothe a lost child. "We'll fix that right quick though. Right quick."

I had no idea what she was referring to and was almost thankful when Nurse Carol cleared her throat. She smiled kindly at Aunt Lizzy while interrupting, telling me that she wasn't offended for having been ignored. On the contrary, it seemed she already knew to be patient with Aunt Lizzy. "I'm heading back now."

"Oh, yes, of course, dear," said Aunt Lizzy, not bothering to hide her disappointment, which again struck me as odd behavior toward a school nurse. Still, she took Nurse Carol's hands before continuing. "Thank you for everything you've done for Jocelyn."

Finally, the curiosity became overwhelming and I asked, "Do you two know each other?"

The women grinned knowingly at each other, in reaction to a joke I clearly wasn't privy to.

"We'll cover that, and more, shortly," said Aunt Lizzy before the airline representative drew her attention to finish the ticketing process.

I said my goodbye to Nurse Carol, with whom I'd never exchanged words until today, and still I saw the beginning of tears in the corner of her eyes as she turned away.

Her final words to me were simple and indicative of a nurse. "Be safe." Even then, I felt as if she were conveying a deeper meaning, a warning of what was to come but I never got the chance to inquire. Instead, I followed Aunt Lizzy through the airport, her pitched voice carrying the entire conversation by herself. By the time I was seated on the airplane, Aunt Lizzy had given me a complete profile on each of my cousins, though her rapid pace didn't allow me to digest any of the information. Instead, I listened quietly stunned that I was heading toward a new, mysterious life when I should have been eating birthday cake, sitting Indian-style, in the middle of my dorm room surrounded by friends.

I drew in a breath as much to calm myself as to vicariously take one for Aunt Lizzy, who continued to talk non-stop, merging one sentence with the next, and without ever taking a breath.

As I tried to keep up, my awareness absentmindedly drifted and I noticed, oddly enough, that every row before us was filled with passengers from the front toward the middle. This left the entire last half of the plane to us, allowing for an incredible amount of privacy. Once I acknowledged this, my patience ran out.

"I'm sorry, Aunt Lizzy, but I've been told that I am in danger and, given the size of this thing on my arm, I'm actually leaning toward believing it. You and Nurse Carol seem to know more about what's going on with me than I do so can you please explain this all to me?"

I was clearly exasperated, so much that she couldn't ignore it any longer.

Then, before my eyes, she transformed in to a completely different person, someone calmer and more thoughtful. She suddenly took on the appearance of someone who had seen too much in her life causing me a flicker of guilt for having brought this out in her. When she spoke her voice softened nearly to a whisper. "Jocelyn, have you ever noticed anything...peculiar about yourself? In other words, have you ever been able to do something that others couldn't?"

I thought back, trying to recall something that would satisfy her. "No," I finally said. "Not really."

Her lips pinched upward as she considered how to continue. "Think along the lines of something..." She paused to search for the most appropriate word before summing up her intended thought in a way I never would have expected, "...mystical."

One of my eyebrows lifted in suspicion.

"Everyone has a little magic in them," she argued, slightly annoyed with me. "Some have a little more than others. You, I imagine, have quite a bit."

I laughed through my nose in disbelief. Playing along, I countered, "Why me?"

Without a flinch or the bat of an eyelash, she replied solemnly, "Because you hail from a line of distinguished witches."

Before I knew it was coming, I sniggered. Then I waited for her to break in to a grin, chuckle, or show any sign she was joking with me. Doing none of these, she opted to stare at me blankly.

"You don't expect me to believe that, do you?" I asked, still grinning.

"You can believe what you want, Jocelyn," she said and turned to gaze out the window.

Only then did my smile fade.

"All right, so you are telling me that my family practices Wicca?" I asked, slightly unnerved by the idea.

Aunt Lizzy held back a grin at my question but she did look my way. "Not necessarily. All types are practiced, not just those in the mainstream." To my perplexed expression, she elaborated, "Witchcraft has been around for centuries and has evolved to fit different personalities and lifestyles. We have evolved with it."

I bit my lip to keep from laughing again and turned to face the front of the plane.

"Think about it, Jocelyn," she urged quietly. "You already know the truth. You are part of that evolution. You only have to accept it and then I can explain everything."

Her carefree demeanor had been completely erased. It was clear from her tone and the fact that she faced the window again that she didn't intend to continue this conversation until I'd come to terms with what she'd told me.

"All right," I replied simply to appease her.

She pivoted her head toward me again, her lips pinched in dissatisfaction. I knew from her expression that she didn't believe me. "All right, what?"

I hesitated then. I knew she was asking for evidence, validation that I believed her, and I could have played along convincingly. Something stopped me though. Not only was she astute enough to see through it but if I were honest with myself, there were memories that singled me out as different…possibly mystical in nature. The first was when I'd touched Elizabeth's plants and brought them back from the dead, sprouting regenerated leaves in only a day. I also recalled the time when Alisa had been unable to overcome a stubborn cold; it was only after she had accidentally taken my water bottle and drank from it overnight that she had completely recovered. Then it was as if a floodgate had opened and memories inundated me. I had to literally shake my head before the thoughts would clear.

My face fell then at the realization, something Aunt Lizzy must have seen because she briefly placed a comforting hand over mine.

"Things…they mend when I'm around," I muttered, speaking more from my subconscious as if someone else were doing the talking.

She nodded expectantly and then mumbled, "Your father was a healer, too."

"He was? My mother never told me…" I mused disconcerted that she'd keep something so personal to herself.

Aunt Lizzy nodded. "There is quite a bit your mother never told you."

That acknowledgement made me wonder what else she hadn't mentioned. I got the feeling it was a lot.

"But," Aunt Lizzy went on, "all of that is starting to be revealed. Your scar, for example…"

I was still slightly stunned at my aunt's assertions so, when my eyes fell to the thing on my arm, I watched it absentmindedly.

Having followed Nurse Carol's instructions to regularly administer the ointment she'd given me the scar's heat had subsided so that it now felt more like what I thought an intense sunburn might feel like.

Then Aunt Lizzy began to speak, mesmerizing me with a history lesson I couldn't have envisioned.

"Your mother sent you to that academy to keep you safe, Jocelyn. She sent you as far away from New Orleans as was possible, while still allowing easy access to you. After your father's death," Aunt Lizzy snorted lightly, "well…there was no convincing her that you were safe after that. So she took you and stowed you away. Then, because your mother is a tenacious woman, she hired someone to protect you, to guard you. And Nurse Carol did a fine job with-"

"Nurse Carol?" I asked, dumbfounded.

"Yes, the very same," said Aunt Lizzy with a firm nod. "She watched and sent reports of your progress to your mother and me over the years so that essentially we've watched you grow up on paper. I have, as I'm sure your mother has, looked for, waited for, expected really, one thing in particular to appear in those reports; An ailment - anything that would tell us that the protection we've placed over you had weakened. That sign, or more precisely, that scar on your arm, tells us that they've found you."

"Found me? Who's found me?"

Aunt Lizzy drew in a shuddered breath but didn't answer immediately. When she did, her expression stiffened and her eyes darkened. "The Caldwells. The Caldwells have found you."

"Who are the Caldwells?" I asked, the scar now competing for my attention with the goose bumps rising on my other arm.

"They are the reason you are on this flight and the reason you have that scar on your arm. They are your enemies, Jocelyn." My goose bumps turned to chills as she continued. "The Caldwells will use all resources necessary to harm, to maim, to kill any Weatherford whenever they can get away with it, and they've proven as much over the years. Because of them, we've lost and been forced to rebuild our family fortune. They nearly killed us off entirely in the 1920s. They even killed your..." She stopped herself short, hesitant to finish her sentence.

"My what?" I persisted.

She hesitated to reassess whether to tell me, finally falling on the side of keeping silent. "They are treacherous, Jocelyn. That's all you need to know."

I waited for her to change her mind, to finish her thought but she was unwilling to offer more. "How could they do all that? And why would they?" I asked disheartened at learning my family came with such a disturbing past.

"The Caldwells have been casting curses against us since as far back as we - the Weatherfords - can remember. The reasons are many and they compound with each effort to hurt us. In turn, we've retaliated as best we could to protect ourselves, to send them a message they never seem to hear. Yet, they continue to wield their powers without thought of the consequences. And they are crafty, Jocelyn, so you'll need to be careful. They cast their most dangerous curses to work in private, coming to fruition when you are unable or unaware of how to protect yourself and they do it in a way that no one can trace it back to them."

My eyes drifted toward the front of the plane where the stewardesses were suddenly taking their seats.

"You've now come to live with us while your mother continues her work at the ministry," Aunt Lizzy went on, seemingly unaware of the commotion at the cockpit. "It is the safest place for you now."

The plane dropped then, deep enough so that my stomach lurched into my throat and violent enough to send Aunt Lizzy in a frenzied effort to search through her purse for a bag of herbs. Harried, once finding it, she took a pinch and swallowed it without chewing. Instantly, she was taking deep, slow breaths, locking her eyes on the bag in case she needed to use it for something else.

"Turbulence," she squeaked. "Never been very..."

While she was unable to finish her explanation, I knew what she meant and I left her alone. Having traveled enough times with my mother on holiday vacations, air sickness was something I'd seen countless times before.

As I sat quietly registering everything I'd been told, with each thought came two more questions. Unfortunately, the turbulence didn't cease for more than an hour and by that time Aunt Lizzy had turned a faint shade of greenish-gray and I just didn't have the heart to badger her for answers.

Finally, my eyelids fell and at some point I drifted to sleep, awakening to Aunt Lizzy's gentle nudges.

I found that her face retained the odd color and her eyes drooped low enough to confirm she hadn't slept at all, not even during the layover in Atlanta.

Without a word to each other, we finally disembarked at Louis Armstrong International airport in New Orleans, walked slowly through the terminal, and found Aunt Lizzy's car, the latest Porsche 911, bright red and in flawless condition. It fit her perfectly, even in her current state.

It was still dark at that time so when she raced down the interstate and through the downtown area of New Orleans, I didn't see more than a blur of buildings and street lights flashing by. In fact, she sped so fast down her street that I was unprepared for the sharp left she made in to her driveway. Aunt Lizzy seemed to be in a hurry, or maybe she just drove fast. Either way, the flight seemed to have taken a toll on her.

Coming to a stop on a brick driveway just outside the back door, she pulled in line with a row of sports cars that gleamed, untainted and dust-free, even in the dead of night.

Then I stepped out, looked up, and found my new home.

The sun was just about to peek over the horizon by then, illuminating the two-story, second empire mansion. Intricately and ornately designed with a mansard roof, iron crest, and boasting paired columns and sculpted petals around the doors, windows, and dormers, it was both imposing and majestic.

Aunt Lizzy motioned me to follow her so I grabbed my photo album and top hat and entered the back door, finding the house equally as sophisticated on the inside. The few lamps and hallway lights left on for us allowed me to see the house was comfortably decorated with furniture that was either plush or highly-polished. Framed pictures covered the walls and luxurious rugs lay across the hardwood floors in every room we passed.

She escorted me to a lavishly-appointed guest room on the second floor and then disappeared down the hall to the master bedroom. As my gaze drifted back toward my new room, it moved across the row of old photographs hanging along the entire hallway, some torn at the edges and others worn with time. In each of them, people stood or sat with regal expressions and not a single one was familiar to me. Yet, I knew they were my family because we all carried one distinct element.

It was so obvious - I couldn't have missed it, not after my mother's quizzing on the significance of specific gems.

Each one wore a crystal quartz stone just like the one in the bracelet my mother had given me, and forbidden me from removing. However, not all of them wore it as a bracelet. Some of the stones were embedded in hair clips and rings, others in belt buckles, and still others were worn as a necklace.

This was when I realized I was not alone.

Turning, I found a stout, swarthy-skinned woman staring at me from an open doorway across the narrow hall. With her hair wrapped in a vividly colorful scarf and her neck, not to be outdone, donned with yarn necklaces from which hung teeth and other small bones, she looked entirely out of place in this home. Leaning to one side on a cane that looked like it could snap in half under her weight, she remained staring at me as if I were an intruder she was about ready to pummel. Then she made the most unexpected comment.

"Wards off evil," she said with a deep southern accent. While her words were cordial, her tone and pinched lips told a different story.

"Excuse me?" I replied with a tilt of my head.

"The stone wards off evil."

"Oh…" I mumbled, giving the pictures an uncomfortable, fleeting look. That feeling of being left out of the loop had returned. "So, the crystal quartz is my family's stone?"

She didn't answer right away, her frown continuing to pucker her fleshy face.

"You're astute," she finally replied, though coming from her it didn't sound like a compliment. It was more of an observation, a line to check off a list of attributes. She continued to openly assess me before changing the subject, stiffly saying, "Welcome back, chil'."

I blinked a few times, processing what she was implying. The long night had slowed me down but I

20

collected myself and refuted, "Oh, no...I've never been here before."

Her eyes widened at my statement before she settled back to her pinched frown. "Well, yer wrong 'bout that. This here's your family." She snapped her cane up, scarcely missing my left ear. "That there's yer Great Aunt Barbara, first patron of the ministry. That there's yer Great Great Uncle Vesper, the last of the local justices...'fo they retired the positions." She continued moving down the row, pointing to each one with her cane and giving a brief description of each in a way that made me think she was bothered with having to explain it all. Then she settled the cane back against her leg and looked at me squarely. "Seein' as how ya don't rememba me, my name's Miss Mabelle. I'm the keeper of this here house. Now..." Her hand swooped out from behind her, startling me. "I need ya to do a little shoppin' fer me."

This threw me a little. It wasn't exactly the most welcoming gesture. Nice to meet you. Now do some shopping for me.

She wiggled her hand at me, insisting I take what she held out, which was a small piece of paper and a wad of cash. When I didn't, she reached out and shoved them into my palm, a rushed sigh showing her frustration with me.

That was when I caught sight of the room behind her. I couldn't have been certain what it was that drew my attention but that didn't stop the goose bumps rising on my arms. It may have been the miniature skulls hanging from the top of her windowsill, clicking as they knocked against one another in the breeze. Or it may have been the flicker of the myriad candles blazing across every possible surface of her furniture. Or maybe...it was simply my intuition telling me that something just wasn't right.

I drew in a quick breath, shocked, but she didn't seem to notice.

Instead, she grabbed hold of the door and shuffled backwards. "Jocelyn," she stated in her most impolite tone yet. "Happy birthday."

With that, she stepped back into her room and slammed her door.

Stunned at her utter disrespect, I dropped my gaze to her shopping list, seriously contemplating whether I should tear it into pieces and shove them under her door. But then I noticed the words on the piece of paper and all thoughts seized.

Just below the directions, she'd written:

Jocelyn's school supplies

Glancing back at where she'd been standing seconds ago, I was now bewildered.

Maybe she was upset because she didn't want to run the errand for me, someone she barely knew? I mused. While I considered this, my intuition told me the shopping excursion was something more. It was a feeling I paid attention to because it steered me right every time. It was the same feeling that told me when the headmistress was walking the halls while my friends and I were trying to sneak back to our dormitory room at night or when a teacher had switched out a test on us after I'd secured the answers in a covert mission the day before.

In short, it was a feeling that left me uneasy.

That feeling lingered as I entered my new room and laid down onto the plush comforter; my thoughts turning toward making a good attempt at falling asleep. As expected, I had no luck. My body tossed and turned until I sat up only a short while later. And there before me was a closet filled with clothes, a note pinned to the sleeve of one shirt. With my interest piqued, I crossed the room to find an unsigned message.

Thought you might want something other than an academy uniform to wear.

I laughed quietly to myself, recognizing the handwriting instantly. It was written by the same person as the shopping list. Miss Mabelle had a softness to her after all, I mused.

Having left my small wardrobe at school, because I hadn't been given any time to request my suitcases from storage, I was thankful for the thoughtfulness. She had even gotten the sizes correct.

Realizing she'd gone to great lengths on my behalf collecting these clothes, the least I could do was her shopping, especially if the items were for me. So, after a quick inventory, I changed into black cotton pants, a white tank top, and a grey vest. To top it off, I settled my black top hat on my head and doused myself in a mixture of silver and gold bracelets and necklaces. It was the exact opposite of what was allowed by the academy's conforming dress code.

Only during midnight attempts to sneak out and on vacations with my mother was I ever given the chance to wear clothes outside the academy's strict dress policy. I loved it and took full advantage of it. On my escapes from the academy grounds, I always wore flowing thigh-high dresses or fitted pants. On travels I was enticed to wear the clothes of the country I was visiting so I could better experience life through the eyes of the natives. Yet even then, I'd choose something that allowed me a sense of identity, a handmade necklace or a patterned scarf, and more color the better.

These clothes, hanging before me, made me smile. They were bold, distinctive, and you wouldn't find them on every street corner. They were perfect for me.

A quick glance at the directions scribbled beneath the shopping list told me how to reach St. Charles Street but even as I approached the door, I hesitated.

With my hand on the doorknob, a single thought ran through my mind: I've been told that I am in danger.

My awareness drifted to the scar, now partially covered by my jewelry as I contemplated it. It was healing so rapidly it looked more like a thick purple line without any puckering and emitted far less heat.

The uneasy feeling returned.

While the prudent person would walk back upstairs and wait for Aunt Lizzy to emerge from her bedroom, that wasn't me. I was the person with red stars on every year of her record at the academy, all for misconduct. I was the one at school who had suffered the customary punishment of assisting the gardeners with their landscaping so much that I knew them each by name. It was me who regularly convinced my friends to sneak out after hours, always with delinquent behavior in mind to glue the classroom doors shut, paint our rival school's sign with our school colors, leave notes for the boys at their academy down the street, and steal the academy car for joy rides. In fact, I was the only one in the student body who had pre-scheduled meetings with the headmistress to review and repent for my digressions.

At the end of my reminiscence, I found myself smiling, a soft giggle shaking my chest.

No, I was not a prudent person. This was my new home and I wouldn't be fearful in it.

With that in mind, I left the house quietly, and after taking the St. Charles streetcar and walking 30 minutes I reached my destination.

My path took me through a neighborhood adjacent to Aunt Lizzy's, a place called the French Quarter, also known as the Vieux Carré. It holds the distinction of being the oldest neighborhood in the city. This not only meant that the rest of New Orleans sprawled out from the French Quarter, its center, but that many of the buildings dated back to the 1700s, built after The Great New Orleans Fire consumed most of the buildings. The Quarter, as the locals call it, boasted aged buildings crowding each other along narrow streets; lush, welcoming courtyards tucked away down narrow alleys and carriageways; and the smell of crawfish etouffee and jambalaya wafting from unseen kitchens. Adding to the neighborhood's mystique, jazz musicians sat in the sheltered entrance of stores that had not yet opened to serenade those walking by. Street performers propped on boxes remained motionless, only launching in to their act once a bill was dropped in the nearby hat. Also along the way, elaborate wrought-iron and cast-iron balconies overhung the sidewalks, offering me shelter from the growing intensity of the sun. Even for September, this city proved it could deliver heat with a kick.

Being such a far stretch away from the cool, pristine academy grounds, I couldn't help feeling like I was on vacation, exploring a new city and culture, this time without my mother.

The directions I followed, took me to a quiet side street lined with worn buildings, and more specifically, to an unmarked, weathered door along a row of doors looking remarkably the same.

Without the typical store sign or even a window to peer in, I didn't know whether I might walk into someone's house. To be on the safe side, I knocked.

The door rattled loosely against its frame and then settled. A few moments passed and no one came, so I knocked again. Again, there was no answer.

Wondering if the directions were wrong, I tried the door handle. It was unlocked, which almost surprised me. Opening it a crack, I peered inside.

While it was incredibly dim inside, lit only by candles held in wall sconces and open lanterns hanging from the ceiling, I could see that it was actually a store. Disheveled and poorly laid out with towering wooden bookshelves stuffed with merchandise, I couldn't see all that far inside.

"Hello?" I called out without receiving an answer back.

Figuring they may be in the storage room, if one even existed, I stepped inside.

"Hello?"

No one responded so I moved farther down the aisle.

This was no regular OfficeMax or OfficeDepot. It didn't even resemble a college bookstore. In the place of textbooks on biology, calculus, and the English dictionary there were witch almanacs, spell books for solitary witches, and tomes on spells and rituals for every purpose. Where pens and paper should have been, there were tarot card stacks and candles of every color, style, and size imaginable. Canisters of countless herbs, stones, and gems replaced impulse-purchase bins of calculators and keychain flashlights.

What exactly am I supposed to buy in here? I wondered.

Then, just as I reached the cash register, which looked like an antique ready for a museum, the store's front door opened, allowing in a thin stretch of light down the side aisle. I listened as the store's most recent patron strolled toward the back, where I now stood when the scratchy voice of an older woman drew my attention away.

She hobbled out from the back room, hunched and bracing herself against the counter as she walked.

"What you lookin' for?" she asked.

Hesitating, I didn't know quite how to explain it and then settled on the most basic of answers. "My school supplies."

She lifted her chin in a brief gesture of acknowledgement and then shuffled down the long counter, stopping at nearly end of it. From there, she withdrew a clothed bundle, tied with twine at the top. Rather than carrying it back to me, she dragged it, drawing up dust where it had settled. Leaving it before me, she then held out her hand for payment.

"Eighty-five dollars."

I placed the cash in her palm and she dropped it in a canvas bag beneath the register, without bothering to count it.

"You got the potent kind," she stated.

"The what?"

"They're dangerous," she warned. "Watch yerself with them."

Interestingly, I wasn't the least bit surprised that whatever the brisk woman sleeping across the hall from me had ordered on my behalf wasn't safe.

"All right," I shrugged. I wasn't quite sure what was in the bundle or how I should treat them to prevent inflicting harm.

Then several things happened simultaneously. Just as I turned around to leave, the person waiting patiently in line behind me spoke. And just as he spoke, the room broke into chaos.

The wall sconce candles flickered first. Next the tarot cards lifted from their spot on the shelves as if a brisk wind had picked up and carried them, disheveled, through the air. Then heavier things began to move. Candles darted off the shelves like projectiles, hitting the walls with enough force to leave wax marks. Books slid off and slammed to the floor or against the bookshelves opposite them. The ceiling lanterns swung fiercely from side to side, slamming against the whitewash to send down chunks of plaster. The glass canisters banged against each other threatening to break.

That was when I felt arms around me, pulling me to the ground, and a body covering me, solid and secure. My top hat was gone and hands now covered my head with elbows pressed against my ears, dimming the sound of the destruction around us. With my face covered by my own hands and my body in a crouched position, only my legs were exposed.

I had to give the person credit. Despite the devastation going on around us, nothing touched me.

It raged for several seconds, prolonging the demolition of this elderly woman's store. Then, just as quickly as it had begun, it came to a screeching halt.

My protector's hands freed my ears and the body stretched across my back moved away. That was when I heard the voice. It was comforting, concerned, and a little uncertain. I was instantly drawn to it, realizing a ridiculous urge to listen to it endlessly. I couldn't help feeling foolish, especially since his question was so understandable given the circumstances.

"Are you hurt?" he asked.

I felt a hand, warm and firm, on my shoulder, coaxing me to react.

Releasing the breath I'd been holding, I stood and blinked a few times, clearing the haziness in my head.

"Never been better," I muttered and when he handed my top hat back I heard him chuckle.

A quick look around told me that the elderly woman had survived unharmed but her store had not. Every piece of merchandise now lay broken, littering the floor.

Without any warning whatsoever, she launched in to a tirade, speaking rapidly and in French, a language I hadn't learned well enough yet. Then she stopped suddenly, to my surprise, with a chuckle, wide eyed and beaming.

I chalked it up to delirium at seeing her store destroyed at some unknown phenomenon until her other patron standing beside me spoke.

"Huh…" he mumbled.

"What?" I asked, still battling the surreal state I was in, watching as the woman shrugged and disappeared into the back room still chuckling.

Then he chuckled to himself, surprised. "She said she's never seen this before. Apparently she's read about it and been told of it but hadn't witnessed it herself."

"Witnessed what?" I asked, taking my sack of school supplies.

He laughed again, farther down in his chest. "Well..." He cleared his throat uncomfortably. "She thinks she just saw the introduction of two fated lovers."

"Really? Who?" I asked, my head swiveling back and forth now, profoundly intrigued and looking for the people they were referring to, the two whom they believed to be the cause of this mess.

He hesitated and then spoke deep, firm, and with certainty. "She meant us."

3. REVEALED

Us?

The word lingered in my consciousness attempting to connect to a clear, concise thought.

Fated lovers...

She meant us...

They simply wouldn't unite.

As I processed the meaning of what this stranger was telling me, I absentmindedly looked up at him and then my awareness changed entirely.

Gazing at me less than a foot away, were breathtakingly beautiful clear green eyes that told me that he was more curious than disturbed by the idea. In fact, he looked like he was evaluating me to determine whether it could be a possibility. The unadulterated intensity of his stare should have made me uncomfortable but it didn't. I felt excited as if a fire had been kindled in my stomach.

He shook his head, seeming to clear his thoughts and I wondered if my evaluation of him might have been correct. Then he opened his mouth to speak but was distracted by the storekeeper who waddled in from the back room carrying a broom and dust pan.

His attention then seemed to be solely on her. "Can I help you?" he offered.

"Pfff," she replied, with a forced exhale. "Out of my store."

Evidently, she was no longer enthralled with us. Instead, she circled the counter and with one hand on each of us, pushed us down the aisle and out the door.

"Come back soon," she added before closing and locking the door behind us.

The entire time I had not looked back at him, instead focusing on leaving the store without tripping over the destruction. Yet, the impact was made, his face burned in my memory. With a single glance, I could have gone a decade and still recognized him on the street.

His sandy blonde hair hung over his forehead, still a little tousled from the store's eruption. His jaw and chin were strong and defined. And he'd been grinning which accentuated the curve of his lips and boasted perfectly-straight, stark-white teeth. His crystal clear green eyes, so innocent, had drawn me in before I even knew it had happened, captivating me. Even his one flaw seemed perfect. A faint scar just above his lip made him ruggedly seductive and real. His white, short-sleeved shirt fit snuggly against the contours of his muscular arms and molded against his chiseled abdomen. The three buttons down the front were left unfastened to a point that exposed his rippled chest muscles. His jeans hung loosely from legs that stretched as tall as mine. All together, he was unassumingly alluring.

Then he said something that, while meaning to be innocent, altered my focus entirely.

"I guess I'll have to come back for my own school supplies," he laughed quietly, shaking his head at the closed shop door.

"School supplies?" I blurted. "You were here for those, too?" My heart leapt at the hope of meeting someone from my class.

"That's right." He nodded.

Ever since I'd stepped foot inside that store one question ran through my subconscious and it had now bubbled to the top of it. I took a brief moment to formulate it and then decided to risk any ridicule my question might bring before asking, "Exactly what type of school are these supplies for?"

His eyebrows shot up then. "You don't know?"

"I wouldn't be asking if I did," I said a little abruptly.

Again, he laughed to himself. "Good point." He drew in a breath, determining the best way to answer. "Why don't you look in your sack? It might give you a hint."

Suspicious, I pulled the string at its opening just enough to peer inside and my confusion grew. Piled in a heap at the bottom were clear bags of what appeared to be herbs, a jar of broken glass, and a cross.

"I think I need a stronger hint," I replied.

He swung his head from side to side, checking the street to make sure no one else was within earshot. Even while we were alone, he still lowered his voice. "Well, based on the fact that you're here outside this specific shop, having bought a bag of those specific items, I'd say that you've enrolled in the school to practice the supernatural arts."

"What…" I started before having to swallow the lump in my throat. "Excuse me. What arts?"

He shrugged and then replied as if it were widely known; something that took me only a second to realize was probably the case within the circles that he spent his time. "Witchcraft and voodoo mostly but the professors will bring up other subjects to keep it interesting."

My gaze quickly fell from his eyes to the cobblestone street as I absorbed this information. If I'd heard him right

– and I was fairly certain given the solitude on the side street where we stood, that I had – I was enrolled in a school to practice mystical forms of magic.

"I take it you didn't know?" he asked, earnestly, his interest keenly on me now, something that made the flame in my stomach grow.

Considering what he'd said briefly, I realized that had I thought of it I might have figured it out. Over the course of my years at the academy, my mother had mailed me books at intervals, typically just prior to an upcoming holiday. It had always annoyed me because it interfered with studying for final quarter exams, compounding my workload. Then she would quiz me on the plane flights to our destination. I now understood why she'd done it. The books had all been studies of gems, stones, herbs, the Latin language, and cultural ideologies of mystical elements, and they had been preparing me for this point in my life without my knowing it.

"Let's just say I didn't know much." I shook my head, angry, finally verbalizing the words that had rung through my head several times over the last eighteen hours.

"Hmm," he mumbled. "Then how did you end up here?"

That is a long story, I thought, but I knew what he was really asking was how I'd found this indiscernible store. Still struggling to contain the irritation that had risen up, I pulled the shopping list from my hip pocket and showed it to him.

He gave it a quick glance before doing a double take. Then, his eyebrows furrowed inquisitively over those exquisite eyes before he dug out a similarly-sized piece of paper from his hip pocket and held it up next to mine.

The messages were exactly the same. His instructions to stop at this shop first, and then move on to several other shops were listed in the same order as my shopping list.

Only the handwriting and the names at the top of the lists differed. Where mine said Jocelyn, his said Jameson.

"The housekeeper where I stay...where I live," I corrected myself, "gave me the list."

He paused before answering guardedly, "So did mine."

"Maybe the school sent everyone the same instructions?" I offered, though I wasn't convinced myself.

"Maybe..." he said skeptically. "I guess we'll have to ask them when we get home." Then his demeanor changed to something more lighthearted. "Good thing we learned of this or I would have thought you were following me around, Jocelyn." He emphasized my name making certain I knew he'd noted it. His mention of it was both charming and stimulating.

Nonetheless, my mouth fell open in offense. "And I would have thought the same thing about you, Jameson," I retorted.

His eyes turned playful when he responded. "And you'd have been right."

Completely unprepared for his comment, my subconscious kicked in again. "Good," I stated before even realizing the word had passed my lips.

I paused then, considering what had just transpired between us. Had we just acknowledged, to a complete stranger, that we were intrigued by each other? While that seemed odd, he appeared to take it in stride. This, I was learning, appeared to be his typical approach to everything.

"Mrs. De Ville, at the next store, isn't as friendly as Olivia," he made a nod toward the store we had just been in. "Don't take it personally. She is the same way with everyone. Just giving you fair warning."

"Thanks," I said and began following him down the street.

Without needing to openly discuss it, it seemed we'd just agreed to shop together. This was fine with me.

Clearly, he had a better idea of where to go in this city than I did and as we walked he offered further insight, this time in regards to the school I'd be attending. "Mr. LaBarre is tough on grading. Ms. Boudreaux will attempt to intimidate you on the first day by pairing you with another student for an exploratory sparring lesson. You'll learn quickly that she likes to test the boundaries of propriety. And be careful of Ms. Roquette. She's just gotten off probation by The Sevens and is more wicked than usual. Can't say I blame her. Being bound from speaking for six months has to be hard on anyone. Not that it wasn't a relief for the rest of us."

"How can someone be bound from speaking for six months?" I asked, a bit skeptical.

He held back a smile while asking, "You're completely new to this, aren't you?"

"Yes," I replied, unabashedly. Besides there was no hiding it.

Jameson's silence caught my attention and when I looked up I found him staring at me. He was reserved but fascinated.

We had just turned right onto a street named Chartres. It was just as quiet as the previous one so his silence made me feel like I was standing in a spotlight.

"Where did you come from?" he asked almost tenderly.

The softness of his tone made my heart skip a beat, something I'd never experienced before. Thrown a bit, I drew in a breath before answering. "Upstate New York."

"I take it you weren't going to this type of school there," he said, motioning to the bag of mystical items I was carrying.

Chuckling under my breath, I shook my head. "No. But I would love to have seen my professors faces if I carried these into class." Then I thought about it and added under my breath, "And if I'd known about them, I would have."

He released a hearty laugh. "I take it you tested the boundaries of conduct there?"

I smiled, unable to contain it. "Oh…I think the headmistress would consider that an understatement."

He nodded, convinced of something. "Then my assessment of you was right on."

His declaration made me ask, "Which was…?"

He stopped in front of an unmarked gate, and one that I would have missed entirely if I'd been walking by myself. Beyond it was a courtyard covered in overgrown vines and tall, potted plants. But he paused there, choosing to answer me before entering.

"At the other store back there…before things started flying off the shelves…Olivia was warning you to take it easy with your supplies because they could be dangerous. But I already knew you could handle it."

"Ah…" I replied, holding back a laugh because I was sure it would sound mocking.

"That's what I was about to tell you when something hit me in the back."

I recalled that moment when he'd opened his mouth to speak but didn't get the chance. I blinked, taken aback that he, being a stranger, had come to this conclusion about me.

"How could you possibly know that?"

When he replied it was as if his explanation would bode no further questions, as if his response was common, a given understanding. He brushed aside a draping vine and pressed a corroding doorbell. "That's what I do. I channel people."

I opened my mouth to question him but deep inside the store a chime echoed back to us and a door groaned open at the end of the courtyard. An elderly, hunched woman wearing thick glasses and a distrustful frown appeared. She moved so slowly that I wondered how she'd reached the door so quickly, considering briefly that she may have been standing there waiting for us.

"Mrs. DeVille," he called out.

She had been looking to her left but at the sound of his voice she swung her head toward the gate where we stood.

"Well come in," she spat. "Come in!"

He pushed open the gate and allowed me to enter first so that I followed Mrs. DeVille inside the rather dusky, grungy room that housed her storefront.

While the other shop had some semblance of organization, this one had absolutely none. Mrs. DeVille wiggled her fingers around the room by way of a brief tour. "Voodoo dolls, gris gris bags, beads, floor washes, oils, candles…" As she went on, I noticed, propped in one corner, a frightening wooden statue of a crouched man screaming. Directly above him was a beautifully decorated cross. Interspersed around the room and settled next to cabinets and rugged wooden tables were striking displays of elaborately decorated altars. While all of that seemed odd, they weren't what stood out to me the most. Candles, spotted around the room, flickered despite the lack of a draft and chimes mounted to the walls and hanging from the ceiling jingled even though nothing visible was touching them.

When Mrs. DeVille was finished, she headed for the back room summing up her tour with one final and unexpected warning. "Don't play with anything! I know how you children are. Always wanting to touch and play. Not in this store. Not with my things. I have eyes out here and they'll tell me if…" Her voice faded to a mutter as she left the room and we were alone again.

Jameson caught my eye and we stifled a chuckle at the woman's expense. Then we withdrew our lists and headed for the first item on it.

A small sign denoted gris gris bags. Even though they were distributed around on various tables, the one beneath the sign had the largest abundance of them.

Still, they didn't intrigue me as much as Jameson's comment outside the gate. "What exactly do you mean - you channel people?" I inquired, sliding up beside him.

He shrugged. "Their abilities mostly."

"I'm still confused," I admitted.

"Right, I forgot you're unfamiliar with all this..." He waved his hand across wall, motioning to the mystical items collected on it. "Everyone has a talent. My mother calls it their gift. Some people never cultivate it, some don't even know they have it. But everyone's born with it, that unique ability that sets you apart from the rest of the world. Mine isn't so rare," he admitted with a slight frown, "but it is powerful. I sense other's abilities from the first time I meet them and, if I'm touching them, I can channel that ability to use as my own."

"I see," I replied, holding back my laughter by picking up one of the bags on the table. "What are these used for?" I asked.

"You don't have to believe me, Jocelyn," he stated, noticing my effort to hold back my disbelief. "Whether you do or not, you'll start to witness it around you."

His lack of insistence made me second-guess my judgment of what he'd said. Typically, when someone is lying they are pushy, unrelenting. The fact that he didn't care if I believed him told me that, even if I didn't accept what he told me as truth, he firmly believed it himself. I figured he could believe whatever he wanted as long as it didn't affect me.

Nonetheless, it seemed he was finished with that revelation because he went on to enlighten me about something far less dramatic, the bold red gris gris bag I held in my hand. "They're used for various purposes. Some are meant to beckon money, others peace, others success. Some are used for fertility."

I shot a look at him and he chuckled. "Not that one." Then he cleared his throat to hold back a smile before adding, "That one is for love."

"Oh," I muttered, uncomfortable under his gaze.

Although I didn't look in his direction, I knew his eyes lingered on me as I awkwardly returned the bag to the table. Then he burst into deep bellows of laughter.

"Quiet out there," barked Mrs. DeVille from the back room, coaxing another, softer, bout of laughter from him.

"Are you teasing me?" I demanded in a lowered voice even as I broke into a smile.

"Yes," he said without the least bit of guilt. "You take it well."

A thought popped into my mind then, one I gave fleeting attention. Could he have been teasing me about the channeling? He seemed to pull off his joking with such grace that I could have missed his playful undertones. Something, intuition maybe, told me no. He had been sincere when describing his gift.

Regardless, I didn't know what to think and sighed in agitation at his playfulness.

"Come on." He grinned, turning toward the next item on our list. Along the way he grabbed two gris gris bags, keeping one for himself and handing me the other one.

A bold red one.

Stifling a grin and enjoying his unspoken flirtation, I met him at the table where he stopped next.

"Voodoo dolls," he stated.

"They seem so innocent and safe," I noted, evaluating them.

"Until you know what they can do."

"Which is…?" They looked like a normal doll to me.

His chest expanded with a deep inhale as if preparing for a lengthy explanation, but he summed it up a simple, candid remark. "Just about anything you want."

He shook then, as if a chill had run through him, swept up the nearest doll from the table, and moved on.

"Last item on our list," he announced, examining the display of candles on the shelves in front of him.

Recalling having seen one elaborately designed somewhere toward the back wall, I spun around and sought it out. There, between an elk horn and a skull, sat a white candle sparkling despite the dim store light. Encrusted with jewels and intricate carvings deep in its wax cylinder, it took my breath away.

Jameson came closer then. "It's perfect for you."

I reached down and picked it up, lifting it overhead to better examine its radiance, paying no attention whatsoever to the bracelets that had slid down my arm to expose the metal one that my mother had given me.

"It's stunning, isn't it?" I breathed.

But he didn't answer and that was when I felt the tension grow around us.

Rotating my head toward him, I noted that his eyes weren't on the candle. They were lower, settled directly on my wrist.

For a moment, I faltered, wondering if he'd caught sight of my scar and how I was going to explain it to him.

But it was my other wrist he'd locked his focus on, the one with my white metal bracelet.

From his position, he could clearly see the stone embedded in it.

Casually, I dropped my arms and placed the candle on the table, noticing that he didn't blink or take his eyes off my bracelet once. It was as if he'd found danger lurking in the darkness and refused to turn from it.

"It's a gift from my mother," I said, twisting my arm so that he could see it clearly, using my right arm to keep the bangles from sliding down over it again. "The stone is a-"

"Crystal quartz," he finished.

"That's right," I replied as steady as I could, a little unnerved that he still hadn't blinked or taken his focus off the stone. "Do you know it?"

His eyes, which now focused on me like a laser, were filled with questions, and most of all apprehension. "What's your last name, Jocelyn?" he asked stiffly, his relaxed manner completely erased now.

"Weatherford."

His stare did not break for several seconds as he remained motionless, his breathing undetectable. He was working something out in his mind. I could see it in his eyes.

"All right," he said slowly, as if the words were a struggle to release. It seemed he was still in the midst of evaluating whatever it was that had caught him off guard.

"Is everything-"

"Yes, everything's fine," he said, gradually relaxing by the time he reached the front desk register.

"That really is the right candle for you, Jocelyn." He gave me a wavering smile before adding, "It's beautiful."

"Thanks," I replied, still on edge. Whatever it was about my bracelet had clearly unnerved him and I wasn't about to let it go. "Is there something wrong with my bracelet?" I stepped up beside him, close enough that he stiffened back up again.

"No," he replied quietly. Then, as if it were an afterthought, he added, "Not with your bracelet." Before I could ask exactly what the problem was – which I was certain he knew would come next – he ended the opportunity by calling toward the backroom door, "Mrs. DeVille? We're ready."

She wobbled out to the front desk, once again as if she'd been propped directly on the opposite side of the door the entire time. I snuck a peek at Jameson and found he was smiling warmly at her, despite the sneer in her expression.

"Thank you, Mrs. DeVille," he said cordially after his transaction was complete and stepped aside for me. I noted the warmth had returned to his eyes and his lips were curled up in a soft smile, both directed at me. His welcoming attitude had returned, thankfully.

Mrs. DeVille, on the other hand, addressed me entirely different.

Her gaze darted to my head and then she grimaced. "Nice hat. Sixty-three dollars."

I ignored her and counted the money in my hand. Then I heard Jameson's voice whisper near my ear. "It is a nice hat."

Jameson was back to his flattery, something that, despite having just met, I actually enjoyed. My time to bask in it, however, was short lived.

"I was being facetious," Mrs. DeVille muttered under her breath.

"Mrs. DeVille," Jameson retorted firmly. "I've known you for several years and I have no doubt that flattery is only found by accident in your irony."

She blinked at him, having found herself twisted by his use of words. In the quiet pause that followed, I took a moment to respond.

"Thank you," I said to him.

"You're welcome." He grinned back. "Ready?"

"Absolutely." I slapped the cash on the counter and slid it toward her before turning, my head held high, and strolling out the door with Jameson directly behind me.

Together we left the courtyard, sharing an exchange of expressions that meant we'd been slightly offended by Mrs. DeVille's attitude but still managed to find the humor in it.

"Mr. Thibodeaux is next. He's nicer," Jameson said understatedly, bringing on another bout of laughter.

That was when I realized that I was actually enjoying myself, something I couldn't possibly have expected having just arrived in a new city without any truly solid acquaintances.

As if reading my thoughts, Jameson asked, after a brief glance at my metal bracelet, "So, Jocelyn Weatherford, when did you arrive in New Orleans?"

"This morning," I said expecting a reaction from him.

I didn't get one. He continued his slow stroll, nodding casually in thought.

"Well, I knew it was recent," he admitted.

"Really? How?" Now I was more surprised than him.

"We would have crossed paths earlier."

"It's one of the largest port cities in the United States," I chuckled. "How could you be so sure?"

"Oh…" He smiled to himself, harboring a joke he clearly wasn't going to share with me. "I'm fairly certain of it."

I was just about to pester him to be included on his inside joke when suddenly, and with deep intrigue, he launched into a series of questions, all focusing on me. From that point forward, until we reached Mr. Thibodeaux's door, I felt as if I were rattling off answers to questions so rapidly I couldn't recall the one I'd answered directly before. What I did recall, or rather what struck me, about his list of questions was that he didn't ask a single one about my family. Nothing about siblings or who I lived with in New Orleans; nothing about my mother or father. He did listen intently, though, seeming to memorize every answer and showing little emotion to any of them.

I'd never been self-conscious before. It simply wasn't in my nature. At an academy assembly, I'd demonstrated my self-defense skills in front of two hundred girls and the entire faculty without breaking a sweat. I'd delivered a thank you address during Parent's Weekend to several hundred attendees and didn't stutter or stumble once. When my skirt unraveled in front of the boys at their academy during a school-sanctioned dance, I simply slid it back over my hips, zipped up, and continued moving to the music.

Yet, I felt self-conscious now. This passed quickly enough though when he came to a stop.

"We're here," he announced because again there was no way to tell there was a store within.

"Do any of these places have a sign?" I asked; searching for one in case I'd missed it.

"No, you'll never see one," he replied flatly. "We keep our world fairly well hidden."

Our world, I mused. I still had little understanding of the world he was referring to and wasn't entirely certain I wanted to be a part of it. It still seemed like a dream-state, a childhood nursery story, something unreal and untouchable. Yet, by birthright alone, I was clearly invited in.

He pulled at a set of wide, wooden doors, opening them to reveal the entrance to what was once a carriageway. The secluded cobblestone entrance was encircled on three sides with faded peach stucco walls, windows opened to the fresh afternoon air, and vines clinging to the clay roof.

"The Thibodeaux family runs one of the oldest shops in the city...at least for the items we're looking for," explained Jameson as we approached a small, inconspicuous door. "They are well respected and have an enormous amount of influence - in our world."

There were those words again. They hung in the air between us, mystical to me, common to him.

Jameson knocked lightly on the door and then stepped back several steps, which seemed odd to me until a few moments later.

The door slowly crept open, outward and directly over where Jameson had been standing. Now I understood why he'd given it clearance. What wasn't obvious to me was how the door could open without anyone touching it.

No one had answered Jameson's knock, at least not in person.

I approached the entrance as Jameson entered, a little suspicious of what I'd find inside.

From the light of flickering candles, an elderly man sat at a weathered table, his legs extending out and crossed at the ankles, his hands clasped across his round belly. While there were no visible signs of an air conditioning unit or even a fan, the air inside was cool and dry. The humidity seemed to halt at the doorway.

Jameson was already speaking with the man in a hushed voice when I reached the table.

"...and Mr. Thibodeaux, I would like to introduce Jocelyn Weatherford," Jameson stated solidly while ushering me closer.

In hearing my name, the man's eyes lit up and then moved, questioningly, between Jameson and myself several times before he even uttered a sound.

Finally, he stood and extended a hand to me. "Ms. Weatherford..." he said with an accent that could only come from living in the south for most of one's life.

"Pleased to meet you, Mr. Thibodeaux," I replied, shaking his hand, noting its softness despite the man's age.

"As it is for me," he replied with a curious smile hovering beneath the surface as he again glanced in Jameson's direction. "Now, you've come for school supplies?"

"We have," said Jameson.

"Excellent, I'll get them for you."

As Mr. Thibodeaux opened the only item on his desk, an aged ledger, and perused the pages, Jameson explained how the Thibodeaux family worked.

"They sell only the best, and rarest, tools - some dating back to the fourth century. Because they are housed in select and highly-secure warehouses, whatever is ordered needs to be bought well ahead of time. Basically if you need something powerful, special, or unique, you come here and then you wait for it to arrive."

"I see," I replied, though I didn't. Not entirely. "So, if these items need to be pre-ordered, how did mine arrive so quickly?"

Jameson, caught unexpectedly by the question, gave me a puzzled stare, which quickly fell to Mr. Thibodeaux.

Without lifting his head from the ledger, he replied, "Your purchase, Jocelyn Weatherford, was made on the day of your birth…exactly sixteen years ago."

Jameson blinked in surprise. "Today is your birthday?"

"Yes," I said hastily before readdressing Mr. Thibodeaux. "But, why was mine ordered so long ago?"

"Most likely to secure the purchase," he muttered, flipping a page. "It's one-of-a-kind."

Mr. Thibodeaux had apparently found what he was looking for because he thumped his finger against the page and stood up to shuffle to a small door a few feet away. Briefly disappearing inside, he returned with a square object wrapped in brown paper and twine and set it in front of Jameson.

Without delay, he then pulled open a drawer in the table between us to withdraw a metal box and slid it across the table, keeping his hand on the lid.

Jameson, who'd been distracted from his own purchase, a book of casts, stepped closer to mine, settling on the more extravagant of the two items Mr. Thibodeaux had brought out.

"Jocelyn, this item has been sought after since it went missing back in the fourth century," said Mr. Thibodeaux. "It is incredibly valuable. The Sevens recently resorted to confiscating my inventory in search of it. Half of my goods are now gone."

Clearly, this was not another book of casts. "I understand."

He hesitated. "You will take extra special care with this purchase," he added for good measure.

"I will."

Only after my reassurance did he release his hand.

I drew the box toward me, glancing up at him. He was fearful, which made no sense to me until I asked a seemingly benign question. "So, who are The Sevens?"

It was their reaction, a tense meeting of wary eyes, which told me I should pay attention to Jameson's answer. "They're the equivalent to our world's judicial and legislative branches combined. Their name comes from the fact that there are seven of them who preside over our welfare." He scoffed, then, before mocking, "Welfare. Right…"

I took it that he didn't agree with that assessment, which only made me more curious as to what the box held. My hand reached out to lift the lid, curious about what I might find, but Mr. Thibodeaux wouldn't allow it.

"You will keep this lid closed until you are safely home," he instructed.

Jameson's eyebrows lifted with interest and I knew he was thinking the same thing as me.

"Well, can you at least tell me what is inside?" I asked. "I mean, it's not a bomb, is it?"

I intended that last part to be a joke but Mr. Thibodeaux didn't share my humor. "It is not. But it is just as dangerous."

I laughed uncomfortably. "Wonderful."

Mr. Thibodeaux ignored my comment, turning instead to wrap our purchases.

As the box was extended to me, Mr. Thibodeaux gave me a final warning…as if I needed one at this point. "This is not a school supply. It is a gift. Don't let anyone know you have it until you are ready to use it."

I placed my hands on the box but Mr. Thibodeaux refused to let go.

"I am allowing you to walk out of my store with this box because your mother insisted you'd be safe. I believe her and that is the only reason."

Still unnerved, I nodded sincerely and slipped the box, now wrapped and unidentifiable in silk fabric, into my canvas shopping bag.

We said our goodbyes and left with Jameson still shaking his head at the item tucked away even as we crossed the carriageway toward the street. Yet by the time we reached the wooden gate Jameson's reaction had turned to concern.

"Do you really think you'll be safe getting home with that..." he paused realizing he didn't know how to refer to whatever was now in my possession "...thing?"

"Yes," I replied decisively.

His eyebrows lifted, still not entirely convinced. "I don't know, Jocelyn."

"I'll be fine," I replied.

While he didn't agree, he did shove open the gate and step out onto the street.

And then he froze.

I nearly collided with him but managed to stop myself.

His worries about the dangers of me carrying my secret merchandise seemed to now be erased as he stared down the street. In fact, based on his stance, the resolute set of his jaw, and the sternness in his eyes, a far greater fear was approaching.

Searching for it, I noted three boys around our age just a few blocks away.

Sighing in agitation, he spun around to face me. "They've seen us. I have to go, Jocelyn. I'm..." His eyes took on an intensity that both stunned and intrigued me. "I'll make sure you get home safely."

"Sure..." I replied, dazed by his sudden need to leave.

He'd been so relaxed the entire time I'd been with him. Not even the chaos in the first store where we'd crossed paths had caused this type of concern in him.

I glanced passed his shoulder at the boys, who were now a short block away. They had the same sandy blonde hair as Jameson and were smiling in our direction as they drew nearer.

They didn't appear to be of any real concern. Still, he gave them a fleeting glance before snapping his head back in my direction. "I'll see you at school, Jocelyn."

What struck me was that his goodbye wasn't jovial or even as carefree as I would have expected between two schoolmates, new or otherwise. No, instead there was an underlying sadness to it. And I got the distinct impression that something between us was about to change.

Then Jameson spun around and hurried to cross between me and the approaching boys.

I watched as he met them, talked briefly in a small huddle, and then motioned toward another side street in the opposite direction.

He's drawing them away from me, I thought. Maybe he isn't ready to introduce us?

I shook my head at him and felt my stomach shake with a small laugh. He was odd - my first friend in New Orleans. Handsome, charming, and odd.

I strolled slowly down the street, no longer seeing him or his friends anywhere in sight.

I was smiling then, happy to have met him and having absolutely no premonition whatsoever that I'd just spent the day with my family's most dangerous enemy.

4. BIRTHDAY

It was late afternoon by the time I returned to Aunt Lizzy's house and, despite the haze stretching just over the buildings, an oppressive heat began to swelter across the city. I wasn't sure if this was unusual for early September in New Orleans or not but hoped it was just a one-day heat wave. After closing the front door behind me, I could have kissed the air conditioning unit.

The house was just as quiet as when I'd left, but as I passed the dining room and found five canvas bags identical to the one I carried from my shopping excursion, I was reminded that it wouldn't be that way for long.

The bags were lined up in a row along the table, waiting for their owners to retrieve them and as I stood there I couldn't help feeling dumbfounded.

They weren't there when I'd left, which meant sometime over the course of the day Miss Mabelle had set them out.

She ordered my niece's and nephew's school supplies but not my own? Giving her the benefit of doubt, I settled on believing she just hadn't had enough time. After all, I had just found out myself as of yesterday that I'd be relocating here.

Carrying my bag upstairs to my room, I closed the door against the silence that weighed down the rest of the house, rubbed another round of Nurse Carol's ointment on my diminishing scar, and then opened my mother's gift.

Withdrawing the silver case, I lifted the lid and found something completely unexpected.

Inside the box, was a simple rope, although I was learning that nothing was truly simple in this new world…It was not manufactured at a factory, I was certain of that much, because it didn't appear to be made of twine but instead consisted of hundreds of strands of hair. Blond. Auburn. Black. Dark brown. It was held together by seven strips of brown leather evenly placed down the length of it.

"All right…" I muttered without a clear indication as to why this rope was in any way significant or why anyone would bother to look for a bundle of hair over the course of centuries.

Regardless, I figured that if someone was looking for it than it must be important in some small way to them. And therefore I should find it a hiding place.

The room was small so I didn't spend much time determining that there wasn't a single spot I'd feel comfortable leaving it. Standing in the middle of the room, hands on my hips, I considered my options.

Then, as if in answer to my search, a small, square sliver of wood dropped from the back corner of the room, just above the floorboard. Stooping beside it, I fitted it back in position and found that whoever had cut it did so in the direction of the wood grain so that when in position it was undetectable. It would be a perfect hiding place. Opening the flap, I found it was empty, notwithstanding the cobwebs that covered it, so clearly it wasn't in use.

Just as I placed the silver box containing The Seven's rope inside and closed the secret compartment, an uproar started downstairs.

Listening from my crouched position, I thought it might be a brawl breaking out but there was laughter and contented squeals in the midst of the commotion.

My cousins were home - and they weren't the quiet-mannered type.

I stood and slipped out my door to the top of the stairs, still listening.

"Purple! Exactly the kind I wanted!" said the voice of a melodic, but authoritative girl.

"Ohhh, this is going to be fun..." came another voice. This one was distinctly male with a deep, rumbling resonance.

I was at the bottom of the stairs by that point and standing only a few feet away. No one noticed me, their focus being entirely on the school supplies that were now littering the dining room table. Then Aunt Lizzy, who was still fighting grogginess, broke the commotion.

"This..." she said, standing off to the side with a weak smile, "is your cousin Jocelyn."

All of them spun around to face me, frozen, stunned, and, most of all, silent.

Then the roar began again, louder this time, just as they launched themselves at me. I was suddenly surrounded, being patted on the shoulders and hugged by arms that came from the crowd, each one talking over one another gleefully.

"Let her breathe!" came Aunt Lizzy's voice. "LET HER BREATHE!" she repeated over my cousins' screams. "I told you they'd be thrilled," she shouted to me.

Nodding back, I was almost carried into the room and dropped beside the dining room table. I am certain the introduction would have gone on longer if it weren't for the loud clap that came from the direction of the kitchen.

My cousins and I quieted down instantly and turned to find Miss Mabelle standing in the open doorway.

"Turtle soup's ready," she declared, never breaking her glare.

"Turtle?" I asked under my breath.

"You'll love it," said Aunt Lizzy. "All right. We have a special dinner prepared tonight. It is Jocelyn's sixteenth birthday so let's make it memorable."

That started another exuberant commotion from my cousins surrounding me until Aunt Lizzy cleared her throat. "Clear off that table and take your seats."

A few minutes later, as I stood awkwardly off to the side, my cousins raced their heavy-laden, supply-filled canvas bags up to their rooms and returned. Then commands were issued by Aunt Lizzy as the commotion continued to swirl around me.

"Placemats. Silverware." She pointed around the room. "Distribute," she said to a short, thin girl with strawberry-blond hair while shoving a stack of plates in her hands.

The girl didn't lift a foot to follow the order.

Instead, she remained in place, whispered something under her breath, and the plates began rising one after the other on their own and moving across the room and landing on a placemat before each chair.

I stood across the room certain I was witnessing an optical illusion or maybe the imperceptible snap of her hand so that the plates landed where she wanted. It occurred in the midst of two boys elbowing each other and another girl shouting for Miss Mabelle to make her soup spicy. No one took a second look at the plates.

As everyone was pulling out their chairs and Miss Mabelle began bringing in the soup bowls, something else caught my attention.

"Oh…" Aunt Lizzy grumbled, realizing she'd forgotten something. "Candles, Estelle."

The girl who had liked the purple candles she'd received in her bag of school supplies earlier, tossed back her dark brown hair, mumbled something that sounded like Latin and pursed her thick lips together before lightly blowing through them. As if it were an everyday occurrence, the rest of the table went about their business while the wicks began to flicker with flame, without a matchstick or a lighter in the room.

As if that wasn't enough to make everyone I know run for the door, with a quick lift of Aunt Lizzy's finger jazz music began filtering softly in from the living room.

Stunned into silence, I tried to rationalize what was happening. Maybe tricks were being played? Wires had carried the dishes and the candles had special timers. And these things had all been set up before they'd left for camp just to fool with me. But I knew this wasn't the case. How could it be? No one knew I'd be coming.

Then it dawned on me…

Jameson had been correct.

I was witnessing the mysticism I had been mocking all day long. This realization stayed with me throughout dinner, which was a four course meal and probably the most delicious food I'd ever tasted. And while I would have preferred to sit quietly throughout the meal, giving me time to enjoy it and to better comprehend what I had observed here and in the French Quarter shops, that turned out to be an impossible expectation. I was peppered with questions about myself, my life to-date, and my mother for the first half of the meal. Only one thing broke the conversation, something that settled in and didn't leave me throughout the meal. When I'd mentioned that Aunt Lizzy had slept the entire day and I'd gone shopping on my own, Miss Mabelle happened to be in the room, collecting empty soup bowls. Overhearing me, she muttered under her breath, "Mmmmhmmm, kin thank me for that…" Then she was gone, the door between the kitchen and dining room swinging back in its place.

It unnerved me.

She had just admitted to ensuring that the only person who could possibly escort me around this unfamiliar city was indisposed; and that during Aunt Lizzy's absence Miss Mabelle had ushered me toward shopping for school supplies that could have been bought in advance, or even piecemealed together from the other school supplies until ones could be bought to replace them. Instead, Miss Mabelle had guaranteed that I would be shopping on my own. What happened to southern hospitality, I wondered.

That aside, dinner was very entertaining, as well as educational. For the last half, I asked them questions and found that I really enjoyed my cousins. This was a relief because they were the only family members I'd ever met. It bode well for the rest.

They were lively and each with their own distinct personality. Estelle was confident, audacious even, with a fondness for asking pointed questions. She favored the colors purple and green, which I was forewarned were the only colors in her wardrobe. Vinnia captured the image of a southern belle perfectly, with softly curled strawberry-blonde hair and large, innocent eyes. She moved very slowly and said very little. Although when she did speak her summation of the topic was amazingly precise. Spencer was short with curly red hair and a boisterous voice that didn't seem right coming from his small frame. Oscar was a year older than me, average in height but built like a train, stiff and sturdy. He reminded me of a union boss with the poise and fairness to negotiate, which he did whenever an argument broke out. Nolan was a talker, fast and impeccably clear, with an almost palpable energy that simmered just below the surface. Besides their hair color, which had varying shades of red in it, and upturned noses, they did have one other thing in common. They all wore a crystal quartz stone somewhere on their body.

After several hours, as the questions lessened, I was just about to ask about Estelle's ability to light candles and Vinnia's ability to carry plates without actually touching them when Aunt Lizzy screeched back her chair.

"Well, your Uncle Lester is about to call and I have a lot to catch up with him."

I'd learned that he was assisting my mother at the ministry and wasn't expected home any time soon.

"And it is eleven o'clock…" she yawned.

I drew in a quiet gasp. The academy would never have allowed dinner to go this late, much less allow us to be outside our rooms at this hour. Still, no one seemed to pay it much attention. Even Aunt Lizzy was leisurely making her way to the stairs without rounding up her children and forcing them to their rooms.

"She does this every time," Oscar pointed out. "The day before school starts-"

"School starts tomorrow?" I asked, feeling my eyes grow wide.

He gave me a nod of affirmation before Estelle started in about her first period teacher.

I watched them blankly, realizing one thing. They weren't moving.

"You don't have a lights out?" I asked, perplexed.

They broke in to smiles, evidently finding humor in my question. But Spencer replied, "This isn't a prison, Jocelyn."

Oscar went on to clarify. "We don't follow the same rules or structure that you might be used to. Brush your teeth, don't brush your teeth. Eat breakfast, don't eat breakfast. Have chocolate for breakfast." He shrugged. "Do what you want. No one will stop you."

I sat quietly stunned, soaking up what he'd just relayed to me. Then, somewhere in the recesses of my mind and without much thought to it, a response formulated. "I think I'm going to like it here."

That brought out laughter from everyone at the table before they began pushing back their chairs, collecting dessert plates and silverware, and bringing them to the kitchen.

I did the same and found Miss Mabelle slumped on a stool in a corner near the pantry, her cane propped against her robust thigh. She appeared to be asleep.

The dishes were arranged next to the sink and the silverware was placed in a bucket of suds as the conversation turned to the next day. Several times the word "school" was mentioned bringing out a yawn each time.

"You should rest," Vinnia encouraged. Apparently, she'd noticed them. "It's going to be a big day for you tomorrow."

As much as I wanted to spend more time with my newly found family, I knew she made a good point. Having been unable to sleep much on the plane, or since we landed, it would be fair to say I'd been awake for almost thirty six hours.

Before I headed upstairs, Spencer revealed that he'd be driving me the next morning and instructed me to be ready by seven o'clock.

Their voices drifted up but became muffled as I closed my door.

This birthday hadn't been at all what I'd expected. There had been no corny song or bundles of gifts. No birthday cake or congratulatory speech. But in its own unique way it had been one of the best. I'd finally met my family. It made me smile knowing I was very slowly coming to terms with my new home, my new life.

Shunning sleep for just a few minutes, I dropped my canvas bag on the bed and slowly emptied it on to the comforter. Shaking my head, I was still confused about what classes would bring tomorrow. Candles, tarot cards, gris gris bags, a voodoo doll, an assortment of stones… Not your typical school supplies.

Then all thoughts about school instantly disappeared as I focused on the items strewn across my bed. One of them shouldn't have been there. It knew it with certainty. It's starkly defined color would have drawn my attention when I'd peeked in the bag at Olivia's store.

The violet candlestick, delicately carved with an intricate curving pattern lay haphazardly across a stack of tarot cards.

Picking it up for inspection, I realized there was only one person who could have put it there.

Jameson.

And my smile returned.

Finding a book of matches and a simple silver candleholder among my school supplies, I assembled them on my nightstand and struck the match, noting with curiosity that it didn't leave the typical, stringent smell of sulfur behind as I touched flame to wick.

A brief crackling followed and then something entirely unexpected happened.

Smoke began billowing from the candle. Enormous clouds of it filled the room within seconds.

In a rush, I blew it out, hoping that none made it to the hallway. A quick glance back told me that it hadn't and I took a seat on the bed, ready to laugh at myself.

But then I looked up…and the laugh caught in my throat.

There in the dim light of the moon filtering through the window, I watched as the smoke collected into letters. The letters then formed words, which I read in a whisper.

I didn't get to say it earlier.
HAPPY BIRTHDAY
-Jameson

5. ENEMY REVEALED

I didn't tell anyone about the candle the next morning, partly because I hadn't mentioned Jameson to them, and partly because there was no time for it.

The house had turned to complete pandemonium.

I was startled awake by the sound of a shout. This, apparently, was Miss Mabelle's way of rousing the household. After slipping out of bed, showering in the bathroom adjacent to my room, and selecting a colorful bohemian dress and brown leather knee-high boots, I was ready for my first day of school.

Downstairs, things became more hectic.

When there wasn't a body rushing by me there was a shout to take its place. Footsteps thudded down the hallway, doors slammed, grunts were made as something was forgotten midway down the stairs.

I waited for Spencer by the door nibbling a croissant I'd found in the kitchen, holding my canvas shopping bag, and trying to stay out of everyone's way, all while recalling the birthday gift Jameson had left me last night. Just the thought of it sent a flood of excitement through me and roused butterflies in my stomach. The affect of it clung to me so that I didn't even think about my new school until we were on our way there.

My cousins each had their own sports car, Spencer having opted for a black Audi R8, and they all drove in a line out the front gate. While it was a short drive to my new school, the Academy of the Immaculate Heart, Spencer had time to inform me that I was one of the lucky ones. Apparently, the old principal greeted new students with a forced introductory meeting but the new one was more leisurely. Therefore, he or one of the other cousins would orient me to the school grounds.

As we pulled into park, I noted that this school resembled my old academy, albeit on a smaller scale. The campus housed red brick buildings dripping with ivy and expansive, lush lawns, bringing on a pang of sadness and the reminder that I needed to make a call to my friends soon.

Spencer found a spot to park in a vacant row and the rest of my cousins' sports cars fell in line next to it. I stepped out, still holding my canvas bag, and taking in the campus.

"Oh no…" Spencer said across the car's roof. "Not that one. That's for later."

Then he swung a laptop bag over his shoulder and rounding the car to replace the canvas bag in my hand with a laptop of my own.

"This," he said heaving the canvas one across the backseat to settle next to his, "won't be needed until after school." He looked up to find my bewildered expression and explained, "That one is used for casting classes in The Quarter which start after school."

"For extracurricular?"

"Sort of," he replied as if having no other way to describe them.

"Come on," Estelle called out, already strolling toward the school's entrance with the rest of my cousins, the sash of her deep purple shirt trailing behind her.

We reached two double glass doors and entered the school's main hall together. Had the doors not been shaded, had the morning light been angled slightly different, what transpired next may never have occurred.

I'd been right behind Oscar, close enough that when he came to a sudden halt just inside I nearly collided with him. Although I'm not sure he would have noticed.

His attention was on six others directly in front of us.

They all had the same sandy blonde hair and were all close in age to each other as well as to me and my cousins. And they all wore an agate stone, one of the oldest stones in recorded history and one thought to be worn for protection.

None of this mattered much to me because the butterflies had returned.

Stepping around Oscar, I came in to full view as Jameson turned to face us.

"Hi," I said, excited to meet again and trying not to show it.

His stunning translucent green eyes settled on me and didn't move. "Jocelyn…" he stated softly, apprehensively.

His tone was different today. It was restricted. And it instantly made me suspicious.

Then all eyes were on us, swinging from me to him and back to me again.

It was Estelle who asked what seemed to be on everyone's mind. "You two know each other?" There was an edge to her voice.

"Yes," I said, having no idea why I felt like I'd just broken a rule.

"How?" Oscar demanded. At the sound of his tone, the feeling I'd crossed a boundary grew more distinct.

"In the French Quarter, yesterday. Jameson showed me around."

"First name terms, ha?" scoffed a girl next to Jameson, who gave her a swift glare for it.

My defensiveness kicked in then. "That's really none of your business."

The girl stepped forward but was also held back.

"You showed her around?" demanded a stout boy on Jameson's side of the line, inquiring just as harshly with him as my cousins were being with me.

Jameson didn't respond right away. He remained rigid, his eyes boring in to me, guilty, seeming to apologize. But there was no reason for it. He'd done nothing wrong.

"Jameson," snapped the girl, insisting on an answer.

"Don't raise your voice to him," I ordered, knowing that I was stirring up the fight.

The girl was about to retort when Jameson responded. It was subdued but stiff and unyielding. "She didn't know who I was."

His eyes never wavered from me.

"Did you know who she was?" urged the girl.

He drew in a deep breath, unwilling to answer.

After another forceful prompt from the girl, he growled in warning, "Enough, Charlotte. Yes, I knew she was a Weatherford."

There were gasps from both sides at his acknowledgement and Nolan took a step forward, reminding me of a soldier advancing toward his enemy.

Oscar's hand came up and stopped Nolan at the chest before asking, "Jocelyn, were you harmed?"

"No," I replied, shocked he'd even think to ask the question. "No, not at all. Jameson was…"

Nolan pressed his chest against Oscar's hand when I hesitated, ready to break through it toward Jameson's side of the line.

"Was what?" Estelle prompted.

I met Jameson's eyes again. The intensity in them made me hesitate. He was waiting to see how I'd characterize him.

"Well...he was a complete gentleman."

This seemed to placate both sides. Nolan lessened his pressure against Oscar's hand and those standing on both sides of Jameson dropped their shoulders.

I got the sense this interaction was about to break up when Vinnia, petite and childlike Vinnia, stepped forward to direct a threat at Jameson. "Stay away from her or you will regret it, Caldwell."

My cousins began to turn and head down the hall, the fight deterred for the time being, when my subconscious registered the name she'd used.

I repeated it slowly. "Caldwell?"

Then I was piecing it all together from the depths of my awareness, his last name screaming through my mind. It was the name of the family who had repressed and endangered the Weatherfords for centuries, the name of our mortal enemy. And it was the name he had not disclosed yesterday when he'd asked for mine.

Jameson remained firm, his expression never flinching and intently trained on me.

"You're..." I swallowed hard, the words barely making it passed my throat. "You're a Caldwell?"

"We're all Caldwells," Charlotte spat vehemently, motioning to the line on both sides of her. Apparently, from her point of view, I should have known this already.

"Easy, Charlotte," Jameson warned again.

She drew in a sharp breath, offended. "You spend the whole day with a Weatherford...knowing she's a Weatherford...endangering yourself...all of us...and you're telling me to take it easy?"

"No one got hurt," he mumbled, contentious, his mouth downturned.

"Not yet..." seethed another one of the girls from his side, one with clear green eyes like Jameson, framed with long dark lashes. Right now they were narrowed and pointed at me.

No one spoke for several seconds and only then did I notice that we'd drawn a crowd. Somewhere inside the swarm people were whispering.

"...starting another fight..."

"...always at it. Can't they just get along?"

"Wonder what they're gonna do this time."

Then Oscar's voice rose above the rest. "Let's go, Weatherfords."

This time, I turned with them to move toward the classrooms, noting that by accident or with intent they'd formed a circle around me.

"That went well," I muttered sarcastically and heard a few of my cousins chuckle.

"You can hold your own," Estelle pointed out, playfully elbowing me.

I avoided it and used the motion to do a visual sweep of the boundary my cousins made. I lingered briefly on the Caldwells who stayed in place watching us leave.

While most of them gradually returned to what they'd been doing before, opening their lockers, digging through their notebooks, Jameson stayed focused on me.

The rigidity in his face had loosened. He no longer seemed alert, tense. But there was something in his expression that I couldn't deny.

He looked disappointed.

That caught me off guard. Here was my enemy who, for every sane reason, should be glaring at my back but he wasn't. It didn't make sense. None of it did. Thinking back over the hours we'd spent together, even after he'd learned that I was a Weatherford, he'd remained friendly, even flirtatious at times. He'd diverted the attention of his family when we nearly met them on the street, which I had a feeling was to help me avoid the tense meeting that had just taken place. He'd defended me against Mrs. DeVille's derogatory remark about my hat. He'd left me an unexpected birthday gift, written in smoke through the air. He'd been concerned for my safety in transporting a dangerous item back home. Even if it had turned out to be a seemingly innocuous rope, he didn't know it. He was supposed to be my greatest adversary and yet he'd done nothing at all to prove it.

This realization stayed with me until we crossed paths again, in my second class, History of the Civil War. As I walked through the door, I saw him seated at the back of the room, his head down, immersed in the words of a textbook.

I found the teacher and introduced myself, quietly so I didn't disturb him. For some reason, I was trying to delay the inevitable acknowledgement between us that we'd be in same room together for an entire semester.

"We sit in order of first name," explained Ms. Wizner, a short, rotund woman with graying hair. "Easier for me to identify you. Now, that means you'll be seated next to Jameson, since your name is Jocelyn."

Right then, at that very moment, his head snapped up.

She and I were at my seat by that point so that she also noticed his reaction.

"Well, well, Jameson. That's what it takes to earn your attention in my class? Sit a pretty girl next to you? If only I'd known last year…"

At that point, I watched my mortal enemy blush.

From then on, the tension flared between us. As the rest of the students filtered in and Ms. Wizner started her lecture, I didn't have to look in Jameson's direction to know his breathing was staggered or that his body remained motionless, rigid. By the end of the hour, the stiffness surrounding us must have been almost palpable.

Feeling it full force, the first deep breath I took was when the bell rang.

Unlike the rest of the students, I didn't rush for the door and, I realized, neither did Jameson.

When the commotion of skidding chairs, rustling bags, and hurried footsteps died down, we sat in a cocoon of quiet. Ms. Wizner had even left the room for a quick bathroom break before her next session started.

Jameson and I sat staring ahead, our arms crossed over our bags set on top of our desks, our feet unmoving. It was almost as if we both had waited for this moment and now that it arrived we didn't know how to react.

I broke the silence. "Thank you for the birthday gift."

He released his breath, which he seemed to have been holding for a good length of time while waiting for either of us to speak. "You're welcome. Did it-"

"You should have told me who you were," I stated in a rush, acknowledging what had held me back, what had kept me in my chair as the room had emptied, before my time ran out and I had to run for my next class.

"I was about to bring that up," he admitted. Then he sighed, seemingly frustrated with himself. "I should have." He nodded. "But I…"

"Yes?" I urged, not really caring my tone was harsh.

"I knew what would have happened, if you learned I was a Caldwell."

"How could you be so sure? You don't know me."

He lifted one eyelid at me, skeptical. "Come on, Jocelyn. The first advice your family would have given you, probably before you even entered the city limits, would be to watch out for the Caldwells. And I'm a Caldwell."

He waited for my response, that intense gaze settling on me once again.

I couldn't deny it wasn't true. It had happened exactly as he'd portrayed. "They're only trying to keep me safe."

"And you know, I don't blame them. My family would have done the same thing."

As I turned my head toward him, our eyes met, stirring something deep inside me. While part of it was the excitement of being within arm's reach of someone who was incredibly dangerous to me, it was also the fact that he'd recognized that our families were, in fact, similar. Albeit, it was that we shared a preservation instinct.

My gaze dropped to my right arm searching for remnants of the scar that had now completely disappeared, that ailment that had brought me to New Orleans, the domino piece that had set in motion my introduction to Jameson. Then my focus drifted to the scar above his lip and I wondered if it had been inflicted by one of my family members. Hadn't both families suffered enough, I wondered. Where did it end?

Ms. Wizner, along with several students from the next class, came through the door then, marking the time had arrived when we'd need to leave.

We stood at the same time, collected our bags, and left the class. But only a few steps from the door, Jameson stopped me.

"Jocelyn." He waited for me to turn and face him. "I'm sorry for not disclosing who I am. That was wrong - but I don't regret it. It gave me a little more time with you before we had to face reality."

I nodded and he started down the opposite end of the hallway. Then I stopped him.

"Jameson." I hesitated, wondering if I'd regret my next words. They seemed so simple but carried such weight. "I'm glad you waited."

And for the first time since I'd left him on the street in the French Quarter, he smiled - that relaxed, charming grin that had captivated me and made me feel so welcome.

No matter what my honesty might bring, ostracism from my family or fury from his, I felt it was worth it to see that smile.

Then, a few more steps down the hall, I wondered what had just happened. Jameson and I, who were both bestowed the duty of being lifelong enemies since our birth into our respective families, had just acknowledged to each other that we'd wanted to spend more time together. It was ethically wrong, certainly unheard of, and very likely dangerous. Worst of all, it was impossible. Our families would never allow it.

I didn't bother to try and stifle the despondency that surfaced with this revelation. In fact, as I glanced back in search of Jameson, I found he'd done the same.

Even though we were far from each other, several rows of lockers to be exact, I knew he'd come to the same conclusion. His shoulders slumped, his head bowed, his lips downturned, his forehead creased with disappointment…all told me the truth.

He disagreed with the position we were in too.

We hesitated, for just a second, our eyes locked on each other, and then we entered our respective classes.

Lunch came and went without a sign from the Caldwells. My cousins, having met me at my classroom door, took me to their eating spot, a table on the outdoor patio overlooking an expansive green lawn. I then surveyed the area for the Caldwells, which Oscar noticed.

"They eat inside," he said, attempting to console me. "They stay well away from us, where they can't start anything." He yawned and stretched out his long, meaty legs. "Nope. Out here there's usually just us, the girl who speaks to the dead, and her boyfriend."

I held back laughter with a grin that told him I didn't believe a word he was saying.

"No kidding," he insisted. "She has a spot in Jackson Square where she sells messages…They were gone most of last semester, something about being in Europe, but they're back and trying to make up classes so they can graduate."

"Which one is she?" I asked and he pointed out a petite, dark-haired girl sitting on the grass.

"This is a strange world I've been let into..." I muttered.

He laughed. "That's an understatement. Anyway, you won't see any of the Caldwells out here."

"They know better," said Vinnia.

"So the ones I met in the hallway this morning...Was that all of them?"

"Pretty much. The tall one, Burke, is quiet but has a good temper," Oscar explained with a snicker, telling me he'd seen it firsthand. "The two girls, Charlotte and Alison, are usually the instigators. They don't mind starting something."

"Or keeping it going," Estelle added wiping her fingers on a purple napkin, specially included in her lunch bag by Miss Mabelle who knew her attachment to the color.

"Yeah, Charlotte and Alison, they're my favorites," I said wryly.

Oscar chuckled before continuing. "The other one, Dillon, is the youngest of the Caldwells so he's stayed clear of us; although I don't expect that to last long. Once his skill level is up I imagine he'll use it. And then there's Jameson," he gave me an inquisitive look, "who you already know."

"Not very well," I corrected. "I just arrived yesterday." I reminded him.

Oscar nodded and then smiled to himself, evidently realizing the truth behind my statement. "Right. Well, he's the most peculiar of the Caldwells. Although they're all similar in that they're patient, persistent, and smart, he doesn't have the same talents as the others. Umm..." Oscar swiftly looked around and realized he wanted to keep whatever he was going to say next as private. Lowering his voice, he continued. "He channels. That's his thing. He's good with kids; they don't seem to see through him like we do. When he sets his mind to something, he does it. No matter what challenge he's facing, no matter how ludicrous. And, once a week, he leaves the city on some kind of errand, which we've never been able to figure out. Tried following him a few times but he always caught on and made sure we lost him."

"Oh," chimed Estelle, "and he doesn't date seriously, has never had a long-term girlfriend."

My head snapped in her direction. "But he's…"

"Gorgeous, right?" Estelle filled in my thought.

"Undeniably," I replied, shaking my head.

"And the girls notice it," she reassured.

"He's waiting for someone," said Vinnia between mouthfuls of crab cake sandwich.

We all looked at her, curious how she might know this, but she simply shrugged, unable to speak beyond the food between her bulging cheeks.

Immediately, I wondered who that someone might be. It couldn't be me. I was a Weatherford - he was a Caldwell. We both knew it wouldn't work, which is why he spent those few extra hours with me. He'd been as interested in me as I was in him and wanted to make the most of our time the day before. This - here - right now was what he meant by "before we had to face reality." This was reality. We would never be able to spend untainted time together again.

Vinnia's statement settled in the back of my subconscious as I went about laying out my lunch. The bag prepared for me by Miss Mabelle once again showed her knowledge of my tastes. Inside I found a sandwich combining bacon-lettuce-tomato and peanut butter-jelly, Kettle chips and freshly squeezed orange juice.

The conversation turned to other topics then. Tough classes. Malicious teachers. But no one else brought up the Caldwells.

Even then, I couldn't stop myself from searching for Jameson throughout the day, between classes or in the library where my cousins met after last class to get a head start on homework and to snack while waiting for the next, more mystical, set of classes to start.

As we worked through the mountain of assignments given to us on the first day of school, I continued to keep my hopes up that Jameson would walk through the door. He never did and a few hours later my cousins and I packed up and headed for the parking lot.

In fact, only Spencer's casual warning got my full attention.

"Get ready for some real lessons," he smirked lightheartedly as we slipped into his car's bucket seats.

The truth was that each of the classes I was enrolled in seemed to be several months behind the academy so I wasn't the least bit concerned about them. My nervousness was reserved for where we were headed and it was only compounded with Spencer's next comment.

"Now, you're going to need the canvas bag."

While I had a number of questions for him, I didn't bother to ask any. The fact was I had a feeling that I already knew the answers.

I was headed for another school, one that would be teaching subjects far outside the Department of Education's mandate.

Inside, I sniggered. If only Alisa and Elizabeth could be here to see it. My physics class at the academy was probably going to pale in comparison.

He left the parking lot, with our cousins behind us, and headed for The Quarter, his speed telling me that he'd been to our destination many times before. Being that it was September, dusk had just begun to settle over New

Orleans and, while the streets were still lit by the dampening sunlight, neon signs now shone brightly above the doorways beckoning tourists with jambalaya, jazz, and cocktails.

Spencer parked on a quiet street just outside the heart of The Quarter so that when I stepped out the tantalizing smell of southern food and the faint sounds of a jazz horn hung in the air. My cousins found parking where they could, as there seemed to be more vehicles parked on this street than most others in The Quarter, and then met us at an obscure wooden door.

We entered together to find ourselves in a long, dark, arched hallway. With the dim light of the courtyard guiding us, reflecting off collected pools of water and wet cobblestones, we made our way toward the opposite opening.

On the other side was a courtyard, which, like most others here in the city, was draped in flourishing vines. Buildings encircled us, sheltering us from the street, with a single balcony running the entire circumference of the second story leading the way to countless more rooms. I wondered if this might have been a secluded apartment building at one time.

After a sweeping glance of my surroundings, I found that others had arrived before us.

Groups stood in cliques beneath the second story balcony and by flickering gas lanterns mounted alongside various doors. In the hazy evening light, I scanned them and found we were all similar in age, some I recognized from the school we'd just left.

Immediately, my cousins merged with the groups, each one seeming to know at least one other person in them.

"Are these all the students?" I asked Spencer after he'd introduced me to a few of his friends and settled in to wait for the class to begin.

"No, there are classes each day of the week here, based on levels of ability. Most families start their kids as young as four-years-old and as they advance in their casting skills they move on to another level, another day."

"Which one are we in?" I asked.

"We," he gestured to the rest of the cousins, "are in the advanced class. You, however, were probably assigned this day to just watch and learn. There's no sense in sticking you in a class with the second graders - Crafty Casters as they're called - when you'll probably pick up skills faster with us."

"Ah," I mumbled. "The advanced class…"

Oscar, who stood nearby, took this as a sign of nervousness and wrapped his arm around my shoulder protectively. "Don't worry, we'll keep you safe."

Actually, I wasn't concerned at all, even though admittedly I should have been. Instead my interest was piqued as to whether Jameson had made it this far in his casting skills.

As it turned out, he had.

I heard scuffling behind me and pivoted just as the Caldwells emerged from the shadowy hallway. I caught sight of Jameson instantly and had to consciously subdue the excitement that ran through me. I also noticed that his eyes quickly examined the courtyard until they landed on me. Then, very briefly, a slight smile lifted his lips.

The courtyard fell silent as the Caldwells made their way to the opposite side from us, fusing with another group of students, while the rest observed both families warily.

Apparently, the Weatherfords and Caldwells had clashed at this school, too.

An elderly woman came through a door then and stopped in the center of the students. She looked Haitian, petite, with thick braids wound up and piled on her head and an orange patterned dress that hung to her ankles.

When she spoke, there was an authority in her voice that, despite her size, gave you the impression not to test her.

"I am Ms. Veilleux, the head of this school. Because of the student number this year, we will separate the class in two."

Although no grumbles escaped from the students, there was an immediate air of surprise. They stood a little straighter, their attention more focused.

"The attendance list is posted on my door. I will give you the next five minutes to review it and to find your respective room. There will be no transfers, no exceptions." With that, she returned through the door where she'd come as the students filtered toward the paper hammered to it.

The Caldwells steered clear of us as the students gathered and we searched for our names.

I found an A next to mine and was about to exit the crowd when a cluster of names drew my attention. The Caldwells. They were bundled into one group - Group A. The same one as me.

We were to meet in the room on the opposite side of the courtyard, well away from the other part of the class.

Instinctually, I straightened my posture, tilted my chin up, and strolled through the crowd. If I was going to face them, I would do it with a show of confidence.

My cousins were waiting for me in the center of the courtyard, where I stopped to ask, "Which group are you in?"

They all replied at once, casually, some with a shrug - "B".

I nodded slowly. "I'm not."

Eyebrows rose as they stepped forward.

"That must be a mistake," Estelle suggested.

"We should tell-" Nolan was saying before being cut off.

"It's no mistake." Ms. Veilleux had returned, standing off to the side where no one had noticed her. She had her hands clasped in front of her as if she'd been calmly waiting for this reaction from my cousins.

"Jocelyn will remain in the group assigned." She paused to look each of us in the eye, seeming to tempt us into a dispute. Apparently, my cousins came to the same conclusion as I had. She wasn't going to budge. When she received no response, she prompted, "Lessons will begin now."

I exchanged looks of suspicion with my cousins but we followed the instructions given and headed for our respective classrooms. As I approached the door, I intentionally straightened my back even further. If I was going to spend the next couple of hours in a room with my enemies, I wouldn't be showing any fear of it.

Then I entered the classroom with them directly behind me.

The room was simple with only small wooden tables set against each wall. The ceiling was low and the floorboards had gaps in them big enough to see the dirt below. They groaned as weight was unevenly distributed on them, an eerie sound in the nearly silent room. A muskiness filled my nose which, oddly enough, gave me a feeling of comfort, something I appreciated with my enemies at my back.

The students stood on the perimeter, against the wall, after stashing their canvas bags on the tables. I did the same, keeping my attention partly on the other students and partly on Jameson.

He crossed the room and dropped his bag on the table and then stepped up beside me. At first, I was flattered. Then I noticed Charlotte, the curt girl who'd given Jameson and me such a hard time in the school hallway, was standing just to his right. He had positioned himself between the two of us, standing so close to me that our arms nearly swept against one another. My stomach, in reaction, did flip flops and it took all my will not to look at him. I was absolutely certain he felt the same when the tension between us rose and I heard his breathing catch as our elbows accidentally came in contact. Unexpectedly, he kept his arm in place for longer than would be considered appropriate and I debated with myself on whether to break contact. He was a Caldwell, a fact I couldn't deny - and I was surrounded by them. Another fact I wished weren't the case. With both of our breaths staggered and our attention limited to that spot on our skin where we were making contact, at that moment nothing else existed. There was no classroom, no students, no teacher. We weren't standing in an aged building surrounded by wood walls. We were alone in our own world. Only when Charlotte began snapping her fingers in front of his nose did he pull away.

The remaining Caldwells were scattered, their agate family stones glinting in the faint light, making me feel surrounded.

The last of the students filed in before a squat woman with gray hair wound in a loose bun and Victorian-style clothing moved from a dark corner to the center of the room.

"For those of you who don't know…" said the woman, pausing to stare at me. "Jocelyn Weatherford, to be precise, my name is Ms. Boudreaux."

I understood the hidden meaning within her message immediately. I was the only new student. Terrific.

"What the rest of you may not know is this…" she continued on. "Why are you here?"

A slender girl in the corner raised her hand and waited for a nod from Ms. Boudreaux before answering. "For spell-casting lessons."

"No," Ms. Boudreaux snapped.

"To advance in the art of magic," offered a boy with a narrow, curved nose reminding me of a beak.

"Again…no." She eyed us, waiting for an answer. "You are here to learn to protect yourself - and others. Injury – Disease – Age - Impairments - Death. How do we defeat these? By breaking curses, by casting protection. Now, " she ambled in a circle just outside the reach of her students, thankfully paying me no more special attention. "Let's assess what we have to work with, shall we? You may use your family stone or tools from your school supplies. And who wants to go first? You and you." She pointed to the girl and boy who had spoken up earlier. "Into the middle of the room."

Their earlier inspiration to impress Ms. Boudreaux apparently disappeared with her request because this time they reluctantly stepped forward with frowns.

"Miranda, you will be Andrew's attacker," Ms. Boudreaux instructed and then stepped back to allow them space.

Neither of the opponents sought out a stone from their canvas bags so I figured they'd be using their family stones. This, I thought, was going to be interesting. How dangerous could a stone be? It might leave a welt if pitched hard enough at their opponent, but stones just didn't sound particularly threatening to me.

Of course, I would be proven wrong, and come away with a new found respect for them after this lesson.

I was so immersed in my thoughts while attempting to hold back my laughter that I almost didn't hear the whisper sent my way. It was terse and somehow I knew it was meant for me.

"I hope I get you."

Glancing in the direction it had come, I saw Charlotte leaned forward in order to better peer around Jameson at me, again her eyes narrowed.

"You'd regret it," I replied in a hushed tone so Ms. Boudreaux wouldn't overhear.

At my retort, Jameson's lips curled up in an almost undetectable smile.

Not wanting her to get the best of me, I said, "I'm told I have impressive abilities." And for a final stab, I added, "Gifts as your mother would call them."

Her eyes darted to Jameson, the only person who could have relayed that fact. His smile was gone as he ignored her gaze.

"You don't know how to use them, Jocelyn," she sneered back. "You're no more a threat than a fly on the wall."

Any retort at this point may backfire, I knew. It would sound defensive, weak. So, instead of giving her the satisfaction in believing she'd won this spat, that I was cowering to her, I countered with the next best approach.

Meeting her eyes, my lips lifted in to a bold and arrogant smirk, one that conveyed her words meant nothing to me, that I see her as harmless as a fly on the wall.

She seethed and snapped her head back to the front of the room. I casually turned my attention from her only to catch sight of Jameson's head rotating in my direction. He was holding down a grin, which I returned. Then, as if I needed further confirmation that he'd supported me in that exchange, he winked at me, congratulatory and admiring.

I wasn't going to deny it. It felt good to have his support, even if we were supposed to be rivals.

Grinning, I gave my attention to Miranda and Andrew, although strangely neither of them had moved or made a sound. They remained, staring at each other, less than a foot apart.

Then, leisurely, Miranda closed her eyes, her fingers uncurling around whatever it was that she held in her hand. With her palm exposed, it revealed a vividly colored turquoise stone in the center of it. Appearing so tiny and insignificant, I watched curiously for that little object to do something, anything.

Miranda followed this with a quiet muttering. "Incantatio frigus incantatores."

It was Latin. My mother had tried to force the language down my throat several summers ago but it never stuck. Still, I could understand one word: cold.

To my astonishment Andrew's arms immediately came up to wrap around his body. His torso began to shake uncontrollably. His teeth began to chatter as he sucked in air between lips that were quickly turning blue. He was already bent at the waist, attempting to harness as much heat from his own body as possible, by the time Ms. Boudreaux stepped in.

"Nice job, Miranda." She stepped forward just as Andrew's teeth quieted and his lips returned to a more normal beige. "And what technique did you use?" she inquired.

"Elemental. I chilled the air around him."

"Excellent," she replied before acknowledging Andrew. "Clearly your protection did not work. We'll need to practice it."

He nodded before eagerly hurrying back to his spot along the wall. Miranda took her time returning to the lineup; clearly enjoying the fact she'd won that sparring match.

Now, I was impressed. Whether that affect came from a stone or otherwise, the potency of it couldn't be refuted.

"Next," Ms. Boudreaux suddenly called out, requesting more volunteers. "No one? Shall I continue selecting you then?" Without waiting for an answer, she called out another name, waiting for that person to come forward. When the person didn't move, she called it again, this time using her last name.

"Jocelyn Weatherford."

"Me?" I asked, dumbfounded. I was only supposed to observe.

"Into the center," replied Ms. Boudreaux. "You will be the defender."

I moved forward, recalling what Jameson had said about this teacher. She liked to test the limits of propriety. Clearly, she was doing it now.

"You understand that I've had no formal training," I mentioned.

"I do," she replied casually, not even bothering to look at me. "Elementary or otherwise, everyone has a skill level. Use yours to the best of your ability."

By this point, Charlotte was nearly jumping up and down with her hand in the air, desperate to be selected as my opponent. Ms. Boudreaux moved passed her, though, selecting the largest boy in the class.

As he stepped up to meet me, he had to duck to avoid the ceiling beams and, when he stopped in front of me, I noted how his arms were so broad they didn't lie against his body but instead bowed outward.

My concern was growing now. Not only had I boasted about my skills to Charlotte, this boy was a mammoth in comparison to me. How was I ever going to spar with him?

I hadn't chosen a stone from my canvas bag – there was no need for it. I didn't know what any of them could do or how to use them. Instead, I looked down at my left wrist where the white bracelet was clasped. In it was my family's stone.

I had little hope it could do much more than glint off the lights.

"Emery," said the boy, extending his hand into my view. This eased me a bit. If he was offering his hand to me I figured he would be friendly, sympathetic to my being new to the class. His next comment dispelled that illusion. "I don't go easy in sparring."

I laughed through my nose, sarcastically, and shook his hand. I was getting the instinct that Ms. Boudreaux already knew this.

"Begin," came her voice, commanding, unwavering.

Emery didn't close his eyes, though it was fairly clear that he didn't need to. He had a solid grasp of his skills and didn't require the extra method of focus. He didn't hold his stone in his hand either. His family stone, a golden rutilated quartz known to affect the respiratory system, hung from his neck on a silver chain. I noticed with irony that it did glint in the light.

I waited, uncomfortable beneath his stare, Jameson's stare, the entire class.

The worst part was that I didn't know what to wait for, having no idea how he might attack. I even paid special attention to the temperature until I started to feel silly.

Having reached the end of my patience, I made a demand that I'd quickly regret.

"Well, come on already," I grumbled. "Let's get on with it."

A few of the students snickered at my blatant attempt to be the instigator until Ms. Boudreaux shushed them.

Emery then spoke in a chilling whisper: "Incantatio clausa faucibus."

Faucibus…faucibus…Half my mind raced to translate it, the other half harangued me for not paying more attention to my mother's Latin quizzes.

Then the word came to me.

Throat.

And that was when I begin to feel it. A pressure at the front of my throat. Gradually worsening, the pressure reached around to the back of my neck until it felt as if hands were fitted around my throat, squeezing closed. On impulse, I made the effort to remove them but my fingers grabbed only air. Quickly, just before my airway was blocked entirely, I drew in a breath, searching for something to stop the sensation.

The pressure tightened.

I made an attempt to draw in air, felt my chest cave in, felt my lungs react, no air entered. My throat remained closed.

My mind raced for an answer, anything that might stop Emery's attack, and it was this effort that I believe distracted me from entirely seeing what happened next.

A commotion started to my left, bodies shuffled to the side though in no particular order. They seemed to be avoiding something. The sound of whatever it was that hit the wall there still resounded through the room, rattling the floorboards and shaking the entire structure we were in.

Then I could breathe again, recognizing this while drawing in a labored, hoarse gulp. Arching my neck back, I took another deep breath, this one filling my lungs with cool, delicious air. I took several more of them while the room steadied.

Regaining my awareness, I looked to my left, curious what had occurred there in the midst of my sparring match. Maybe another one broke out? I wondered.

I couldn't have been more wrong.

I found my opponent there slumped against the wall. His limbs sprawled out, his head wobbling, eyes blinking to recover his sight. The movement I'd seen in that direction had been from the other students dodging Emery's body as it had been flung toward them.

Unable to understand how he'd gotten there, I searched for the reason. Only then did I realize that no one was staring at me any longer. All heads were turned in the opposite direction, to where I'd been standing before entering the circle of students.

I followed their concentration to where Jameson was poised in a lunge. His right arm was extended, his palm facing me. No…facing Emery. His other hand clutched Charlotte's arm, channeling her ability.

Then I pieced together what had happened…

Jameson had just stepped in and defended me.

6. THE PLEA

He hadn't planned it.

That much I was certain of as Jameson rocked back to a standing position and released Charlotte's arm. Yet, he retained his firm stance, his head tilted up defiantly, his expression taut and unyielding.

While I was still processing all that took place, I was certain of two things. What he'd done was by instinct and he had no regrets for it.

When his eyes locked with mine they stayed there briefly, only to confirm that I was breathing again, before moving down my body to ensure I hadn't endured any other injury.

Only after he was confident I was safe did his expression loosen.

Charlotte remained at her brother's side but with the same amazed and disgusted expression the rest of the class held.

It was obvious this had never taken place before. I was fairly confident no one had stepped in to defend another during a sparring match before and I was absolutely certain that a Caldwell had never protected a Weatherford.

These insights, however, were discarded immediately as the room erupted.

I started toward Emery, concerned about what injuries he might have sustained. Ms. Boudreaux brushed by me to reach him first, an herbal remedy already in her hand. She stooped and tucked it under his nose until he reacted to it with a shudder.

In the midst of the commotion, as I watched Emery's eyelids flutter, I reacted with the only solution I could offer.

"I'm a healer," I said in a shallow, hushed breath. And then my mouth snapped shut, realizing what I'd just done. I'd made an announcement that the class had just heard, and about which I wasn't entirely certain of…and I was furious at myself for it.

Several heads turned and once again I felt in the spotlight but it was Ms. Boudreaux who reacted. She yanked me forward and down to a crouched position, giving me the approval to work on him.

Completely uncertain of what I was doing and irate with myself for having proposed my assistance in the first place, I hesitated. Emery's eyelids fluttered and without another thought I placed my hand on him.

"Incantatio sana," Ms. Boudreaux instructed.

While I'd never spoken this particular phrase before, or any really, and the objects I'd touched had still healed, I figured it couldn't hurt.

"Incantatio sana," I whispered hastily.

There was no movement from Emery other than his fluttering lids.

"Incantatio sana," I repeated more firmly, more loudly. "Incantatio sana."

Emery's eyes settled, closed momentarily, and then reopened. His mouth twisted upward in a half-smile before he drew in a breath. Then, in the silence, his voice gruff, he asked, "Well? Did I win?"

"No," I replied flatly.

Only then did Ms. Boudreaux relax, rolling back to an upright sit. A few students laughed and stepped away, the incident over now. I stood, drew in a deep breath, and headed back to the edge of the room where I had been before the sparring session.

Now I was the one in the flustered state. I had just openly acknowledged that I had healing capabilities and they had just been demonstrated on my opponent. How could that be, I thought. Then I surmised that there was really only one conclusion. He had already been on his way to recovery. I had nothing to do with it other than placing my hands on him and speaking a quirky phrase at the opportune time.

Somehow, this realization made me feel better.

Jameson still stood where he'd been, his stance still readied. It looked like he'd take on the entire class if needed.

Emery didn't seem to take any offense though.

Whatever Ms. Boudreaux had done, it worked. By the time he was on his feet, he clapped his hands readily and belted, "Who's next?"

He even argued with those insisting he sit the next one out. That took place as Ms. Boudreaux wiggled a finger at Jameson, beckoning him to the corner of the room.

Clearly, he was going to be punished which made me wonder what that meant in a school like this one. Although I tried to listen without making it obvious, she kept her voice low and what I deduced from the conversation wasn't much. When he collected his canvas bag and left the room, I figured he was heading for the principal's office, or whatever the equivalent was here.

The sparring lesson resumed but not without stares from the Caldwells. I figured they were each planning a different end to my demise. To take my mind off it, I focused on learning as much as I could, picking up a few spell incantations and learning how a voodoo doll and a few more stones could be used.

Jameson still hadn't returned by the end of the two-hour class, which made me start to wonder if he'd been expelled from it, a thought that made me feel guilty even though I had been a bystander during the incident. He'd been defending me, and if I were honest with myself I'd have to admit I was flattered. Eventually, Ms. Boudreaux would have stopped Emery but Jameson couldn't wait that long, he couldn't bear to see me in pain. I knew this for certain without him having to tell me.

For this reason, I sought him out after class was dismissed. While the rest of the students left through the archway toward the street, my direction took me toward the only other lit window in the courtyard.

But I didn't get very far.

I found Alison was suddenly in my way.

How she'd gotten around me without my noticing was actually remarkable. Even in the darkness, I should have seen some movement, along the walkway to my left or around the planter to my right. There had been none. I made a mental note that she had the ability, the gift to move fast and without sound.

Her glare conveyed her thoughts adequately but she insisted on voicing them. "You've done enough. Leave him alone."

"You're blocking me. Get out of my way," I demanded, making an effort to move around her. She didn't allow it.

Then Charlotte was beside her, forming another human wall between Jameson and me.

"You heard her," she said, the anger visible in her as well.

Then the Caldwell boys appeared on both sides of the girls, coming around me from both sides.

I scanned the line, seeing no genial expressions.

"You don't scare me," I stated. "None of you do."

"Let's test that theory, shall we?" Charlotte hissed, a smirk rising up, already stepping forward.

"Let's not," came Estelle's voice behind me.

I rotated and noticed my cousins had lined up beside me. This was getting out of hand.

"All right. All right," I said, holding up my hands. I didn't want to see a fight break out over something that could be said to Jameson in private during class tomorrow. More importantly, I needed to get my family out of here. If Jameson appeared, that would definitely upset the delicate balance we'd reached.

Slowly, as one would in the presence of a snake, I moved to the side, toward the archway. Thankfully, my cousins followed.

With the exit in sight, it appeared that disaster had been avoided...that was until I heard my name.

"Jocelyn, Jameson called out.

A simple word, but what he didn't realize was that with everyone's nerves flared and tensions heightened, he'd just set the fire to a brewing conflict.

Suddenly, I found Vinnia and Nolan suspended above my head, their legs curled behind them, their arms at their sides, readied for whatever might come.

My jaw fell and I believe a sigh was released but I couldn't be sure. I was watching their feet dangle over my head.

Then Charlotte and Alison were in the air, hovering at the same height as my cousins. Apparently, they have the same ability, I thought, feeling surreal as I watched it.

Then there was scuffling, mumbles as those on the ground took their positions, poising themselves for the coming attack.

A line of defense formed on both sides, in the air and on the ground, all five of my cousins pairing up with all five of the Caldwells.

Shouting began, voices rising over each other so that words were obscured in one long, intermingled utterance.

Jameson, stunned by the abrupt, unexplainable conflict rushed in to the center of it, crossing the courtyard in only a few lunges. He came directly for me, swerving and barely missing Oscar's effort to seize him. While it seemed from every aspect that he was narrowing his assault on me, my attention was locked on his expression, one that no one had the vantage point to see but me.

He wasn't attacking. He was coming to my aid, again.

But he never reached me.

I watched in horrified amazement as the bodies of each Caldwell was slammed backwards, their limbs flailing out in front of them, as if they'd been hit by an explosion. My cousins did the same, ending up on the other side of the courtyard, their feet dangling just above my head. Although no one appeared to be hurt, they were clearly seething with anger, mostly at the opposite family. Jameson was the exception. He hung in the air, patiently waiting to be released, his focus flickering between me and his siblings.

He was still on alert.

With bodies cleared from the center and hanging throughout the air, it revealed the two women just beneath the eaves, standing directly across from me.

Ms. Veilleux placed a calm hand on Ms. Boudreaux's arm, silently telling her to remain where she was, before moving out to the center of the conflict.

I thought at first that she was strolling but noticed her feet never actually touched the cobblestones. She stopped directly between us and the Caldwells before settling to the ground.

She spoke serenely with a melody to her voice that contradicted the words she chose. "You have now threatened your acceptance into this school." She paused to allow that message to sink in. "This school dates back to

1720. It is a place that has trained some of the most powerful casters to ever exist. We have offered our students the knowledge and skills required to protect them within the boundaries of our world." She fell silent, taking time to watch for her audience's reaction at her next statement. "Never did we intend our lessons to be exercised in combat within the sanctity of our school." This summoned guilty, downcast eyes from nearly everyone in the group. Jameson and I were the exception. Our eyes met and held each other.

"This is a place of learning, a place to test your abilities, to improve upon them. It is here that I learned the art of levitation, as you well can see." Her hand gestured to those still hanging in the air and I wondered how many others had this same ability. I certainly didn't. "This school is a place to seek refuge, wisdom, enlightenment. It is not a battlefield. Do not turn it in to one." Her next words were a demand and not a request. "You will not fail in this effort."

A few of the Caldwell's exchanged looks of doubt and I wondered if the same nonverbal message was being communicated between those above my head.

As if Ms. Veilleux anticipated this reaction, she chose that moment to render their punishment. "This will be the final conflict between your families. You will learn to appreciate each other, to accept one another or you will suffer a fate worse than any I could deliver." She withdrew a piece of parchment paper in which words had been scribbled in ink and held it up. "You have earned the attention of The Sevens and they have responded with a missive. It states any further altercations between the Caldwells and the Weatherfords, on these premises or any other, will result in protective services. I do not want this. You do not want this." Her voice dropped then, from the placating softness to an unquestionable command. "Coexistence…is not a choice."

With that, she spun on her heel and marched back passed Ms. Boudreaux, who trailed her inside the office and closed the door behind them. Those hovering were slowly lowered to the ground, no one daring to say a word.

With the Weatherfords closest to the archway, we collected our canvas bags previously dropped randomly around the courtyard in our haste to prepare for the conflict. The Caldwells watched, motionless and silent, and then did the same before following us out to the street. Although they waited before we'd reached the end of the tunnel before entering it.

I noted how both families appeared deflated, the fight leaked from them after Ms. Veilleux's chastising. I had a strong feeling it was also because of The Seven's threat. Spencer was deep in thought while driving back to the house and I didn't think disturbing him with annoying questions about The Sevens or how to levitate would help.

But my notion was confirmed back at the house.

When we entered the kitchen, jambalaya, comfort food I noticed, was waiting for us at a long wooden table spanning the length of the room. Miss Mabelle had also prepared an abundance of desserts, from various cakes to soufflés to bread pudding of all types. Miss Mabelle had been busy, it seemed.

With Aunt Lizzy at an evening meeting, which I learned was common due to her many volunteer duties, there would be no formal dining this time. And we took advantage of it. Oscar swung his chair around so that he ate over the back of it. Estelle plated dessert first. Vinnia ate on the counter, her feet tapping the cabinet below. Nolan leaned his chair back against the counter and ate from the plate in his lap. I stood across from Vinnia, leaning against the counter there, watching my cousins reminisce about the altercation. They were enjoying it so much, I couldn't help but come to the judgment that my cousins not only liked to fight, they invited it.

As I watched them, I thought about Jameson and wondered if the Caldwells were engaged in a celebration, too.

Estelle chuckled as she slid a piece of chocolate cake with purple frosting onto her plate, a slice I knew she'd chosen for the color. "Did you see Charlotte's face? Her nostrils were flaring. It was perfect."

Nolan shook his head, a broad grin admitting his enjoyment in taking part in the fight. "And Dillon…I think he just learned that the Weatherford's don't put up with harassment."

"Good," said Spencer, his mouth stuffed with mashed potatoes.

Oscar, however, sat quietly chewing, his head bowed in thought.

Noticing it too, Nolan elbowed him. "You all right?"

"Huh," he looked up, his eyes glassed over. "Sure, I just…"

The room fell silent as they waited to instantly refute whatever was dampening his good spirits.

"I think it's important to celebrate victories but I'm not convinced this was one of them."

"None of us got hurt," Nolan rebutted. "No one was even punished, Oscar."

He looked torn as to how to convey the concern pressing him. "That doesn't mean our actions didn't invite The Sevens here."

The very sound of that name brought a visible depression over the group.

"They don't even know about what happened tonight," Estelle challenged.

Oscar tilted his head at her, giving her an unspoken gesture to consider that statement further. "They have emissaries in this area and you know it. It's just a matter of time."

The fall of her head confirmed that she agreed.

"Like I said, I'm not sure this is a victory."

Spencer released a sigh, shaking his head. "The Sevens…"

"They have no right to impose rules on us," Vinnia fumed, her reaction again belying her innocent appearance. "Or to bring in their Vires."

"But they will," insisted Spencer. "If they see cause for it. I heard recently that they infiltrated - relocated as they called it - their Vires to villages near Chicago and St. Louis."

"What are Vires?" I inquired.

"Security forces," explained Oscar. "Vire means forces in Latin. Their army was established centuries ago when Latin was the predominant language."

I nodded, understanding. "Their Vires have been confiscating artifacts from Mr. Thibodeaux. He told us…me yesterday at his store." Thankfully, no one seemed to catch when I cited being with someone else, namely Jameson.

Instead, Nolan nodded. "Their Vires have been collecting weapons."

"They're overstepping their bounds," Oscar mused, his eyes downcast. "The Sevens must be getting more confident."

"Or more intimidated," Estelle pointed out.

"Don't you mean intimidating?" Nolan asked his tone edged with irony.

A brief silence hung over us, tension so thick it was almost a physical presence in the room. Then Oscar made a suggestion that wasn't immediately popular. "Maybe, for the sake of everyone, the entire province in fact, we should do our best to prevent any fights with the Caldwells for a while."

"We already do that," said Estelle sternly.

"They came at us tonight," Vinnia added.

He ignored her tone and replied evenly, "I know. I'm saying that if they should try to start something, anything at all, we need to prevent it. Turn and walk away, call for one of us, but do not engage and do not cast." He glanced around the room at the discouraged expressions. "It's either that or we start dealing with a bigger threat."

"The Vires," muttered Nolan.

Oscar shook his head. "Not their security forces...The Sevens themselves," he corrected the caution in his voice intentional.

His point, it seemed, had finally sunk in. After a brief, disgruntled silence, heads began to nod. They were downcast but at least they were nodding.

As I watched this entire discussion take place, a question lingered in the back of my mind. I felt a little guilty for it, in fact, because it directly went against what my cousins had all agreed to. I wondered if I'd ever get the chance to interact with Jameson again under these new conditions, beyond the brief hello before our classes started.

As if Estelle was on a similar train of thought, she frowned before disclosing, "Guess I won't be hexing them tonight then. Was going to conjure a boil mark."

Nolan beamed at her. "You were going to hex them?"

She shrugged, giving him a fleeting guilty smile.

"Don't," insisted Oscar.

"I just said that I wouldn't," she replied defensively.

With that irritation hanging in the air, we fell quiet, returning to our plates of half-eaten food.

"Sorry," Estelle mumbled a few minutes later, apologizing for her impertinence.

Oscar grinned to himself, conjuring a retort under his breath that sounded like "incantatio gurgite" and making a quick circular motion in the air. Although I couldn't understand him, I soon inferred his incantation from the result.

The water in the glass before her began to churn until a whirlpool was created to slosh over the edges and spray across Estelle's plate.

She gasped, offended but smiling. "Oh, that was bold. You do understand it calls for retaliation."

"Umhmm," he confirmed, grinning deeper.

"Neat magic-" I said and stopped myself. I'd almost added the word trick at the end and that would have been derogatory.

"Thanks," said Oscar proudly.

As if to prove my point, Spencer admired, "You really are getting better with the elements, Oscar."

"I've been practicing," he admitted a little sheepishly.

Oscars transgression temporarily forgotten, Estelle slid a jar of salt across the table toward him while suggesting, "Try this…"

And soon the kitchen erupted into an impromptu study session that lasted late into the night.

In fact, the next morning, when the scream resounded down the hallway outside my room, I wasn't certain if it was real or a figment of my foggy dream state. If the former, it didn't sound good.

I leapt out of bed, pulled on a white lace top, jeans, and a pair of brown leather boots while in a rush for the door.

Someone moved in a blur down the hallway, so rushed I couldn't make out who it was until I recognized the whimper.

Estelle landed with a thud against Aunt Lizzy's door just as the rest of the household was emerging from their rooms.

"Who's screa-" Spencer was in the midst of saying as he opened his door.

Then Estelle's arm was under his nose because Aunt Lizzy hadn't emerged yet. "Boil," she stated.

"Did you cast incorrectly?" asked Spencer. "Did it come back on us?

95

Oscar growled. "You said you wouldn't-"

"I didn't!" Estelle retorted, furious at their insinuations. "It was the Caldwells."

A second later, I heard synchronous gasps run down the hallway and found my cousins staring at their left forearm. On each one, a boil stretched the entire width, rising several inches off the skin surface.

Instinctually, I looked down at my own arm expecting to see the same affect. There was nothing. Where the boil should have been was my ever-present white bracelet.

Although I didn't entirely subscribe to all that I was seeing or learning in this new world I'd become privy to, always believing in the back of my mind that there was an explanation for it all, I felt relieved to be wearing my bracelet and thankful my mother had given it to me. But I realized it couldn't be my defense because my cousins wore their crystal quartz's as well and theirs didn't protect them. Then it occurred to me what it was that had prevented the affects of the Caldwell's hex. I was a healer, my body naturally prone to correct any ailments. Yet, the Caldwells had gotten beyond that layer of protection before, with the scar that had brought me here to New Orleans.

Finally, it struck me. The source of my protection wasn't my family stone or my inherent ability to heal.

It was Jameson.

"Apparently, they came up with the same hex," Spencer muttered, assessing his new ailment.

"We need something to counter it," said Vinnia flatly.

"Well, I have an ointment," I offered. "It should work."

I saw a few hopeful shrugs and then Oscar said, "Then let's try it."

After I administered the ointment on each of their boils, we finished getting ready for school, took muffins Miss Mabelle had left out for us, and headed out the door.

By the time we reached the main hallway, Estelle brushed up beside me and held out her arm, beaming. "Gone," she stated. "Completely."

I confirmed it with a quick glance. The skin was back to its smooth, flat surface.

"And then," she pulled up her other sleeve to show a minor wound. "I took some of the ointment you gave to me and rubbed it on this…" When I didn't respond to what she thought was an evident hint, she persisted, "And it's still there."

"I see that," I replied, still confused.

"It wasn't the ointment, Jocelyn. It was you administering it. It was your touch." She stated this so resolutely that it seemed hard to dispute. Then she drew my finger to the wound that still existed and rubbed it hastily against its surface before flipping her purple scarf over her shoulder and sauntered toward her next class.

I then headed for my classroom where I sat transfixed by several notions. First, she knew I fought the belief in my ability. Second, while I'd seen that ability materialize at times throughout my life, I'd snubbed it, never spending the time to develop it. The incident in which I helped Emery revive after being thrown against the wall was just another time I had to question my own suspicion. Third, if I were to acknowledge this ability in me than it would require me to accept the one belief I'd been denying since I'd been introduced to this world of witches. I would need to accept that it wasn't an act or a series of hoaxes, that it wasn't fabricated but that it was, in fact, real.

Staggered by these revelations, I entered my second class unprepared to handle seeing Jameson again. Not after what had happened last night between our families or this morning's hexing incident. So when my eyes landed on him, a flood of emotion rushed through me but only one settled in and took hold.

Anticipation.

He, on the other hand, looked tired. His eyes were dark and sunken, his shoulders drooped forward.

As I slipped into my seat, he spoke and I learned why.

"Your arm seems to be fine," he said, his voice croaky.

"It is," I replied. "My family's, however, weren't."

He nodded, slowly. "I couldn't stop theirs. Took me the whole night to prevent yours. Charlotte can be powerful."

My intuition had been correct. His ragged appearance and hoarse voice told me so. Realizing this, I had an immediate urge to comfort him.

"Thank you...for all of it," I said alluding to his protections against Emery's choking and his sister's cast.

Before I even realized it, I reached my hand across the aisle and placed it on his arm.

He drew in a quick breath and held it, reacting to my touch.

Certain I'd made him feel uncomfortable, I began to withdraw my hand when he placed his over mine, pressing it against his bicep. Now I was the one reacting to his touch. A heat coursed through me unlike any I'd ever experienced, tickling my stomach.

Jameson's chest expanded as he inhaled deeply and I knew he was having a similar reaction. I could feel his muscles flex beneath my fingers as he debated whether to keep his hand in place. Then, very slowly, his fingers curled beneath mine delicately lifting my hand away.

I'd crossed a boundary, touched an enemy who I shouldn't even be acknowledging. Something in me registered that he was stronger than me, acting ethically and removing my hand.

But he didn't release me. Instead his hand curled around mine until we were holding each other's hands.

Our eyes locked, questioning, exploring, wondering what might be behind the other's. I was stunned by what I found in his. We were asking the same questions. Do we want to pursue this? Is this right? Where will it lead?

His eyes held longing, a resonance of hope, possibility…

Then Shelby Taylor, a girl from my first period class, came up the aisle and we instantly released each other. It went without saying that neither of us had mentioned to our families that we shared a class together. Eventually it would become known, but we wanted to prevent it as long as possible. If anyone saw a single interaction between the two of us, positive or negative, the gossip would literally fly through the school hallways.

For the remainder of the hour, my entire concentration was on Jameson and when I caught him out of the corner of my eye casually looking my way a few times, I knew it was the same for him. I doubted that either one of us could have repeated one word of Ms. Wizner's lesson.

When the class ended and the room emptied, Jameson and I remained seated once again, eyes forward, bags on our table, hands folded over them. I wondered if this might become a tradition.

"So," he said, twisting in his seat the moment the last person was out the door. "You have a question for me."

I lifted my eyebrows in surprise. "And how did you know that? I know you're not a mind reader," I said reminding him that I knew of his channeling ability.

He chuckled. "I'm attentive."

"Ah, I'll have to remember that."

"I'm sure you will," he stated with a teasing grin. "Your question?"

"Right. Why did you call my name last night from across the courtyard?"

"The action that started the minor battle?" he mused lightheartedly.

I smiled at his irony. "Yes, that one."

Then his smile fell away and he seemed hesitant to answer.

I wondered if I shouldn't have asked and then realized it was perfectly legitimate. He'd called my name. I had a rightful interest in knowing why. For this reason, I remained quiet, waiting for his answer.

"I don't want you to think less of my family," he admitted and then added under his breath, "Although I doubt they have much margin to lose."

"Well, I can't promise that I won't judge them without knowing what it is you haven't told me," I admitted openly. "But I can commit to giving them a fair ruling based on what you do say."

He gave me a single, rigid nod. "So choose my words carefully."

"That would be wise."

"Fair enough. As you know, there isn't much trust between our families." We paused to both chuckle at his understatement. "The last time the Weatherfords met us in that particular courtyard, there was no one around to stop us and we...well, the fight destroyed the planters, broke several railings, you get the point." He cleared his throat uncomfortably before continuing. "So, when I saw my family lined up facing the Weatherfords it looked like the same scenario all over again. Only this time you were in the middle of it."

"So," I said slowly.

"So, it made me react."

"Why would my presence in that fight be any different? I'm still a Weatherford."

"You are," he agreed slowly, as if unwilling to disclose anything further.

Yet I persisted. "I don't understand," I said cautiously. "Why did my involvement concern you?"

He shook his head, his eyes searching mine for an answer. "I don't know. I've considered that you are new to our world and have no idea how to protect yourself. But you have your family for that. I've considered Olivia's belief - that we are fated lovers." His hesitancy in making that statement made me realize how much he actually believed it to be true. "But I'm not sure I have the same philosophy…The only thing I really am sure of, Jocelyn, is that I want to get to know you, your likes and dislikes, your beliefs, who you really are. Not just as a Weatherford, but you as a person."

There it was; his honest feelings hanging in the air between us. He was leaned over now, his elbows on his knees, his body halfway across the aisle, the scent of him surrounding us, like a blend of fresh air and sunshine.

Then Ms. Wizner entered the room, in a heated discussion with a student who appeared to be begging to be allowed out of her class.

Knowing we had no more time, he spoke low but in a rush. "I know you don't trust me. You have reason not to. I'm a Caldwell. But if you…if you give me a chance…"

I opened my mouth to answer but another student had already entered and was coming down Jameson's aisle toward us. By the time we'd stood, he had taken a seat directly in front of Jameson so there was no way to speak without him overhearing.

Jameson followed me out of the room and into a hallway that was far too busy still for an answer. Then the crowd of students rushing to their next class overtook us and I lost sight of him.

His plea still hung in my ears. Give me a chance. It competed with another plea running through my mind. It was an echo from Oscar's vow the night before. Turn and walk away.

It would have helped prevent inciting a volatile feud that simmered beneath a thin, delicate surface.

It would have been the prudent thing to do in a world of sinister, supernatural influence.

It would have been…

7. RETALIATION

The gift was wrapped in a big red bow, which was quickly removed in order to open its doors.

It was in the form of a blue, off road vehicle by the name Audi Q5. Spencer strolled its perimeter while articulating the nuances of my very first vehicle. With a turbocharged V6 engine, nimble performance, upgraded navigation, and heated seats, it was casual, sporty, and stylish. The vehicle was perfect for me, and the best birthday gift I'd ever received, late or otherwise.

The rest of my cousins sat inside during Spencer's tour, admiring the new addition to our lineup of sports cars.

"It'll be nice to have a vehicle in the family that doesn't scrape the speed bumps," said Oscar. Given his size, I wondered if that happened often.

"It'll be nice to have leg room," I commented, openly jesting with Spencer, whose vehicle's dashboard had been steadily wearing down the skin on my knee caps.

"Ouch," he retorted despite grinning through the open passenger window.

"It's one of the reasons we didn't select a sports car," admitted Aunt Lizzy. "You have your mother's legs."

I knew this, recalling how she'd always buy first class tickets to our holiday destinations simply for the leg room.

While Miss Mabelle and Aunt Lizzy both claimed to have picked it out, I had a feeling it was mostly Miss Mabelle with the insight that led them to this particular choice. Her assumptions of me so far had been unpredictably accurate.

The inspection of it over, someone suggested a quick ride around the Garden District. So I slipped into the front seat and started the engine. It purred.

With everyone piled in, we drove through the streets focused more on the vehicle than on where we were going - at least until I turned down a particular street.

"Not this one," Spencer shouted but it was too late.

I had turned the corner.

In reaction, I slowed only to be told to go faster.

"Why?" I asked, puzzled by their frenzy.

If they answered, I didn't hear them. I'd already found it myself.

In the driveway of one particular house, a peaceful, well kept, two-story that reminded me a lot of where I now lived, sat a row of luxury off-road vehicles, the same ones I'd seen a few Caldwells driving off the school parking lot. As if that weren't enough, the synchronous turn of my cousin's heads to the opposite side of the street was enough confirmation.

"The Caldwell house," I stated.

"Yes," said Estelle through clenched teeth, reminding me of someone who was getting a vaccination.

Painful or not, I had to keep driving passed the house. Turning at this point would make it obvious we were here. Just like my cousins, they parked in a cohesive line along the front of the house and they each drove a sporty vehicle.

I wasn't the only one to realize it either.

"They look so normal," Vinnia noted in her typical precise estimation of others after having been daring enough to look.

Estelle shook her head in astonishment. "I know."

"Haven't you seen it before?" I inquired, a little confused. "You must have done intel on your mortal enemies." I meant this humorously but no one laughed.

"We have," Oscar said tightly. "We know just about everything there is to know about each of them."

By this point, the house was behind us and, even though the joy of the ride ended at the sight of the Caldwell home, I kept driving, hoping they would disclose more. And they did.

"Their father is an investment banker, their mother volunteers like ours," said Oscar. "They're not around much so the kids were raised by their Haitian housekeeper, Miss…"

"Celia," Estelle filled in.

"Yes, the one who practices voodoo."

"Voodoo?" I said impulsively.

"That's right," Oscar said as if it were a common occurrence. "She's one of the most sought after in the city - next to Miss Mabelle."

It dawned on me that this was what the hanging skulls and countless candles were in her room. It should have concerned me, which would have been the logical reaction. But other than her surly attitude, which apparently was a core part of her personality and not solely directed at me, she'd done her best to fit things to my needs. It was what I imagined Miss Celia did for the Caldwells.

"They're wealthy," Oscar continued, drawing my attention back to him and returning the subject to the Caldwells. "But they rarely spend money, their cars being the exception. No big parties, no family vacations."

"No expensive toys," said Estelle. "You, Oscar, would never survive in that family."

"It's a good thing you're stuck with me than," he ribbed.

I turned on to our street then wondering if the Caldwells had the same bond, same camaraderie as my cousins.

When we reached the house we found that dinner was ready, something that I didn't know was gumbo until Spencer congratulated Miss Mabelle on it being her best dish. I had two servings, it was so good.

Afterwards, as Miss Mabelle cleaned the dishes, my cousins and I sat at the kitchen table with books assigned to us from the normal school. None of us touched them though. I had questions nagging me and this was my first opportunity to ask them.

"Vinnia," I said, keeping my voice low so I didn't disturb the others, even though I found out quickly they weren't actually dedicated to their studies. She looked up, inquisitive. "How do you...How do you fly?"

In jest, she lifted her shoulders in a shrug and the book in front of her rose in unison.

I gave her a frustrated look and she giggled. "I'm sorry. Couldn't resist... It's called levitation." She placed the pencil in her hand on the table and leaned back. "Back when witches were being burned at the stake here and in Europe, there were a lot of misconceptions about us. One, however, was correct. We are able to...fly, as you called it. We don't need a broomstick. And we aren't restricted to using it on All Hallows Eve or Halloween. The only limitation is that those of us who can do it are born with it. No one can learn to levitate, unfortunately."

I nodded. "Right. Everyone's born with their own unique abilities," I replied, recalling what Jameson had told me while buying school supplies.

"Exactly," said Vinnia. "Mother and I levitate. Estelle and Oscar manipulate elements. Well, Oscar to some extent," she teased and received a scowl for it. "Spencer and Nolan channel."

"But everyone has the aptitude to learn other skills," clarified Spencer. "You can learn to manipulate the elements or channel. But you'll never be as good at them as you are with your principal talent."

"That's right," said Vinnia. "You can learn to channel energy, thoughts, or knowledge of the future, commonly called intuition by those outside our world, but others will always be better at it than you." At the mention of channeling, I immediately thought of Jameson and a pang of excitement lit up my stomach.

"There are really only two abilities that cannot be learned," Vinnia continued to explain. "Levitation and-"

"Healing," said Estelle pointedly.

"Is that your talent?" asked Nolan.

I shrugged, refusing to vocalize it. I still wasn't entirely embracing the idea of me having a talent of any mystical sort.

"You still haven't accepted it yet, have you?" asked Estelle, observantly.

Not wanting to be refuted, I simply smiled back at her.

After a brief silence in which my cousins exchanged looks of concern, Miss Mabelle cleared her throat and said, "Goin' upstairs now. Keep it quiet or I'll be back down ta knock heads."

We said our goodnights and she left as Spencer stretched his legs out, laid his hands across his belly, and said, "But then, of course, there are The Sevens. They've been around so long that they have acquired special talents. They can transfer abilities or energy between them. While that may not sound so impressive, think of centuries of knowledge and practical exercise in leveraging energy to do as you wish and then think about transferring all that power in to a single person. It would make them virtually indestructible."

"Which is why they've lived for centuries," said Estelle.

As if I weren't amazed enough already, Vinnia added, "And if seven individuals were able to transfer those powers among one another, in part or as a whole, whenever one or more of them were at risk - that would make all of them virtually indestructible."

"For example, consider that most of us are not born able to levitate and are forever grounded. Each one of The Sevens can levitate."

"And channel…"

"And heal…"

"And manipulate the elements…"

"And they are experts in each one."

I now understood Mr. Thibodeaux's anxiety about The Sevens seeking the rope I had stored upstairs and how Ms. Roquette could be disabled from speaking for six months as punishment by The Sevens. The Sevens were impenetrable.

As the topic moved to something more lighthearted, like why Oscar's attempt to start a flame typically resulted in setting the object next to it on fire, a realization overcame me. I had entered a world that was just as dark as it was mystical. I appreciated the fact that my mother had removed me from it until I was prepared to learn to defend myself and that Nurse Carol had recognized this was the time to do it. If, of course, any of it were actually real.

Several charred remains later, Oscar gave up his attempt to control the flames he conjured, all of us holding back our laughter at his attempts, and we collected our school books and untouched assignments to head upstairs.

I slept well that night, even waking up early and venturing downstairs after hearing someone noisily clanging cookware together.

"Good Lord, Miss Lizzy. Why you always got ta be so loud?" Miss Mabelle's voice drifted around down the hall toward me.

"Jocelyn, you're up!"

"Hi, Aunt Lizzy," I said and then glanced in Miss Mabelle's direction, who sat on her stool in the corner again, cane leaning in its spot against her thigh. She tilted her head and looked up at me under her lashes as I asked, "Joyful as always this morning?"

She harrumphed and rolled her eyes in response.

"Can you get your cousins up too?" Aunt Lizzy asked in a rush around the kitchen, flour drawn across her cheek, her apron askew and dirtied with paste.

"Voice box broken, Miss Mabelle?" I asked, knowing full well that it wasn't. It was just getting more entertaining to tease her.

"Don't make me use it this monin', chil'," she replied snidely.

Smiling, I left the kitchen to wake the rest of the household.

"Mabelle, come help me with these fritters," I heard Aunt Lizzy behind me and then came Miss Mabelle's subsequent snap "I'm old n' tired!" But as I reached the stairs, Miss Mabelle was back to criticizing my aunt for not turning the fritters fast enough, which confirmed she did indeed lend a hand.

I knocked on everyone's bedroom door until I heard a reply and then found a phone to make a quick call to my friends in New York. They were in class, but I left a message to let them know everything was fine. Then I went to my room to get ready for school.

I was in a particularly energetic mood today and I knew exactly the reason. In my mind, pieces of my conversation with Jameson the day before came back to me. While his words were compelling, it was his actions that defined his intentions - the intensity of his translucent green eyes, the urgency in his tone, the lean of his body toward me. I was eager for today's class to start but first there was the obligatory dressing, breakfast, drive, and first class. Hoping it would pass quickly, and this would be an impossible feat, I went about changing my nightclothes to a sundress, knee-high boots, and lots of jewelry. This time, however, I kept the bracelets to my right hand only, leaving my mother's bracelet completely visible. Whereas before it was just a piece of jewelry, it was now becoming a source of pride, an unspoken acknowledgement that I was a Weatherford.

At breakfast, Aunt Lizzy proudly presented us with a platter of steaming fritters, all of varying degrees of burnt. I chose the closest one to me, not caring so much about the black. I didn't think anything could bring down my mood today. However, I was proven wrong when we reached the main hallway at school.

Jameson's locker, along with Charlotte's and Burke's, were located at the entrance so that they couldn't be missed when I stepped inside.

Right then, my happiness dissolved.

Charlotte rotated around, having closed her locker, to talk with Jameson when she saw us. Instantly, she stepped toward us, her lip curled in a glare.

"No," Jameson barked and held her back.

Bewildered, I watched as she attempted to shrug him off, her narrowed eyes still pinned on me and my cousins - but Jameson held on to her.

My cousins and I had stopped in the middle of the hallway at this point, preparing for an assault that seemed inevitable. Burke assisted Jameson in quelling Charlotte and almost dragging her back to the other side of the walkway.

"I wouldn't stick around if I were you," Jameson warned, still subduing his sister, his eyes on me, seeming to speak directly to me.

Leaving did seem like a good idea. Already a crowd was forming. So I headed down the hall with my cousins but not before I saw the cause of Charlotte's anger.

As she was spun around, her hair picked up and slid over her shoulder exposing the swollen red spots along the length of her neck. Hundreds of them. A fleeting glance at Burke, who was still restraining her, told me that he'd been afflicted, too. The rash had crept out from his hairline and across his temple. My eyes flitted to Jameson just before the crowd swallowed me and I breathed a sigh of relief when I didn't see any evident sign of the spots on him.

"That was you, Estelle. Wasn't it?" Oscar asked behind me.

"It was a good one," she said proudly. "Those voodoo dolls really do work!"

Oscar sighed loudly in frustration.

"What?" she countered. "They deserved it. Now they'll reconsider retaliating again."

"All you did was provoke them, Estelle," Oscar retorted.

"He's right," said Spencer. "Charlotte won't back down from that one."

"Ah, she can't do anything," Estelle brushed it off. Then she lowered her voice before supporting her statement. "It's forbidden to cast in public."

"She just might break that rule," Oscar warned, shaking his head while recalling Charlotte's reaction.

"And if she doesn't, expect something else in private," warned Vinnia.

Estelle released a loud exhale, evidently disagreeing with them, and disappeared through the door of her first class without a goodbye.

The conversation between my cousins lingered in my mind all through first period. There would be another retaliation, this time from the Caldwell's side. The disturbing fact was that I didn't really blame them. But I didn't blame Estelle either for retaliating. I saw both sides equally and as much as I was a Weatherford I felt like an outsider, unable to participate and helpless with any efforts toward prevention.

My mind spinning at how destructive this cycle of revenge could get, I entered my second period far more solemn than when I'd woken up this morning. My attitude was buoyed, however, at the sight of Jameson.

He was already at his desk and attentively watching the door. Dressed in jeans and a fitted black, long-sleeved shirt, and his hair falling over his forehead, I felt a burning sensation take hold of me.

A flicker of a smile lifted his face, accentuating his features, as I recognized that we were alone again in the room. As usual when no one else was nearby, the excitement grew around us, something similar to almost palpable stimulation, a questioning tease over who would speak first, what might be said, and what might be the response.

I slid into my seat keeping my eyes straight ahead. Somehow, I knew if I looked in his direction, the passion would increase. "Interesting morning…" I muttered to which I heard him chuckle.

"Jocelyn," he said quietly and I turned my head toward him. I was correct. The excitement intensified. What I also noticed was that when our eyes met, his breath caught just before saying, "You look great in that dress."

And the exhilaration escalated.

I never got the chance to thank him. Ms. Wizner and the rest of the class began filing through the door so Jameson swung his head forward, trying to appear as if we hadn't been talking.

Then Ms. Wizner's lecture began on the Battle of Baton Rouge and I gave my attention, partly to her and partly to Jameson's presence beside me. I noticed every movement, the scuff of his foot, the shift of his legs, the scratch of his pen against the textbook.

Throughout it, I thought about what he'd said. He'd complimented my dress but he'd also done something more distinct. By ignoring what had happened in the hallway between our two families, he was sending me a signal that he didn't want it to affect us. He was behaving exactly as he'd inferred the day before, as if we were two individuals who didn't have anything to lose, who didn't need to deal with feuding families, courtyard brawls or life and death risks. We were two average people awkward but interested when in sight of each other.

Near the end of class, I couldn't hold back any longer and I slowly twisted my ducked head toward him. He made the very same move proving that his focus had been on me too.

Ms. Wizner must have caught sight of us because she raised her voice. "...and the Caldwells and Weatherfords actually fought side-by-side during this pivotal battle, the battle to take New Orleans."

A few students snickered, recognizing that two of them sat in the classroom.

"Imagine that," Ms. Wizner went on. "It is believed this was the only time in history when both families united. Let's hope it will happen again someday."

She paused to stare each of us in the eye, confirming she'd acquired our attention before restarting her lecture. I did my best not to laugh at being singled out when I saw Jameson's shoulders tremble in a silent chuckle, too. I don't think Ms. Wizner had any idea how close her hope was to being met.

At the end of class she stayed back, delaying her traditional bathroom break, as she went about fiddling with her computer. Clearly, she was interested in ensuring an argument didn't break out between Jameson and me.

We collected our books and laptops slower than usual, biding time, but there was no avoiding it. She wasn't leaving.

Jameson must have come to the same conclusion because he walked down the aisle at the same time as I did. He stopped at the end to let me pass by as I headed for the door. In an effort to take one final look at him before our separation for the remainder of the day and through the weekend, I peeked over my shoulder expecting to say thank you.

He wasn't looking at me. He was preoccupied with his arm, which had been covered throughout the class. With the sleeve now shoved up, the rash was clearly visible; thousands of red, swollen dots ran from his wrist to his elbow.

I drew in a sharp breath and he quickly pulled his sleeve down again.

I opened my mouth to speak, to tell him how sorry I was, to ask if I could do anything, but his responding gesture said that I should forget it. It wasn't a big deal. It would pass.

Still, as we entered the hallway and went in opposite directions, I had the uncomfortable feeling this latest battle between our feuding families was about to get much worse.

8. THE HEALING

At dinner my fears were validated.

Midway through Miss Mabelle's shrimp gumbo, everyone's right hand went numb. All except for mine. We discovered this when a nearly simultaneous drop of all the spoons onto the table occurred.

Anyone not privy to the feud raging between the Caldwells and the Weatherfords might have thought my cousins had acquired a sudden and mysterious affliction. But it was evident to me, and I quickly set my spoon down, not wanting to have to explain why I was left untouched by this latest retaliation.

"The Caldwells," muttered Vinnia, slapping her limp hand against the table in an attempt to regain feeling. It didn't work and she resorted to an irritated sigh as she leaned back against her chair.

Vinnia lifted one of her shoulders in a leisurely shrug. "That's a good one," she commented, referring to the hex. Unencumbered, she'd already started eating again.

Unlike Vinnia, who had the aptitude to levitate her spoon, the rest of us ate our dinner with our left hand, me included as I played along. This, I learned, was not easy.

"How long do these last?" I asked, not certain I really wanted to know.

"They range. But for these little hexes, usually about a day," said Oscar, his hand askew as he brought his utensil to his lips.

"And the big ones?" I persisted.

"Big ones are permanent," Estelle replied stiffly.

I knew immediately what she meant. The big ones resulted in death.

By Sunday night, their hands began functioning again, but it was a slow process. In general, the weekend was long. Memories of Jameson crept into my head and each time my yearning to see him again would grow. His stunning translucent green eyes, his efforts to keep me out of harm's way, his flattering comments - all made me eager for Monday morning.

When second period did arrive and for the next two days, we stole glances at each other, hidden smiles, the intentional touch of our arms as we crossed in the aisles. Ms. Wizner made sure she remained in class at the end and was there at the start of it to prevent any issue from arising, which limited Jameson and me. It was ironic that her efforts were meant to prevent a fight when our intentions were the exact opposite.

In fact, it was the rest of our families who should have been kept apart. On Monday, the Caldwells were each seen with a limp and by Tuesday each of my cousins had swollen, enflamed ears. I didn't suffer from the reprisals and I knew it was Jameson I had to thank. That, however, didn't last long. The Caldwells must have realized at some point that Jameson was blocking their hexes because they changed tactics and came at me directly.

It started on Tuesday morning between third and fourth period. The hall was moderately busy so I didn't see her immediately, not until the chill ran up my spine and my skin began to prick from the coolness now present in the air. Instinctually, I wrapped my arms around my body and lifted my shoulders to unconsciously block my neck from the breeze that now ran through the hall. Then I realized no one else appeared to be affected.

That was when I saw Charlotte, half-covered by the corner of a set of lockers. She had her arms crossed, her chin down, and her eyes pinned on me. And her lips were moving rapidly. Although her words didn't carry across the noise in the hall, I knew which ones she was speaking in rapid succession.

Incantatio frigus incantatores.

It was the same cast Miranda had made against Andrew in evening class.

Furious, I fought back the urge to stop and curl against the cold as he had done and instead marched directly toward her.

Her lips moved faster.

Halfway there, her lips became a blur. She was trying to beat me before I reached her, but I wasn't going to allow it.

"I may not be able to cast yet but I can think of ways around that," I said. A traditional punch in the face would feel the most rewarding.

Charlotte concluded sometime before the gap between us closed that I could actually be serious and her lips stopped. Then she spun and fled through the students, putting as much distance between us as possible.

Almost instantly, the chill surrounding me was gone, her energy now focused on her attempt to avoid me. Despite this, I was on the verge of shouting that she'd better run when a teacher appeared in his doorway. Clearly, he'd heard my threat and I prepared myself for being reprimanded when he noticed that I was alone. His face confirmed he'd thought I was talking to myself and I was certain he made a mental note that the newest Weatherford in school might have a problem. I didn't pay him much attention though. I was watching Charlotte flee down the hallway.

From then on, the Caldwells stayed hidden while casting against me. I knew this because when the wind whipped around just me and the sprinklers suddenly rotated in my direction, they couldn't be seen.

I made the decision not to mention it, or any future attempts at me, to Jameson. Having a distinct feeling that if I was to inform him than it would cause conflict between him and his siblings. In turn, they would then take their anger out on me and my cousins and the entire situation would easily and rapidly escalate.

On Wednesday, as I entered the evening class, canvas bag of mystical supplies in hand, I wondered if it was ever going to end. They only cast when Jameson wasn't present so I figured evening class would keep me safe from stray spouts of water and drenching heat spells. But I couldn't be certain.

Ms. Boudreaux was already standing in the middle of the room, hands dropped before her and clasped together. She had a serene expression, but I didn't trust it. Jameson had said she was one of the professors to watch out for.

The Caldwells were already there, in a group, Jameson included. He stood across the room, more interested in me than in what his siblings were discussing.

Ms. Boudreaux spoke up when the last student had entered and the door was closed. "Combinations make you more powerful. Using multiple tools in your casting, for example, will bind the energies and magnify the results. Some casters won't work with less than three tools. For the next two hours, and each evening until our next class, you will practice using multiple tools. As always, use them without ill intent and cast only on inanimate objects. Do not affect your classmates or others. If you wish, you may pair up and benefit by using your tools collectively."

The second Ms. Boudreaux's instructions ended, Jameson was crossing the room toward me; his family, who he had his back to, were speechless and disgusted.

"Hi," he said softly.

"Hi…" I tried to sound casual but it was difficult beneath his family's stare.

"Don't worry about them," he said apparently already knowing they were watching. "I need a partner and so do you."

"I'll partner with you," Alison offered from behind him. She was now only a few feet away, having approached without us noticing.

Jameson's mouth closed and his eyes rolled up toward the ceiling in agitation. Without having to be told, I knew this was a showdown between siblings, a contest to determine who Jameson was most faithful to.

Alison's hands were on her hips, her head tilted to the side, a smirk planted on her petite face.

"Thanks, Alison," he said, spinning to face her. "I'm going to work with Jocelyn."

Very slowly, her smirk fell away and her eyes darkened.

Others in the class had stopped what they were doing now and started watching us.

"You're starting something," Jameson cautioned. "We all agreed that we would avoid what you are doing right now."

So, I thought, the Caldwells did discuss Ms. Veilleux's warning and they'd come to the same conclusion we had - that it would be best not to pick any more fights - in public at least.

"Turn around and walk away, remember?" Jameson said and my eyes shot up at him.

Those were the very same words Oscar had used. Once again, the similarities between the families amazed me.

"You are the one starting it," hissed Alison.

"Then I alone will handle it."

They stared at each other for several long seconds, testing who would admit defeat first. It was Alison, as she spun and marched back. Either because the scene was over now or because they didn't want to encourage it to continue, the Caldwells quickly went about selecting their tools for the class. Still, I wondered what retaliatory element hex awaited me in the future.

Interestingly, Ms. Boudreaux remained in the corner the entire quarrel, watching with curiosity.

Jameson had taken a stand, countered his family, and he'd done it for a Weatherford. That didn't go unnoticed. The rest of the class returned to what they were doing but not without shocked, tense expressions or commenting about it in a whisper.

"So..." He clapped his hands softly. "Which tools should we use first?"

"Are you sure you're all right with partnering?" I whispered with a lean forward.

He smiled and leaned in to meet me, whispering in the same manner, "Yes." He was downplaying what had just happened but I knew he'd face criticism for it from his family. "Maybe we should start with the basics," he suggested, already skirting me to drop his supplies on the table behind me.

Two students were already using the table, Kendra and Ian. They looked up skeptically first at the Weatherford, me, and then at the Caldwell, him, before going back to assessing their combined supplies. Seeing them react made me wonder if Jameson and I would be ostracized by others, too, and then I deduced they were only concerned about being too close to a fight if one should break out.

"Mind if we use this table too?" Jameson asked.

"We promise not to cast on each other," I added referencing our feuding predicament.

Kendra actually smiled. And Ian retorted with a smile, "Or us, right?"

"Can't promise that. Sorry," I said playfully.

That started a whole banter of teasing insults between the four of us and before long I'd forgotten that the rest of the Caldwells were probably glaring at my back.

By the time our humorous sarcasm dissipated, Jameson and I had laid out our tools across the table, grouping them by type.

"Incantatio adolebit," Jameson said under his breath, quickly, as if he didn't think it would actually work.

My guess turned out to be correct because when one of the candle's wicks suddenly lit he stood back smugly, gesturing proudly toward it.

"I've been practicing that." His excited declaration drew laughs from Kendra and Ian, both of whom had advanced far enough in their cast that each of their candles was already lit.

"Very nice," I commented, impressed. I certainly couldn't do that.

"Now you try," he insisted.

I shrugged, knowing already that I'd fail since I had no idea what sparked his candle in the first place.

To appear as if I was making a good attempt at it, I bent down and stared at another, unlit, candle. "Incantatio adolebit," I said quietly.

Nothing happened, of course.

"You're worse than me," Jameson said with a grin.

"Thanks…"

"Let's move on. You might find something that works better for you," he said hopeful.

We tried simple casts until the class was almost over, laughing at my failed attempts.

At the end, I stood back in a huff. "Jameson, this is the advanced class," I reminded him. "You all have been practicing for years. You know the tricks."

He sighed. "They're not tricks, Jocelyn."

"Casts," I corrected hastily. "Casts, I meant."

He thought for a moment, his lips curling in and accentuating the scar above his lip. I was temporarily mesmerized by its rugged appeal until he started talking again.

"Will you try something with me?" he asked tenuously, unsure of my answer.

I shrugged. "What have we got to lose?"

"Yes, good point," he said through a laugh before growing serious again. "I'm wondering if we would have any progress if you were to use a skill you have already tapped. Your primary one." He paused and waited for me to speak. "Which is…" he prompted.

"Oh, I'm sorry." I never thought of myself as having a primary skill so I was puzzled for a second. "Uh, my family says it's healing."

He blinked at me, surprised. "Really?"

"Yes. Why?"

"That's…That's a very unique gift."

It still didn't mean much to me though.

I had no premonition that my opinion of it would change within the next few minutes.

"Well, we'll need something to heal." He glanced around the room and then leaned in to whisper, "Think anyone will admit to a disease?"

I belted out a laugh, receiving a few looks from the others. Dropping my voice to a whisper, I replied emphatically, "No."

Containing our amusement, we thought further.

"We can't use anything you have," he muttered.

"No, I have nothing to cure."

He shook his head. "You wouldn't. Healers automatically heal themselves."

It dawned on me then that this must be the reason why I've never been sick, never had a blemish, never suffered any ailments, until the scar. The scar - which I thought had been healed by Nurse Carol's ointment. If Jameson was correct, she would have given me the ointment as a placebo when it was me healing the scar all along. And I discerned immediately why she would have kept this from me. Because she knew that had she'd told me the truth, I wouldn't have believed her.

In the recesses of my mind I quickly pieced something together. Glancing at the other Caldwells, I dropped my voice so only Jameson could hear me. "So why do you block your family's hexes against me than?"

He nodded absentmindedly, only half of his attention on my question and the other half on finding a test case. "Healers aren't immune to hexes. They're just capable of healing once they're afflicted by one." What he didn't say specifically, but what I understood through his answer, was that he blocked the hexes because he didn't want me to suffer for even a second.

He shrugged then, seeming to concede. "I guess it'll have to be me."

He pulled up his shirt sleeve, on the same arm where I'd seen his rash, and revealed that the affects of it were still visible. Only now there were fewer spots and they had transformed into pink circles.

"Jameson," I breathed. "I'm so sorry." I didn't want to bring it up but the rash looked incredibly painful. And it had lasted longer than Charlotte's hex which told me that Estelle was slightly more powerful - if, of course, it wasn't just a rash he picked up somewhere.

He shrugged it off. "It's healing...You're just going to speed it up."

"I am?" I asked, doubtful.

He was undeterred. "The incantation you'll want to use is - incantatio sana."

I nodded, feeling miserable already for failing, and I hadn't even started.

Nonetheless, I closed my eyes and repeated with authority, "Incantatio sana."

After hearing no sound from Jameson, I repeated it again…and again…and again.

"Stop," he said and I opened my eyes to find him shaking his head. "You need to focus. And keep your eyes open. Your energy will direct to wherever it is you're looking."

"Got it."

I was about to recite the incantation again when he interrupted my concentration.

"Think…Think of a child who needs surgery. He's scared. He's hurting. He's floating in and out of consciousness because of the pain. He's sick from the drugs they've given him. His body is shaking from the stress. He's vulnerable, helpless…"

As Jameson continued describing the example, I sensed desperation, a need to help the child, this fictitious child. And then something stirred in me, something deep and powerful, something that had been locked inside, sleeping, but was now rousing.

It was a palpable thing, stretching, expanding, and then suddenly coursing its way up until I felt it in my chest, pressing at my insides. Then it was emitting from my torso, a strong, unstoppable flow of energy releasing outward into the room.

Instinctually, I seized Jameson's arm, drawing it closer, my eyes locking on his ailment.

I didn't notice the gasps or the fact that the class was now watching us. I was only aware of the force emanating from within me.

This lasted several seconds until the feeling ran out, like it had run on a tank of gas that was now empty.

Exhausted, I dropped my hand from his to brace it on the table and took in deep breaths, recovering.

The room was silent. No one was working on their castings in hushed whispers. There was no scuffing of tools against the wooden tables. There was nothing.

I looked up and found the remnants of the rash Estelle had cast were gone completely from Jameson's arm. But something else had happened. The scar above his lip had lessened too. Lifting my head farther, I found Karin's hair had turned from blonde to brown, her natural shade judging from the color of her eyebrows. Ms. Boudreaux stood straighter. A girl near the door was staring in amazement at her palm muttering, "It's gone." The Caldwells no longer had any signs of a rash ever having occurred.

"What…What just happened?" I asked tentatively.

Jameson, who had been holding his breath, let it out in a rush. "That wasn't me, Jocelyn. It was you. It came from you."

"It was both of you," Ms. Boudreaux corrected, suddenly standing next to us. "Jameson channeled your core ability, Jocelyn. He enhanced the energy but it was you who produced it." She was about to turn and head back to her spot in the corner but hesitated. "Thank you." Then she loosened her limbs and strolled to her seat.

Only then did I understand what had taken place. Jameson and I, together, had healed the entire class.

9. ACCEPTANCE

I'm a witch.

I...am...a...witch. The realization repeated in my head like a constant, blinking light as I lay in bed, unable to sleep.

The house was silent now, Miss Mabelle being the last to make any noise and that had been over an hour ago. Even the soothing blues music someone had been playing in a nearby house had ended.

I was alone with my thoughts now, or just one to be precise.

I am a witch.

Images of pointy hats, black cats, and broomsticks entered my mind but I hadn't seen a single one of these since arriving in New Orleans, making it more difficult to accept this new found understanding of who I really am. Maybe a cauldron on the stove or a wand stowed away in a drawer would have made it easier on me. There were none of these things here.

The witch world had been hard to swallow because they didn't appear to be anything other than normal. There was nothing in their clothes or overt behavior that would identify them as having any kind of supernatural ability or sharing a lineage with those who do. As Jameson had told me on the first day I'd arrived, they attempted to hide this secret culture that I unknowingly hailed from.

But it was undeniable to me now. I'd snubbed this fact, the truth about my ability and my ancestry, because there had always been an explanation for the unexplainable. It was an illusion…a hoax…a magic trick.

Tonight had changed all that…

Not only had I seen the results, I'd felt the source of it and it had come from inside me.

And still that rational part in me struggled with its acceptance of this new fate, uttering alternate reasons, contesting the reality of it until I concluded that the truest test, the greatest confirmation, would be to repeat it.

I kicked off the covers and headed downstairs and out to the garden. The moon was full. The crickets chirped a melody broken only by the bellow of a frog. Most importantly, I was alone.

Settling the screen door back in place quietly, I stepped down to the grass and surveyed the backyard. The grass was lush, without a single patch of dryness. The trees were strong and full of leaves. The herb patch was abundant and growing. On the bushes a multitude of fragrant flowers hung, proving their health. There seemed to be only one place that might offer a good test subject…Miss Mabelle's potting shed.

Crossing the yard left blades of dewy grass on the bottoms of my feet, uncomfortable adhesions that I paid little attention to. There was something of far greater consequence on my mind.

The door was unlocked, thankfully, so I stepped inside and found the light switch. Clay pots, both filled and empty, lined the counter. Gardening tools, all of which were pathetically familiar to me, hung from the walls and were stowed beneath the workbench. But in the back corner, where the light didn't reach so well, were containers of dying, withered plants.

Drawing a deep, unsteady breath, I moved into the shadow and lifted my hand.

"Please…" I said under my breath, hoping this worked because it would prove that I wasn't insane, that my family and those I'd met in this city weren't completely off their rocker.

"Please…"

My hand seemed to move by its self toward the bare, hard branches, stopping when it's sharp, wrinkled edges met my skin. I had to steady my hand because its shaking kept the branch from remaining in contact with my fingers but a few deep breaths later I was ready.

Focusing on that place deep inside, where the power had stirred, I drew it toward me, conjured it, called to it, coaxed it upwards.

The branches turned first. Slowly, the putrid brown changed to a fertile, dark auburn. Then the leaves sprouted, reaching out and uncurling as if I were watching a time delayed recording. Lastly, the blooms emerged, hundreds of them in a stunning bright blue.

My jaw dropped when I realized what I was seeing. Then I grasped the pot and spun it toward the light for a better look.

It was no wonder the gardeners at the academy had told me that I had a green thumb but I'd never done anything like this before. But then, I'd never put forth the same effort either.

It was breathtaking. Not just the plant but the veracity of this talent I'd denied for so long…Yet, here it was, to its due credit. Evidently it was still in its infancy because a glance back at the rest of the pots told me that I hadn't healed them all, as I'd done in class. Those still remained shriveled and clinging to life.

What was the difference, I wondered. Then it came to me. The explanation Ms. Boudreaux had given in class.

"Jameson," I whispered to myself.

He was the key. He was the channel to enhancing this ability.

Still, I had done it. This was my confirmation...

I am a witch. And a descendant of powerful practitioners. Aunt Lizzy had told me the truth on the plane. I just wasn't ready to hear it. Now, though, I found new respect for my family.

The next few minutes were spent healing the remaining plants so that when I left the far corner overflowed with lush green leaves and colorful blooms. My body was finally growing tired so I left the potting shed and crossed the lawn back to the house. Then my feet stopped and I focused in on the porch without really seeing it.

A realization came to me, a feeling actually.

I felt shame for not having acknowledged the ability to heal sooner. Instead of using it, I ignored it, gave it no respect and definitely no room to grow. All that time it could have helped so many...

There, in that moment, with the full moon overhead, the crickets stopped suddenly as if they sensed a life-altering change had taken place. One had. I made the decision to accept this fate, to develop it, and to use it to its fullest capacity.

Standing there, feet sinking into the moist earth, my mind locked on this new sense of purpose, I realized I'd already accomplished the first step.

Now I needed to develop it. And I knew exactly who to turn to. With a plan in place, I went back to my room, crawled into bed, and fell right to sleep.

The next morning arrived with Miss Mabelle's traditional shout but I was already awake, eager to get the day started. After slipping on a patterned dress, leggings, and black boots, I headed for the kitchen and found only

Miss Mabelle, Aunt Lizzy having decided it wasn't worth the effort to attempt another batch of fritters.

Somehow she knew it was me without having to look. "Found some plants in my shed come back to life last night." She was fishing for the truth and wasn't bothering to hide it. Yet, I had an inclination she already knew what it was.

I could have allowed her to assume without confirmation but to what end? Instead, I took a seat at the table and replied, "They weren't completely dead."

"Don't go touchin' my things now, ya hear?" she said and only then did she turn her head toward me. She waited several seconds, staring coolly as she was prone to do, before replying, "'Bout time ya embraced it."

We both knew what she meant and that it didn't require a response. So all I did was smile but her attention was back on the stove by then anyways.

For the rest of the morning, and up until second period, I had a difficult time paying attention. My focus was almost entirely on a constant search of my surroundings for something to heal. On the pathway to the main entrance a bush beside the door was drying so as I waited for my turn to enter I reached out a hand to it. A glance back told me that by the time I was stepping inside it had begun to recover, fresh green sprouts already budding. In my first period, Mr. Treme kept a potted plant on his desk, a small cactus that he playfully threatened as a tool for punishment should anyone disobey during his class. As I passed by it, I brushed my fingers against the pot and by the time I'd sat down it had flowered. I didn't even immediately detect the sweltering temperature on my way to second period until a bead of perspiration dripped from my elbow. A Caldwell was nearby but I ignored it and continued to class, where it disappeared.

"You doing okay?" Jameson asked, genuinely concerned as I took a seat beside him.

Ms. Wizner had been caught in the hallway and wrapped up in a discussion with another teacher, which gave Jameson and me a few minutes alone.

"Yes, I'm still thinking about what happened last night…" Although I was now torn between it and the fact that Jameson's arm muscles were carving shadows in his shirt.

He didn't seem to notice my distraction because he replied, "What we did in class was impressive." Then he glanced toward the door to ensure we had privacy before continuing. "I've never seen anything channel at that frequency before. It'll affect one, maybe two objects in the vicinity but you never see the reach you did last night. It-It's unheard of…"

"Huh," I muttered contemplating it. Then I said something under my breath that I hadn't really intended which brought out a smile in Jameson. "We work well together."

"Yes…we do." His voice was soft, serious. "Talking about Wednesday night, interested in partnering again?" he asked evidently without thought to how his family might react this time.

That, I was going to leave up to him.

"Can't get enough of me?" I asked, teasing instead.

He leaned forward and his voice dipped but the sincerity of it took my breath away. "Not really…"

I stifled a smile at his flirtation and he leaned back, proud he'd gotten a response from me. I ignored his intentions and said, "Actually, I was wondering if we could meet sooner? Do you have anything planned after school?"

His grin turned arrogant before he replied, "Now who can't get enough of whom?"

I sighed in frustration at him and he chuckled. "All right. What did you have in mind?"

"Well…how do you feel about hospitals?"

130

His eyebrows creased. "Not exactly the most romantic spot I can think of…"

I groaned. "That's not my intention, Jameson."

"Too bad…"

"Can you be serious?"

He shrugged. "I am." He drew in a breath, conceding. "Where do you want to meet?"

"I can pick you up on the backside of the gym after last class."

"Still trying to avoid telling your family?" he asked, insinuating two thoughts. First, I was trying to keep my family from learning about our interactions. Second, and far more impactful, that he knew I liked him.

"You're blushing, Jocelyn," he boasted.

No, I thought. I've never done that before in my life. Yet, the heat crawling up my cheeks told me something was amiss and I figured it was for exactly the reason he'd mentioned.

"You do like me, don't you, Jocelyn?"

Ms. Wizner entered then and I instantly fell into our routine of acting like we are ignoring each other.

Yet Jameson remained motionless, his body directed at me, his eyes appraising me as he waited for my answer.

A student came through the door and did a double take at us, then suspiciously kept peeking back at us after taking a seat as if a quarrel were about to be started.

Still, Jameson didn't budge.

"Yes," I whispered hastily across the aisle before more students could approach us.

Satisfied, he spun in his seat and went about logging on to his laptop, not bothering to hide his mischievous grin.

Jameson, true to his word, was sitting on a bench at the back of the overflow parking lot when I drove up. When he stood, I got a full view of him and my stomach tightened in reaction. His shirt fit snugly against his chiseled torso and his jeans hung perfectly from his hips.

He was stunning and didn't seem to notice it. He slid into the passenger seat and said, "So…What exactly is your plan?"

On impulse, my eyes were drawn to the scar above his lip, the one I'd accidentally healed a bit in class. It was a constant sign of his sturdiness, another mark of his stunning features, and I had to deliberately look away.

"Don't you trust me?" I smirked in order to overcome the reaction I was having to him.

"Well, you being a Weatherford, I probably shouldn't. But here I am…" he replied wistfully with humor beneath his words. "And what exactly am I here for?"

I laughed through a sigh. "I want to work on my ability to heal."

"Well it's about time," he said casually.

I turned to stare at him in amazement. "You knew?"

"That you didn't take it seriously? Sure. When I met you on the street outside Olivia's shop you didn't believe in any of us. Not in yourself or others."

I hadn't. Instead I'd mocked it. And he'd known.

"Yes, well…I see it now. And I'd like your help in perfecting it."

"And you plan to do that at a hospital?" he asked referring to our earlier conversation.

"Hospitals, clinics, veterinarian offices, wherever there's a need."

He blew air out his lips and shook his head. "We're gonna be busy."

"So you're interested?" I asked, hopeful.

"Well, it does give new meaning to the term 'spending quality time together' but, sure, I'm onboard."

I laughed at his false begrudging and headed for the first hospital on the list I'd made during lunch, at the same time I'd mentioned to my cousins that I'd practice healing after school. They stared back, perplexed for a few seconds and then agreed that it would be a good idea.

Their perspective would change had they known I would be doing it with Jameson Caldwell so I didn't volunteer that detail.

The next few hours were spent moving from one location to the next. When arriving, Jameson and I would find the waiting room, strike up a conversation with those who appeared ill, and then I would reach out and connect with them, either through a handshake, a pat on the arm, or a brush of my hand. In that brief interaction, I did my best to stifle the potency of my ability in my expression while focusing on conjuring the power within me and whispering "incantatio sana" at an inaudible level while making that contact. A few minutes later, they would get a curious expression, or their animal would end its sign of suffering, and then they would leave. We couldn't help but notice that those nearby were somehow cured of their complaint too.

The other side of this process was the requirement to be somehow touching Jameson. As the channel worked as the enhancement to the healing, I needed to be holding him. Neither of us realized this until we reached the first stop and took a seat in the uncomfortable, sloped plastic chairs. Then, as I surveyed the room, my eyes finished its scan and landed on Jameson. That was when I realized he had his hand out, ready for me to take.

For reasons unknown to me, excitement flared and coursed through my stomach, searing it with a pleasurable pain.

I braced myself and then moved my arm, the one with the bracelet of my family stone, toward him. His face was serene, his hand patiently waiting as if he knew this would be a difficult move for me to make. My eyes lifted briefly to his family stone hanging from around his neck and then I slid our palms together. Our fingers entwined and a peace came over me, a feeling that nothing in the world could go wrong.

It became easier, holding hands with someone who I was told only a few days ago was my enemy, until our last stop arrived.

Then I didn't want to let him go.

Apparently, he didn't either because we didn't release each other until we breached the outside where we were visible to those we wanted to avoid seeing us. For reinforcement, when I dropped him off in the school parking lot, he muttered a comment about his hand feeling empty. I didn't tell him but I could associate with that feeling.

We repeated our practice sessions the next day, Friday, but postponed them for the weekend and resumed them on Monday. And our awareness of each other never lessened. He continued to hold his breath for the first few seconds our hands came in contact and his fingers unconsciously squeezed tighter around mine, signs that he was still affected by my touch. I, on the other hand, just tried to keep the butterflies from batting in my stomach. It helped to focus elsewhere and I began asking him questions about growing up in a house full of curious, rambunctious siblings, how he developed his channeling skills, what he thought of growing up in a lively city like New Orleans, everything I could think of to get to know this assumed enemy of mine. He, in turn, asked me questions, listening intently and making insightful comments.

Ironically, as he and I healed the city of New Orleans and learned about each other, our families were continuing their attacks on one another. If one family came to school with a pimple on each of their cheeks, the other family suffered from a wart in the same spot the very next day. It was the concept of eye-for-an-eye. I just hoped the feud didn't get to the point of actually taking an eye. Because of this, Jameson and I started a tradition in which he would enter second period, reach out his arm, and without needing to be asked I would heal him of my family's latest hex.

While I knew my cousins weren't aware yet of my spending time with Jameson, his siblings appeared to be catching on and heartedly disagreed. Whenever I saw one of them, a frown was always on the other end. I ignored it, having no recourse, and really no motivation for one. I understood their concern. It was the same as I would have been if our roles were reversed.

Still, Jameson tested their patience by standing beside me when Wednesday's evening class arrived, ready to choose me as a partner if the opportunity arose.

"This lesson will be less hands on," stated Ms. Boudreaux in her typical authoritative tone. "And with your hands at rest, I expect your ears open. This will be information covered on your final exam."

A wooden table had been placed in the middle of the room where objects were aligned down the center. Ms. Boudreaux stood at one end and ushered us forward with a wave of her hand.

Jameson and I approached along with the rest of the class. Unlike others, however, we stood close enough that our arms connected, neither one of us bothering to move away. A fleeting look at him told me that while his eyes were down, appearing to assess what was on the table, a hint of a smile lingered on his lips.

My own smile crept up too, despite the feeling that the rest of the Caldwells were scowling at us. Whatever reprisal they cast for my public interaction with their brother would be worth it.

"The Tristan Talisman," said Ms. Boudreaux theatrically, holding up a mound of fabric and unwrapping it to reveal a circular pendant made of pound metal. "Those who touch it with bare hands find themselves temporarily without ability, thereby protecting the one who gives it from the recipient's powers. Note the fabric it is carried in to prevent accidental disablement. Created in the seventeenth century during the time of major advancements in the sciences - alongside the first submarine, the barometer, and the reflecting telescope - the Tristan was invented. While its creator and its exact date and place of origin are unknown, the Tristan was discovered cupped in the hands of a man long since deceased."

"So it could be much older," Emery pointed out.

"Not likely," she muttered with a hint of sarcasm. "The Sevens would have known about it. As we are well aware, they don't like objects of assumed danger floating about. The only reason they've released this one into the provinces is that its power is steadily dissipating."

She gently placed it on the table and picked up the next closest object. "The Quinox Amulet...a melding of stones that is said to bring good luck to those who carry it. Its origin dates back to the thirteenth century during The Crusades. It was designed as a source of protection for an entire family, making it assumedly a potent artifact. It is said to have been traded for their lives and has been henceforth traded around the world. Mr. Thibodeaux recently purchased it for a good sum of money and has given it to us on loan.

Ms. Boudreaux finished defining the rest of the items on the table, which took nearly the entire class. At the end, we were transfixed, some even hesitant to pick up the objects she'd brought into class. But it was the artifact she ended the lesson with that brought a chill to me.

"Can anyone tell me what the most powerful artifact of all is?" She surveyed the students, finding wide eyes and shaking heads. Apparently, they'd been humbled by the evidence of the others on the table no one wanted to take a chance in answering. "The Rope of The Sevens...made of The Sevens hair, bound by their skin."

There were audibly sounds of disgust from around the room.

"Why was it made of body parts…or their hair?" asked Karin, her own hair having remained its natural brown after I'd accidentally altered it during the last session.

"It was the surest method," said Ms. Boudreaux simply and then went on to explain. "The rope was created with the intention of ensuring that no single one of them could overpower the others. It was to be used to trounce any one of The Seven's willpower should it misalign with their endeavor."

"Which is?" asked Emery, riveted.

She looked surprised, as if we should already know the answer. "To dominate our world." Evidently, she quickly realized how corrupt this sounded and corrected herself. "To better control…or stabilize rather…our world." Then, just as rapidly, she changed the subject. "However, the loss of the rope during the fourth century sent the prospect of that effort into question."

That was when I froze, my body becoming immobile, my lungs barely drawing air. Only vaguely, I realized Ms. Boudreaux had pinned her eyes on me.

I have a rope lost in the fourth century - the thought screamed through my mind. It was made of hair bound in between leather straps, hair that was from the heads of The Sevens, leather not from animal skin but from The Sevens' skins.

My eyes flitted around the room from student to student concerned for no viable reason that they would deduce I possessed the rope. I forced myself to stop and listen to Ms. Boudreaux, whose voice was rambling now. "The Sevens have been searching for their artifact since. Numerous people, those in our world and those excluded from it, have lost their lives in the process."

Swallowing back my nerves, I asked in my most steady voice, "What exactly does the rope do?"

Ms. Boudreaux seemed pleased that I asked. "The possibilities are limitless. With it you can cast anything from a head cold to death. But only The Sevens are affected. So, obviously, it's something they had intended to keep close by and secure."

But they hadn't and I now owned it. It made me wonder who, besides my mother and Mr. Thibodeaux, might know this.

"Needless to say," she went on. "Anyone who now has this rope in his or her possession is extremely influential. They are also in great danger and must keep it hidden until the time comes for using it."

Those were the same instructions I'd received at Mr. Thibodeaux's store, just before I carried it out the door with Jameson beside me. Ms. Boudreaux stared directly at me while make these statements but she wasn't the only one.

Jameson's eyes were on me, too.

I looked at him expecting to find his expression curious, dubious.

But it wasn't.

It was worried.

While I downplayed my interest of the rope the remainder of the lesson by asking alternative questions about the other artifacts, Jameson didn't appear to believe my efforts.

By the time Ms. Boudreaux excused us from class, I got the distinct impression that he already knew the truth.

10. SECRET RENDEVOUS

Later that night, when arriving home with my cousins from our evening class, I found that I had visitors.

Other than my family and a few students at either of my new schools, I knew no one in this city. So, I was surprised when my name was called while passing the room's entrance.

"They've come to see you," Aunt Lizzy clarified.

They sat in the living room, a man and woman, both professionally dressed in pant suits. Only the woman seemed unusual. She had a white sign hung around her neck where faded remnants of words had been erased. Over them was a single one written in blue.

It said Jocelyn.

They evaluated me expectantly before standing and introducing themselves.

Their name was Carr and they'd heard about my ability to heal from Mrs. DeVille, who'd heard it from Olivia, who'd heard it from someone else, who'd heard it from the mother of someone who attended the same evening class as me.

Apparently, in the witch world, where supernatural abilities were commonplace, I was a little out of the ordinary.

"What can I do for you?" I asked the Carrs, wishing instantly that Jameson was here. He was not only able to enhance my ability but he calmed me, readied me for the task.

This time, however, I'd have to do it alone and my nerves were on edge because of it.

"Mrs. Carr," said the man motioning toward his wife "has been battling a virus - in her throat - that has taken away her voice. We've tried incantations, balms, rituals. We tried Western doctors. Nothing has worked. Can you help her?"

"I can try," I replied attempting to project confidence.

Taking a seat next to her, I reached out and took her hand, and then I looked up. While I'd meant to focus on her throat, it was her eyes that gave me the motivation I needed. They were fearful, desperate, and conveying the plea that her voice could not.

She was my first patient, the first who knew it anyway. The others had no idea I'd been involved, simply feeling their limb heal or finding their gash had closed up. This woman would recognize it if I failed.

That realization and the look in her eyes were all I needed to conjure the force inside me.

"Incantatio sana," I said, rigidly.

It flared up unexpectedly fast this time but I was able to harness and direct it outward, through my hand and toward her throat.

Seconds passed before I saw her swallow and then her mouth opened.

"You…" she tested her voice. It came out in a whisper, broken, but we all heard it. And then she laughed, a melodious one that filled the room.

She rotated quickly on the sofa and flung her arms around her husband. "I love you," she murmured and then repeated it with more vigor as if she'd been unable to say it for far too long.

Now it was her husband who was struggling to speak. Yet, he summoned the energy to thank me over her shoulder.

"When did she become ill," I asked genuinely curious.

"Three years ago." He shook his head. "Three years and this sign has been our only means of communicating. Not anymore." He lifted it from her neck proudly.

They then offered me money but it just didn't seem right. I had plenty to make up for not having taken advantage of this ability earlier.

Anyway, all I really wanted was sleep. It had been a long and tiring day so I said goodbye and went upstairs. Nolan's door was still open, since he didn't seem to need as much sleep as the others, his mind always moving too fast to allow for it. His head emerged as I reached the top step and he asked, "All healed?"

I nodded.

"Nice job."

"Thanks," I said, realizing that he, and probably the rest of my family, felt these types of incidences were commonplace and it still stunned me a bit.

While curing a woman of throat illness didn't seem like a big deal, it did keep me up a few minutes longer. Not because I'd done it alone, without Jameson's help, but because it told me that my ability to heal was getting around this new world that I was now embedded in and I wondered how many more would be arriving on our doorstep.

The next day, in second period, I learned just how fast word did travel.

"So should we buy you an appointment book?" Jameson asked, playfully.

"What for?"

"Your growing clientele."

My eyes widened at him. "How did you hear?"

His head moved back and forth slowly. "Not many haven't by this point. I told you…it's a rare gift."

I realized he'd chosen this subject over the more volatile one - whether I did actually own The Rope of The Sevens. Intended or not, I appreciated it.

"By the way, would you mind…" he questioned, holding out his hand to me. There, in the middle was an open wound.

"Should I bother asking where this one came from?" I muttered.

He smirked and shook his head, confirming it had been one of my cousins.

I performed quickly on him, finishing just before a student entered the room. Then Jameson and I were back to acting as if we didn't know each other for the next hour. At the end of it, when students left the classroom and Ms. Wizner was pulled away at the request of another teacher, Jameson and I were finally alone again.

"Did you hear a word she said?" he asked, implying I was spending more time concentrating on him than on the lesson.

"No," I replied flatly. "Did you?"

He chuckled. "I don't remember a single one from her since you sat beside me that first day of class," he admitted.

I laughed with him and then his mood changed and he stiffened slightly.

"Look," he said, dubiously, his eyes drifting toward the window briefly as if he were still considering whether he should be bringing up whatever it was on his mind. Then his focus came back to me and he said, "If you want to heal others, there's a place I can take you where people need your help."

I gave him a quizzical look.

"It's…It's not a place I can tell you about, exactly. We, those in our world, keep it private." His lips pinched closed and he momentarily looked irritated. "They shun it really."

I blinked back my aversion toward that statement. From the sound of it, these people in need were victims or criminals. Either way, it was clear from Jameson's behavior that they needed our help and quickly.

With that in mind, I responded without much contemplation behind it, "When?"

He seemed relieved. "Tomorrow night? Meet me at Olivia's store? Eleven o'clock?"

"That late?" I asked, surprised.

"It's the safest time to go."

My eyebrows lifted at hearing the word safest.

"Who exactly are these people, Jameson?"

His mind had been racing, which was clear to me as his eyes locked on the floor without blinking and his expression stiffened, but my question broke his trance.

"They aren't the ones you need to worry about. They're the outcasts."

Ms. Wizner appeared in the door, but with her back to us as she finished her conversation we were allowed a few extra seconds.

"Thank you," he said hastily, in a way that made me feel as if I was doing him a favor.

"We can talk more after school," I offered collecting my laptop.

"Oh no…" He shook his head. "Going to have to skip our errands today. You'll need to rest. It'll be harder to heal them than the others."

That made me curious. I was just about to ask why when Ms. Wizner turned fully into the room. So, instead, my head snapped forward and I stood to follow Jameson out in the hall. Of course, there were students and faculty still roaming so my chance to ask more about this mysterious excursion to heal the outcasts was over.

I was left wondering why Jameson was thankful I'd agree to help them. That, I figured, was a foregone conclusion. Also on my list of questions was how they'd become outcasts, why we needed to meet them so late at night, why it would be harder to heal them, and who exactly made it unsafe? These questions remained in the back of my mind until the next day, when Jameson didn't appear in class.

Then my attention turned to his whereabouts…and the clock couldn't move faster toward the eleven o'clock hour. Every few minutes, I checked it and found it didn't appear to be moving. Yet, when one class ended and the other began I knew time had not stood still, contrary to my perception. Then came dinner, which was just as antagonizing. But the worst of it came after. When our traditional after-dinner practice of the mystical arts had ended and everyone had gone to sleep, including Nolan, I sat staring at the clock.

When it came time to sneak out, I was fully prepared. Not only because I'd been thinking about it for the last half of the day but also I was well versed in the effort. It had been me at the academy in New York who went first through the window or down the hall or out the door late at night. It was me with the talent for avoiding the headmistress and the security guard who walked the grounds. Applying my knowledge here, gave me the foresight to distinguish the sounds of everyone's sleep habits, the odd creaky floorboard, and how much the front door could be opened before reaching the point where it squeaked. Sneaking out here was fairly easy, in fact, and I was soon on my way to Olivia's shop.

The French Quarter streets were filled with tourists and locals, beads hanging from their necks and cups of fruity liquor called Hurricanes clutched in their hands. I had to swerve to avoid several of them as they darted in front of my car. Otherwise I would have needed to use my healing abilities and that would have drawn questions I had no interest in answering. It quieted, thankfully, as I reached the street where Olivia's shop could be found.

Having only been here once, I initially questioned whether I'd gotten the directions wrong. Expecting to find a group of people loitering around Olivia's door, I was surprised that the street was vacant.

Pulling up beside her door, I turned off the engine and then waited. The sound of a harmonious jazz rhythm floated through the streets, soothing me like only this particular music could.

While I hadn't been happy to leave the academy in New York as fast as I was forced to, New Orleans was a pretty good place to end up.

No more than a minute passed when headlights came around the corner behind me. They stopped at my bumper and the driver side door opened.

Then he was there, walking toward me, his sturdy frame being carried by a confident swagger that had come to spark a reaction in me every instance I saw it. This time, however, it wasn't a swell of warmth or the trigger of an extra heartbeat. I felt the muscles that had contracted slowly throughout the day during his absence finally relax.

The recognition of it almost made me laugh. Here I was meeting a Caldwell on a dark street who will be introducing me to an admittedly unsafe group of people without any mention of it to my family…and I was more at peace now than I had been the entire day.

"Smiling? I see you didn't miss me much…" came Jameson's playful tone next to my ear. He'd reached my car window and was now an inch from me, so close that his eyes filled my sight.

"No," I replied as frankly as I could while my heart picked up its pace. Somehow it always reacted the same way to him. "Ms. Wizner was in tears though."

He chuckled and then said, "I figured you'd want to drive yourself, my being a Caldwell and all…"

"I think I've made my mind up about that one," I replied.

"Really?" He was intrigued. "And the verdict is?"

"I think you're all right."

His eyes widened in offense. "Just all right?" he scoffed.

"You're going to need to work for more than that," I said with a smirk.

"You're tough…" he said under his breath before stopping to grin. "It's a good thing I already have a few ideas in mind. If you don't run from me tonight, after where we're going, I'm pretty sure you'll let me take you on a date."

Two things made me freeze then. First, he'd hinted again that tonight would be dangerous. Second, and far more shocking, was the suggestion of a date.

"You haven't thought about it?" he asked, noticing my reaction, and I wasn't sure if he were seriously offended or mockingly playful.

"I just…I didn't think it was an option."

"Our families never need to know," he replied cautiously.

"So we would meet somewhere late at night?"

"Like we are now." His lips turned down. "Not the way I planned it in my head."

That admission made my heart skip a beat. Evidently, he'd been considering asking me on a date for a while. A Caldwell asking a Weatherford on a date - the first one in history, no doubt. It was a big deal. No wonder he was putting some thought into it.

As if that weren't enough to cause the burning excitement now coursing through me, the words 'not the way I planned it' repeated in my mind, which meant one thing. As much as I didn't want to admit it, I had a traditional streak in me and I was flattered at the idea that he wanted to pick me up.

Yeah, I thought, that wouldn't go over so well at my house.

"Um, Jameson?" I asked, distracting him from thoughts that didn't seem all that pleasant. "Where are all the people I'm supposed to heal tonight?" He had mentioned something about driving.

"Right," he said, jumping into action. "Did you want to leave your car and come with me?"

As much as every muscle in my body was magnetically moving in that direction, I forced myself to decline. "I can't imagine leaving it here unattended."

He nodded thoughtfully, disappointment evident in his expression. "I'll make sure you can follow."

With that, he took me out of the French Quarter, down the I-10, and exited at an off ramp that looked as if it had been forgotten by the rest of society. From there, we jostled over rough pavement and then along a dirt road where my headlights caught pieces of my surroundings. An abundance of trees hid whatever was beyond them but infrequent patches revealed a swamp stretched along the left side of us.

About forty minutes into our woodland expedition, his taillight began blinking and he turned off the road, which made me laugh. We were in the middle of nowhere without any reason to abide by the laws of the road and here he was using his blinker. He was being courteous, I knew, and it was sweet. He had no understanding of my driving skills and couldn't have known that I had once outrun the security guard through the backwoods of our academy back east.

I pulled up beside him and stepped out.

The air around us had transformed from soot and smog so typical in the city to fresh air layered with the hint of sweet moss. The warm night had inspired the wildlife to emerge. The frogs' bellowing echoed off the still water and bats darted between cypress trees that stood like soldiers against the moonless sky.

With our headlights now off, he used a flashlight to guide me to the water's edge and then to show me why we'd stopped.

A dock extended out into the water, one that looked like it hadn't been used since the Civil War. I didn't pay it much attention though. The twelve-foot, flat bottomed boat tied to it was far more fascinating. Overflowing with bags and boxes, it had clearly been left there for us.

"This," said Jameson, "is why I was absent from school today. The supplies came in late."

"Ah," I said playfully, acting like it all made sense. "Of course they did."

He suppressed a laugh. "I have you guessing, don't I?"

"Yes…you do."

"You'll get your answers soon," he reassured and walked down the dock, stopping at the boat. Lifting his foot, he placed it on the edge and then swung his hand out to me. "Ready?"

"For what exactly?"

"To heal those who need it," he replied soft but emphatically.

"Right…" I whispered to myself and then treaded lightly toward him, unwilling to back out now. Even if the dock swayed beneath my feet and there was no map in his hand to tell us how to find our destination in this maze of waterways.

Yet, a few seconds later, I found myself sitting on a hard wooden bench in the hull of the boat and Jameson taking a seat beside me. He then untied us, pulled the cord on the outboard motor, and the hum of an engine rose up around us. Then we were moving, the soft, moist breeze picking up strands of my hair to toss them over my shoulder.

Then I figured it out. The boat. The discretion. The night time excursion.

"This is the secret trip you take every week…" I said loud enough to be heard over the engine.

His head dipped leisurely in a nod.

"The supplies are for the outcasts," I went on.

"Yes."

Then I demonstrated just how well I knew him. "This is where your family spends its money. Not on elaborate vacations or parties but here on these people…"

Again he nodded. "You're more insightful than the others," Jameson said, referring to my family.

"Why didn't you bring me here sooner?" I asked with a confused shrug. "We could have been helping them already."

He slowed the motor then, allowing us to drop our voices to a more practical level.

"I know what I feel for you, Jocelyn. And it's strong. I didn't want that emotion to blind me in my opinion of whether I could trust you."

My lips almost lifted in a smile at his acknowledgement but I held it back. His explanation sounded levelheaded, exactly what I would expect from Jameson, but I still didn't understand. "Trust me for what reason? Why the secrecy?"

We'd been steering around cypress stumps and down the waterway we were now moving along when we reached a bend. Slowly, as Jameson curved around it, lights began to shine through clusters of trees along the embankments. From there, I could smell wood fires burning and see boats moored in the water.

Without having to be told, I knew we had arrived. My time was running out to get an answer from him.

Jameson slowed the boat more, allowing him to speak in a regular tone. Even then, his voice was husky, restrained. "It puts everyone here in danger, if you were to talk about this place."

"Me? Specifically me?" I lifted my shoulders in confusion. "I don't understand what I have to do with this place..."

"Your mother works for the ministry," he replied, pulling alongside another weathered dock.

"So?" I persisted.

"So the ministry sent them here."

11. THE VILLAGE

The shacks were built on stilts that dripped with moss, giving them the illusion of hovering above the water. Lanterns flickered at the end of the docks and below the rafters, illuminating nets, crates, and fishing poles, which were found in abundance at every shack we stopped. Some had rocking chairs beside their doors or at the edge of the water where I knew the residents cast their lines during the day. In summary, the place we'd entered was a village hidden in the hollows of a swamp, a place for those intentionally forgotten.

We stopped at the first few shacks and Jameson heaved either a bag or a box from the boat to the edge of the dock, whether windows were lit from within or not. It was immediately clear to me that this was not a new routine and I couldn't help notice the feeling this stirred in me, something along the lines of admiration. He'd given up his nights to deliver goods to people in need and didn't appear to ask for anything in return.

If only my family could see him now…

On one delivery in particular the bag opened and spilled some of its contents across the wooden planks. As I rushed to help Jameson collect them before the items fell in the water, I was surprised at what I found. Canned food, fishing hooks, bait, candles, a knife and sharpener.

Evidently, they didn't have the freedom or the money to acquire the basic necessities themselves. This understanding made me pause and wonder what kind of establishment imposed a punishment like this one. Then I froze.

It was the kind where my mother worked.

This realization settled over me like an uncomfortable blanket so I was partly glad when we didn't see anyone outside for the first few shacks. It gave me time to allow this fact to sink in.

If any of the recipients knew we were there, they didn't acknowledge it by coming out to greet us. They were there though. The laughter and music coming through the walls confirmed it. We moved from shack to shack making me feel as if I were standing outside a party I hadn't been invited to. Which was a fairly accurate depiction of the situation Jameson and I were currently in.

Then we came across the fifth shack and he tied us to a post, signaling that we would be visiting this one. It was quieter than the others, playing soft blues music on what sounded like a scratchy, dated record player.

Hauling a bag to his side as he stepped up to the dock, Jameson explained, "You should know that healing will be harder here."

"Why?" This was no less disconcerting from when he'd mentioned it the first time.

Jameson stood over me, hands on his hips, looking out over the water. "When someone is sent here two things happen. First, they suffer the worst punishment our world can invoke. They are bound, unable to use their abilities. This is to make certain they cannot protect themselves by revoking their punishment or exercise their powers to improve their situation. Second, the closer you get to them, the greater your energy will dissipate. That cast is to prevent anyone else from helping them. It's the reason why I suggested we take a break yesterday in order for you to rest. Because you'll need it."

"Can I get around it?" I asked, uncertain.

"We're going to find out."

I scoffed in return. "Great. Sounds easy."

He had offered his hand to me by this point and I had taken it to step up to the dock. "It won't be," he assured once my feet were firmly under me. "But I know the level of frequency where your energy vibrates. When you healed our whole class, Jocelyn, that just doesn't happen. No one has that ability. No one but you." He caught my gaze and held it, his hands still holding mine. "You can do this," he stated with unwavering conviction.

I knew what he'd been doing, taking another look inside me, assessing me. It would have been natural to feel my privacy was violated but I didn't have this reaction. Instead, I appreciated the vote of confidence because I wasn't so sure myself.

We were on our way to the door when I asked in a whisper, so those inside couldn't overhear, "How do they do all of that? Bind these people and those who visit them?" Then I realized I already knew the answer. "Channeling."

"Yes, that's right," he said, impressed. "It's the only way to cast from one source to another, the only way to displace something." He grinned and pointed out, "You're getting to know us."

I scoffed, not having nearly as much confidence in that statement as he did and wishing once again that I'd given this world its due credence earlier.

We reached the door and Jameson knocked lightly, then he did something completely unexpected. He slipped his hand into mine and squeezed. It was comforting and thrilling at the same time.

153

The door opened to a woman well in to her nineties. She was frail and hunched with wiry arms and a pile of gray hair wound into a bun. Stones of all kinds hung around her neck and in bracelets on both arms. Her skin, which fit loosely around her bones, was tawny, indicating that she was Creole. But it was her eyes that struck me. Although they were framed with creases demonstrating her age, they were, above everything else, gentle.

She didn't appear to be a convict and definitely not one that posed a threat.

"Isadora," said Jameson kindly.

She smiled at him, her eyes lighting up, and she moved aside to allow us in.

The room, I found, was sparse. In the far corner stood a metal-framed bed with a bumpy mattress and thin blanket. In the center was a wooden table with four chairs around it. A wood-burning stove stood in the corner to our left alongside a built-in hutch where food was stored.

Jameson set the bag on the table and immediately began putting the items away, knowing where each item was supposed to be stored without having to be told. He'd done this before, and often.

"This is Jocelyn," he said while stooping down to place canned food in the bottom drawer, but Isadora was already greeting me, in her own unique way.

She'd shifted to stand directly in front of me, her back arched enough so that her eyes could meet mine. I stared down at her, a smile hovering lightly.

"Jocelyn," I said, extending my hand.

She didn't move, no breathes, no blinks, and I let my hand fall. Her steady focus remained on me, speculating, wondering, gazing into me.

"She's the healer," Jameson said over his shoulder while unloading more supplies onto the table, having already determined that she was attempting to distinguish my ability. Clearly, Isadora had channeled at one point because she was applying those same techniques to me now. While her ability had been removed, she still remained observant, critical.

But she shook her head, apparently disagreeing. Then, almost imperceptibly, her eyebrows rose as if she'd seen something that stood out to her.

"Residue…" she breathed and then exhaled in a rush. Whatever that meant, it was shocking to her.

Then she dropped her gaze to my left arm, where my mother's bracelet lay. Her fingers, rough to the touch but gentle, came around my wrist and lifted it for a better view of the stone embedded in the metal.

I hadn't noticed that Jameson was now beside us, motionless, concentrating on our exchange, and then he spoke tenuously. "Yes…She's a Weatherford."

Isadora remained quietly staring at my family stone for the next several seconds and then she released my arm.

"We will need to hide that fact," said Isadora evenly as she turned from me to hobble toward the hutch. It was the first time she'd spoken at length and I picked up the hint of an accent, one of French origins.

"You're right," Jameson concluded. Then he saw my confusion and he explained, "Weatherford's aren't welcome here. They know your mother had a hand in…" he stopped himself. "They know she works for the ministry."

I nodded. "So we don't have the best reputation?" I joked sarcastically.

He smiled, and then reinforced the significance of our subject. "That would be putting it lightly."

Conceding, I said, "All right. How do we do it?" While I wasn't concerned about the backlash, I didn't want to make my patients feel worse than they already did.

Isadora approached holding out a red bandana, which she wrapped around my wrist, effectively concealing my bracelet. In spite of her age and weakened condition, she did it deftly as if she were a surgeon at the operating table, and I wondered if she really was as feeble as she made herself appear.

"That works," I muttered, twisting my arm to ensure it was entirely covered.

"Perfect," said Jameson. Then his following statements made me realize that he and Isadora had already discussed my involvement prior to my arrival here, probably before Jameson even asked me. "Isadora will bring us to the homes of those who are sick. She'll introduce you by first name only and then we can work on healing them."

"Good plan," I replied realizing that he'd done everything he could to make sure this night would go smoothly.

So, with this in the back of my mind, as we headed for Jameson's boat, I reminded myself to take extra special care not to mention my last name or members of my family.

Isadora directed us to a shack across the waterway from hers and Jameson glided us there. It appeared dark from a distance but as we grew closer there were faint shadows moving inside.

We tied the boat and Jameson and I helped Isadora to the dock and then we headed for the door. It opened before we reached it.

A man, balding but with a bit of facial hair, popped his head outside, looking for those he knew had stopped at his dock. When he recognized Jameson and Isadora, a smile stretched across his tanned, seasoned skin.

"Come in," he said affably.

"These are the Duparts," Jameson whispered quickly.

"An entire family?" I replied hastily, keeping my voice low. "The ministry penalizes children, too?"

Jameson gave me a silent response, the look of someone conveying they, too, entirely disapproved.

When I'd first heard of the village I had wondered if the people I was going to help were victims or criminals.

Now I knew they were both.

The Duparts lived in a shack just as meager as Isadora but there was an additional bed, where a little girl lay. She was pale and curled into a ball but her eyes were open and consciously watching everything around her.

Someone, who I assumed to be Mrs. Dupart, rushed to Isadora as we entered. "The healer? Did you bring him?" she asked, wide-eyed.

"Her," Jameson corrected gently. "Jocelyn?"

I stepped forward, getting the impression that the Duparts had been forewarned of our arrival but certain details had been excluded.

I introduced myself and then they brought me to their daughter's bedside. It turned out that she wasn't just pale but a faint shade of greenish-gray.

"It's La Terreur," said Mrs. Dupart, gently brushing strands of hair from her daughter's damp forehead.

I knew that word. It meant terror in French. But the illness, I'd never heard before.

"What is La Terreur?" I asked.

"That's what they're calling whatever it is working its way through the swamp," explained Jameson. "It started a few weeks ago, just before you moved to Louisiana. Symptoms include weakness, labored breathing, and a change in your skin color. But the first sign of it comes as a scream that wakes you from your sleep."

A scream of terror, I thought, which is where it got its name.

My eyes turned toward the little girl. She looked so frail, so vulnerable, undeserving of this thing that had infiltrated her body. I knelt down so that we were eye-level. "What's your name?"

"Marie," she said and then a shudder hit her. Lips pinched, eyes clamped shut. It was evident that she was in pain.

Unable to let it pass without doing something, I took hold of her hand and stated in a rush, "Incantatio sana." I spoke the words before even feeling the force rise. For good measure, I said it again. "Incantatio sana."

Marie's shudder did lessen but it didn't end. Jameson had been right. It was harder to heal here.

Instinctually, I reached my free hand back and found his. Clutching it, I repeated my incantation. When it didn't work, I repeated it again, my teeth grinding against each other, my breathing strained, my own forehead beginning to perspire as the force overwhelmed me.

I was on the verge of insisting they call a doctor when Marie opened her eyes. And they were lucid, alert, alive.

"Momma." She chocked back a sob, pushing herself to a sitting position.

Then the Duparts rushed forward to embrace their little girl.

Between tears, darting glances at me and hurried thanks, we said our goodbyes to the Duparts and started for the next home in which my healing was needed.

We visited fifteen more shacks and each of them had at least one person stricken with La Terreur. In some lived only a single person, too weak or unaware to answer their door. We entered anyway. By the time we left, they were revived, weak still but healed of the condition La Terreur left them in.

Then we visited the last shack…

Similar to the other ones, it had a dock, fishing equipment piled against the shack's wall, and a chair propped against the wall with a fishing pole set across the arms. There were no lights and no music in this particular residence making it seem lonely, forgotten.

Isadora, already sensing something was amiss, didn't bother to knock. Even in the other dwellings where only one person lived there was some sign of life. There was none here.

We entered a darkened room, only a light from across the waterway and through the trees left a shadow on the wall. It was just enough to see the body curled beneath the covers. A candle set on the ground below the person's head had extinguished. In Isadora's haste to light it, she rushed through an incantation and blew on the wick only to be reminded that her abilities didn't work here. Releasing a quick sigh, she dug in her pocket for matches, lighting the candle quickly.

Jameson and I were at the bed throughout her efforts to illuminate the room, but we were having difficulty wakening my next patient.

"What's his name, Isadora?" Jameson asked anxiously.

The room flickered and then illuminated the man. Only his head could be seen, the covers having been pulled to his chin. His head was shaved and glistening with perspiration. Beads of sweat ran across his face as he lay on his side, leaving trails from his cheek and across the bridge of his nose. His color was the same as the others. Even through his swarthy skin, he appeared green.

"His name, Isadora," Jameson demanded.

When she spoke, it was to the man. "Gustave…" she urged.

He didn't flinch, didn't open his eyes. But he did draw a breath, albeit a shallow one.

I didn't see the point in delaying any longer so I took hold of his hand and Jameson's simultaneously to conjure the force I was now intimately familiar with inside me.

Suddenly Gustave's body jolted.

Taken aback, I almost released him but kept my grasp.

"Incantatio sana," I breathed, repeating it again and again, working my way through the barrier that the ministry, my mother had created. "Come on, Gustave!"

Then he exhaled, raspy, extended, and I knew it would be his last one. And he then went still.

Vaguely, I registered that I fell back, sitting on my folded legs, but I wouldn't...I couldn't release Gustave's hand. I wanted to tell him I was sorry, apologize to him for failing, for not having gotten here sooner, for waiting too long before accepting my ability. But I couldn't. All I could do was hold him.

"It's not your fault..." Jameson's voice was in my ear, tender, coaxing. "This isn't your fault, Jocelyn."

His arms came around me, pulling me from behind up against the shelter of his chest, his cheek coming over my shoulder to press against mine, the warmth of him surrounding me from the cold reality of what had just happened.

"You can't blame yourself," he whispered. "You tried. We both tried..."

It didn't matter. The tears fell anyway.

Jameson held me throughout it, pacifying me until my body stopped shaking and the sobs quieted. Only then did I open my eyes and what I saw wasn't what I expected.

Items around his home had risen a foot or more off the ground. A coffee can tilted slightly as it hovered over the table. Two pieces of firewood were suspended near the stove, knocking against each other in midair. The single chair he owned had lifted all four legs off the ground. The candle Isadora had lit hung over our heads, its flame disturbed by the breeze while it hovered unsteadily above.

"Who here can levitate?" I asked under my breath, still keeping Jameson close. Something wasn't quite right...

Watching our reactions closely, Isadora replied, "Gustave."

I inhaled sharply and rotated back toward him, hoping desperately that he'd revived. But he laid as I'd left him, quiet, peaceful, lifeless.

"Could he…Could it…I don't understand," I muttered, aggravated.

"Me neither…" said Jameson examining Gustave from afar.

It was Isadora who enlightened us. She hobbled closer and placed a hand on my shoulder, her French accent coming through as she spoke.

"Jocelyn, Gustave is gone - and you have picked up his residue."

12. RESIDUE

Residue.

I'd heard this word used in commercials and by the cleaning staff at the academy. It had been in connection to soap scum and tire tread, so I didn't particularly like the fact it was being applied to me now. Then I looked back at Gustave, who had died in front of me just moments earlier, and I realized how little a word describing me really meant.

There was something far more important I needed to understand.

If Isadora was correct, I now had the ability to levitate, which didn't make sense. Vinnia had mentioned that there were only two capabilities in the witch world that could not be learned or acquired: healing and levitation. But I suddenly had both.

Throughout the time I was considering all this, Gustave's possessions that I'd unwittingly lifted had collapsed to the floor, the coffee can spilling ground beans across the wooden planks and wood chips shedding from the logs near the stove on impact.

At that point, Jameson had jumped up and I'd thought at first that he was preparing to defend us. But I was wrong. He wasn't concerned as much as excited.

"She's the one, isn't she?" he asked, facing Isadora. When she didn't answer, he prompted, "Isadora?"

"The one?" I asked, pushing myself to a standing position. Jameson noticed and helped me up, reluctant to release my hand after I was on my feet again. That was just fine with me.

He looked at me, eyes wide and bright, while explaining, "The earliest channelers recorded their writings, what they foresaw, in journals." He paused to make a comparison to something I could relate to. "Much like Homer's "Iliad and Odyssey," except for the channelers' passages were dedicated to the future. They were designed to give us an understanding of what to expect. One forethought mentioned a person born with the capability to possess all of our powers - healing, levitation, channeling, and control of the elements."

"Wait," I muttered, waving my free hand in front of me, trying to slow down the information coming at me. "Can't The Sevens already do all of those things? Levitate, heal…"

He scoffed, shaking his head. "They'd like you to believe that…and have done a good job convincing a lot of people of it. But the truth is they've only learned to distribute their energy between each other. None of them was actually born with the capability to acquire residue. That's why they've tried to destroy the belief in this one mythical person."

Still trying to piece it all together, I stopped him again to ask, "And what exactly is residue?"

"It's the energy left behind when someone passes on. Gustave, for example…" he waved his hand toward the man in the bed, noticed he was still uncovered and pulled the sheet over his head before continuing. "Gustave had the ability to levitate, something you weren't able to do just a few minutes ago. When he died, when his soul left his body, you were holding his hand and his power passed on to you."

"So if I'm holding the hand of someone when they die, I acquire a bit of their power?" I asked, unsure whether to laugh in denial or grimace and accept the truth.

"Yes, that's how it's done. The power is sent through touch in the same way that you heal through touch. At least that's how the channelers wrote it would be done. I remember that because when Charlotte was little she'd try to visit funeral homes to hold the hands of the deceased and see if she could acquire their abilities."

That made Charlotte far more odd than I ever imagined.

"And you think this person, the one able to acquire the residue, is me?" I asked dubiously.

"Yes," he replied, emphatically.

I glanced at Isadora, who had been watching this exchange the entire time. More precisely, she'd been evaluating my reaction. When she witnessed my wavering, she shuffled forward, stopping directly in front of me.

"When your father died, what were you doing?" she asked pointedly without any allusion toward compassion.

I felt my body go numb, as it always did when his death was brought up. The story I'd heard only once from my mother on a flight from New York to Tahiti. She'd kept the details sparse and I didn't push her after seeing her distress over the memory of it. What I did know was that my father had died while trying to protect me during an abduction.

I swallowed once to clear my throat and then replied, "I was in his arms. He died holding me to his chest."

Whether in reaction or as a show of support, I felt Jameson's hand squeeze mine.

"And when Gustave died, what were you doing?" she persisted.

164

This answer I spoke much quieter. "Holding his hand."
She waited for me to piece this together.

"You're saying that I picked up my ability to heal others from my father and I picked up the ability to levitate from Gustave?"

Very slowly, she nodded confirmation.

A silence fell over us then, Jameson breaking it a few long seconds later.

"This is going to take you time to accept, too, isn't it?" he asked, referring to my initial denial on healing. After I shrugged, he recommended, "When you do...keep it private. Don't announce it until you know how to protect yourself."

"Why?" I asked innocently.

He glanced warily at Isadora before answering, which didn't leave me all that reassured. "Because there are those who will want to take advantage of that power - or kill you because of it."

"Right..." I said grasping the severity of this unique asset they assumed I had. "Wonderful."

Isadora began ambling toward the door then, seeming to have come to the conclusion for all of us that only time would allow me to understand and acknowledge this larger fate. As Jameson and I followed, his eyes never left me and as I glanced at him I could see them filled with amazement, his head shaking in disbelief.

We took Isadora back to her home where she and Jameson briefly discussed contacting the Vires. The Seven's security forces would need to come and collect the body, for confirmation that Gustave was indeed dead and hadn't figured a way to break the punishment they'd cast. Then we were heading back to the cars, the boat empty now that the supplies had been delivered.

"That was a lot to be told in one night," he said, after we'd reached land and were standing at my driver's side door. "What can I do to make it easier?"

I shook my head. "Nothing," I replied slowly, thinking it through.

He gave me a grim smile and then said, "Sometime, not right now because it would be suspect, but sometime soon - I'd like to kiss you, Jocelyn."

My heart skipped a beat at his acknowledgement.

We didn't move, didn't breath as we stared into each other's eyes. Then the world fell away, the crickets were muted, the sloshing of the water against the boat was silenced, and there was only him left.

For the first time since we'd met it became apparent how much we both felt for each other.

Unable to summon any other words, I replied in a whisper with the only ones that came to mind, "I'd like that."

His face tightened then as he struggled to inhibit his own passion from swelling. Momentarily losing that fight, he brought his hand to my cheek. "Who would have thought that a Caldwell would fall for a Weatherford?"

"Or that a Weatherford would fall for a Caldwell..."

A smile stretched across his face, brightening at my admission. His hand dropped then and he took a step back, blinking once, hard, to stifle the rest of the stimulating rush surging through him.

"I won't say sleep well because I know that'll be impossible," he said and then chuckled.

"Yes, it will be..." I said, not looking forward to the hours I'd be spending tossing and turning.

The sun had already lightened the horizon as he opened my car door for me and I slipped inside. He told me that he'd keep me in his rearview mirror as he closed it and then we drove toward New Orleans.

Once home, I crept upstairs and fell into bed just as others started to stir awake. Soon there were footsteps on creaking floorboards, voices, and slamming doors.

No, I reminded myself again. My cousins are not the quiet kind.

Still, I didn't move. I lay on the covers, partly speculating on what Jameson's lips would feel like and partly judging the weight of a pencil I'd left on my nightstand, wondering if I might be able to lift it.

Simply to protect my sanity, the pencil won. I rolled over and attempted to stir the force I used when healing but didn't feel anything. So I sat up cross legged. Again, this failed. So I swung my legs over the bed and placed my hands on the edge of the mattress. That was when I felt it stir, the force inside me. Soon I was clutching the sheets, bent forward, breathing deeply, and completely unaware of my surroundings.

"What are you doing?" asked Estelle from the doorway.

I released my grip and started to laugh at myself, my shoulders shaking with the effort. Then she joined in until the rest of the cousins appeared in my doorway too, all of them curious.

"Going to tell us what's so funny?" asked Spencer over our bawling.

"I…" I made a good attempt to calm myself but still had to explain through bursts. "I…was trying…to levitate the pencil."

That was when Estelle's giggles ceased and the rest of my cousin's mouths fell open.

"What?" I asked, wondering what I could have possibly done so wrong to warrant the expressions on their faces.

The only motion that came from that side of the room was Estelle's finger. It lifted off the doorknob to point in my direction. Glancing around I nearly missed it and had to look back again.

The pencil was floating just above the nightstand's lamp.

"Vinnia..." I sighed, knowing she was playing a joke on me.

She shook her head, lips pinched closed but opening them just long enough to admit, "That's not me."

Then the pencil dropped and my cousins rushed inside my room, everyone speaking at once.

"You have the..." Nolan was saying, snapping his fingers like someone does when they've forgotten something.

"That thing that's written about in the journals..." said Estelle.

"That thing the first channelers saw..." said Oscar.

"You're the person with..." Vinnia began.

But Spencer, the book smart one, finally concluded it. "Residue. She has the ability to pick up residue."

Then they fell silent, gawking at me in admiration.

I didn't give up the fact that I already knew what it was called or that I'd known I had it for approximately three hours now.

"Come on," I said, feeling undeserving of it. "I'm not a celebrity."

Oscar chuckled under his breath. "You are in our world."

"You need to tell your mother," Vinnia declared.

The rest of them nodded vehemently.

"I will," I said, realizing just how significant this ability was to their world, my world. "I will." I didn't mention that first I'd give myself time to fully accept it. "But until I do, can you keep it to yourselves? I think she should find out from me instead of some stranger on the street." I knew this was an exaggerated scenario, to assume any stranger on any street might have any interest to talk about me. But if this ability were as impactful as everyone has made it out to be, I could rightfully imagine this scenario playing out. Evidently, so could they because they began nodding.

Estelle sat on the edge of the bed beside me. "And when I opened your door I thought you'd lost your mind…" she admitted, giggling. "This is so much better."

"Thanks," I said at her unintentional backhanded compliment.

"So," said Estelle, tapping my knee merrily. "How did you find out you could levitate?"

That sent a bolt of nerves through me. I couldn't tell them I'd been in a swamp attempting to save a man who transferred his power to me while Jameson Caldwell watched.

Instead, I shrugged and shook my head, unable to actually speak words that would mislead them.

"Maybe you've always had it…" offered Nolan. "You just didn't know it."

I gave the same gesture. "Vinnia, now that I know I'm able to levitate, could you show me how you do it?" I asked changing the subject.

Her head jerked back in surprise. "Of course."

A few minutes later we were in the kitchen, with items of varying weights lined up down the middle of the table. Next to my pencil, lay a book, a container of cooking utensils, the toaster, and, lastly, a sack of flour.

"Now," said Vinnia, looking at the clock. "We have about an hour before mother and Miss Mabelle get back from the farmers market. But if you can't do it right away, don't worry. It took me several years to actually control the object I was levitating. That said you could pick it up quicker."

"Nice pun," said Spencer. He stood along the counter to left of me with the rest of my cousins.

"I know," she said proudly and then readdressed me. "Now, the same energy that we use to levitate is the same used for all the other casts. The exact same," she insisted. "You already heal so you know what it feels like. This is where I ran into trouble while I was learning and why I

169

think you'll have better luck and quicker results because you've done it before."

"Are you ever going to let her attempt it?" asked Nolan irritably. "Or are you gonna wait until mother's coming through the door?"

She paused to glare at him sharply. Then, she turned to me and suggested demurely "Go ahead."

I appreciated her instruction though. This would be my first controlled attempt, ever, to lift something without touching it and the more advice the better.

I tried and my cousins patiently waited but after ten minutes. Nothing happened.

"Sometimes," said Vinnia, on the verge of frustration, "it's helpful to use your hand - to direct the energy through."

I raised my hand limply and said, "Like this?"

"No, no, not really," she said and then sighed. "Like this."

Then she took my hand, straightened my arm at the elbow, and pulled at my index finger. "Think of this as your own personal fire hose, only you're bursting energy instead of water."

That helped quite a bit and soon the pencil was rolling back and forth across the table.

"Good!" Estelle commented from the counter amidst my cousins nodding heads of approval.

"Now," said Vinnia, "use your fingers. Like…"

She pivoted my hand around so that it was face up and then wiggled my finger, as if I could coax the pencil upward.

To my shock, it actually worked. First the pencil tip lifted and, once it was at a slant, the eraser end rose from the table, too. It drifted through the air a few inches above the table and then I set it down.

For that, I received a round of applause.

The remaining items weren't as easy. Despite my focused efforts, by the time we heard Aunt Lizzy's Porsche pull into the driveway, the book had done no more than flapped a few pages, the container of cooking utensils lay on its side, the toaster's cord had wound its self into a ball, and the bag of flour had exploded.

We hurried to clean up the evidence in the kitchen but it was no use. On their trip through the door, Miss Mabelle barked, "Whatchu doin' in this hea kitchen? Hmmm?"

Before we had the chance to give her a reasonable excuse, she saw the flour and released a subsequent gasp. "You cleanin' that up now, ya hea?"

That ended our lesson for the day as we spent the next hour cleaning. Then there was normal school work to get done. So while everyone else found a quiet spot at the kitchen table, I noisily practiced my new ability. Once in a while their heads would jerk up at the sound of a spoon falling to the floor or a cookbook slamming against the wall. Only once did either Aunt Lizzy or Miss Mabelle enter the kitchen during that time and neither appeared to notice the spatula floating near the ceiling fan. By the time Miss Mabelle had to start dinner, I was lifting Oscar and his chair off the ground. It was unsteady so that he had to keep his hands on the table for support but it was an undeniable accomplishment. I barely had time to set him down when the door opened and Miss Mabelle came through, catching him on the side and nearly tossing him off, which brought a round of laughter from everyone.

As Miss Mabelle prepared our food, we collected our books and headed upstairs. But I wasn't ready to stop. There was an itch that made me slip back downstairs and out to the backyard, where I was alone and enclosed.

It was humid, as it had been every day since I'd arrived in the South, but temperate. A lawn mower ran off in the distance and I smelled apple pie baking from a house nearby. These were perfect distractions, comforting but not overwhelming to the point it drew my attention away entirely.

Sitting on the steps, I was able to rearrange Miss Mabelle's flower pots and water her hanging ferns without moving more than my finger. We'll see whether she notices, I mused.

At some point, a comment Vinnia had made floated through my mind, one that had implied I had more control over this ability than most did right when they recognize that they have it. And with that confidence in mind, I had the urge to really test my levitation skills, to see just how far I could take it.

Standing, I walked to a part of the yard not visible from the kitchen and slipped off my shoes. If I was going to do this, I wanted to know right when my feet left the ground.

Figuring that my finger wiggle wouldn't be much help, since the object I was about to move was me, I kept my hands next to my hips. The evening was approaching so that the shadows covered most of the yard. Birds shifted among the branches, which drew me away from what I was doing. So, this time, I closed my eyes.

The grass tickled the sides of my feet but other than the blades I sensed no other feeling. Then, as I concentrated, the force rose up stronger than it ever had, swelling my chest and causing me to inhale deeply. Then, as my lungs filled with the sultry air of New Orleans, I felt the grass leave my heels.

"Wow..." I whispered through my exhale.

I noticed two things instantly. First, my arms and legs felt like dead weight. The force came from my torso so that it didn't seem like my limbs served any purpose. Second, my spine felt weightless, as if sacks of air between my vertebrae served as balloons, lifting me off the ground.

I figured that my body had left the ground only a few inches so when I opened my eyes and found I was peering over our neighbor's roof, my body jolted. It was enough to send me down a few feet but not plummet to the ground. Although the drop was fast enough to stir a breeze and ruffle my clothes as I descended. I stopped a few feet above the ground and floated, attempting to balance myself with my arms.

While what I'd done so far was notable, I knew I could go further with this capability.

With Miss Mabelle's potting shed directly in front of me, I narrowed my aim for it and soon the tops of grass blades brushed my toes as I floated toward it. Ceasing just before the door was easy, what wasn't so much was my effort to spin around. Flailing my arms around didn't do any good, rotating my hips did nothing. After several minutes, I found the only way to turn directions was envisioning it. Soon, I was back to the other side of the yard, flipping as if I were on a jungle gym set, only one without bars, trying to contain my laughter so I didn't call attention to myself.

Only when I heard Miss Mabelle's shout that dinner was beginning did I lower myself to the ground and stroll inside, a private grin stretched across my face.

Miss Mabelle saw me coming and gave me a suspicious look. "Mmmmhmmm..." she muttered as I entered the dining room. If she noticed anything peculiar out the kitchen window she didn't mention it. To be honest, if she had I wouldn't have been so concerned. Unlike Aunt Lizzy, who didn't seem capable of keeping anything to herself, Miss Mabelle never seemed to say much at all.

Dinner was quick and conversation centered on the upcoming holiday, Samhain or Halloween as I knew it. Apparently, our evening school threw one party a year and it was on this day. Everyone would be required to wear a costume, no exceptions. While this sounded fine, I really wasn't one to dress up and after one complaint they spent the rest of the time trying to convince me it would be fun.

They would have been remiss if they found out that I didn't give it any more thought when dinner was over and we headed for our rooms. A school celebration didn't sound nearly as exciting as a midnight flight around New Orleans. And that was exactly what I had in mind as I crept back downstairs and out the back door.

The night was cooler now and the humidity had lessened so I was glad I'd pulled on a jacket and jeans for my first flight. The frogs and crickets seemed to fight over each other's volume as I stepped out to the grass again.

Using the same process as before, I lifted myself into the air, my legs dangling awkwardly below me. Before elevating, I took a trip around the backyard to get my equilibrium. Then I rose higher until the rooftops were beneath me, and the chorus of frogs and crickets no longer reached me. I made a quick note of how the streets below me looked like the replica of a miniature town, and then I allowed myself a quiet scream of excitement before taking off over the houses.

Not a single person noticed me as I soared over the city, along the Riverwalk and up over the French Quarter. Keeping my hands at my sides made me more aerodynamic and helped me balance, I noticed. You would think that temperature would be more of a problem than balance when considering the height I was at but that wasn't the case. Maybe this levitation thing had some sort of built-in temperature control because for reasons I couldn't quite pinpoint there was no fluctuation in the chill of the air or wind velocity. It was as if I were sitting in front of a fan set on low speed.

My tour of the city took me over Bourbon Street where I found it packed with people. From the air, it was very different. The near constant aroma of decrepit buildings and southern food didn't reach this high. It was quieter here too. The jazz, thumping bar music, and voices couldn't be heard. Still, it was just as beautiful as on the ground with flashing signs radiating Mardi Gras colors off the wet pavement and gas lamp street lights flickering across the cobblestones.

I was enjoying my trip, wishing Jameson could be here to see it with me, when I passed over the building where our evening classes are held.

Then, the thrill of it ended.

My flight overhead had been completely unintentional. In fact, I hadn't even realized where I was until recognizing the courtyard. But what drew my attention were the people in it.

The courtyard should have been empty.

I dropped closer and deduced from the colorful dress and hair wound into a bun that one of them was Ms. Veilleux. The other two I couldn't identify right away. I'd never seen them before tonight. Wearing black, hooded cloaks, they stood opposite Ms. Veilleux as the three engaged in a conversation.

There was no telling at this distance, several feet above the rooftops, what their topic could be but I knew it turned serious when Ms. Veilleux tried to leave and they didn't allow it.

She was halfway rotated when one seized her elbow. While she stood her ground, tilting her chin up, she didn't force the issue and remained in place. Only when the person finished what they had to say was Ms. Veilleux released.

Then, in unison, the two figures spun and disappeared down the courtyard's tunnel toward the street. I watched as Ms. Veilleux wrapped her arms around her torso and rubbed her shoulders, a clear sign that whatever she'd been discussing wasn't good.

I stayed long enough to watch the other two step into a waiting vehicle and disappear through the city streets.

On my way home, as I flew over Jameson's house it dawned on me who they were, Ms. Veilleux's mysterious cloaked visitors. I noticed that the Caldwell lights were off though, and I wasn't sure if I could get away with stopping there anyway.

I would need to wait until Monday to tell Jameson that Ms. Veilleux had been paid a visit by the Vires.

13. VIRES

Sunday morning's breakfast was left almost untouched after I mentioned the Vires. After I got a good scolding for being out alone, the speculations began and none of them were positive.

"The Caldwells are planning a serious retaliation…"

"The Vires are moving into our province…"

"The school is closing…"

Estelle was the first to place her fork to the side and the others quickly followed. "Most likely, they're checking in again, making sure we haven't disobeyed their command to avoid the Caldwells."

"Like we are their wards," Vinnia scoffed.

In an attempt to help us face reality, Spencer mentioned, "To them…we are their wards."

That made us pause, some of us shaking our heads.

"Maybe it had nothing to do with us," suggested Oscar, always the level headed one. "Could be they had something else to talk about with Ms. Veilleux. There was that thing with the Monteux kid last month - where he almost burnt down the school with his cast - incantatio flamus-"

"Incantatio flamma ignire," corrected Spencer. "You have to study your Latin if you want to pass practical exams next year. I'm telling you, Mr. Mercier isn't called The Merciless for no reason."

Oscar responded to Spencer's chastising with a roll of his eyes.

"Anyway," said Estelle, "I still think there's something wrong. The Monteux kid isn't it. He was punished already."

"Well, whatever it is, it wasn't good," I said. "It looked like they were warning her - and she didn't want to hear it."

"Why'd you get that impression," asked Nolan, who'd been nervously crouched over his plate since I had brought it up.

"Because she tried to walk away and they stopped her." I delivered this news flatly, emotions about it broiling so deeply I wouldn't allow them to surface.

"Sounds like the Vires..." sighed Vinnia.

The room went silent as tensions rose.

"Remember that family over in the northwest province?" said Estelle. "They were in Seattle, right?"

"Portland," corrected Spencer.

The rest of the table had their heads down now, remembering. There was heaviness in the air as if the energy around us had become depressed.

"What happened?" I asked disturbed but intrigued.

Oscar leaned back in his chair, the thought of breakfast seeming to leave him nauseous. "They were caught casting in the woods, deep in the woods where you don't cross paths with anyone else for days. They took extra precaution not to be seen in fact. Anyway, it was some sort of family ritual meant to renew their protection." He stopped and pinched his lips before continuing, his tone more subdued. "And it didn't work."

After a few seconds of apprehensive silence, I persisted, "Did the Vires find them?"

"No, they were turned in." He drew in a deep breath. "Turned in and punished. Almost everyone said they were used as an example, but there are those of us who know better. They weren't examples - they were trophies. The Vire used them for recreational casting and when they were good and tortured they strung them up at the ministry and kept them alive until the story could reach every province."

I swallowed back the bile that rose in my throat. "The ministry?"

"Your mother fought on the family's behalf," said Vinnia, deducing my thoughts. "She just didn't have anyone else on her side at that time to help."

"Yep..." said Estelle, staring out the kitchen window at nothing in particular, "it's the first rule you learn. Don't get caught casting in public."

I thought about the Caldwells and their attempts to freeze, overheat, or drench me in the hallways of our school during the day. But, other than Charlotte's first try, none of their efforts were so obvious it couldn't be traced back to them. And that was exactly what Aunt Lizzy had forewarned me about on the plane here. They were sneaky. Regardless, the very fact they were casting in public made me realize just how dedicated they were to affecting me.

"If they try anything like that on Ms. Veilleux..." threatened Vinnia, again amazing me that the smallest of the Weatherfords had the most nerve.

"Nah," denounced Oscar. "Won't need to. She keeps that school obscure enough. Her neighbors still think she tutors wealthy delinquents."

Now I understood the secrecy.

"That's why I'm so surprised the Vires contacted her last night," said Estelle exasperated. "It has to be because of us and the Caldwells."

The rest of the table shrugged or frowned but Oscar spoke for us all. "If it is, we'll know soon enough."

The conjecture and assumptions lasted the rest of the day, someone throwing out a possibility every few hours. But it wasn't until Monday that I heard the most reasonable explanation.

I was on my way to second period, keeping my eyes moving through the crowd in case I ran into a Caldwell and hoping if I did it would be Jameson. As it turned out, we did cross paths but not the way I expected.

The fast-paced footsteps caught my attention first. Then the crowd around me was running, sharply brushing my shoulders in an effort to get around me, and closer to whatever was ahead. Shouts started about then and they were along the lines of…

"Fight!"

"They're girls!"

"It's a Weatherford and a Caldwell!"

That last one launched me into a sprint.

I followed the flow of the crowd until reaching the part where they clustered together around a vacant center in which two heads were positioned only a foot apart.

I recognized them instantly.

Estelle and Alison…

Shoving my way through the swarm of students, I reached the center and found them pitted silently against each other, mouths turned down, eyes locked on each other, daring the other to make the first move. Their book bags were hanging at their sides, straps gripped between clenched fingers, and I knew they would become weapons if given the chance. Without the option to cast here in the hallway, it was the only tool they had.

Jameson broke through the circle on the opposite side at the same time I did and our eyes met. His were the same as mine…deeply apprehensive.

We each stepped across the opening, closing in on our relatives, and meeting them at the same time.

"Let's go Alison," said Jameson, his voice commanding.

She didn't respond. Not even a flinch was made at the sound of his voice.

"Estelle, this can't happen."

There was no sign of her withdrawing either.

I looked up at Jameson and shook my head, perplexed on what to do next.

His expression had turned by then, not to anger or frustration. It was telling me to leave, to get out of here before something was said or a move was made and I was caught in the middle of it.

Very slowly, I shook my head from one side to the other and back again, denying him.

I knew he understood as his shoulders dropped and he sighed in frustration.

"Alison, not here," Jameson warned. "Not now."

The only movement made was an almost imperceptible raise of her lip, into a snarl.

"What started this?" I demanded and then I saw it - the water down the front of Alison's shirt and the flattened, bent cup inside Estelle's fist.

"Estelle!" I sighed.

"It was an accident," she seethed to me and then reiterated it sharply for Alison's benefit. "An accident."

"A manufactured accident," Alison hissed. "Weatherford's are professionals at displacing blame."

I paused, realizing that was exactly the belief held in my family toward theirs. How could two families be so similar and still be at odds, I wondered. Without the time to evaluate it, I simply used this notion to turn the fight around.

"Jameson," I said cautiously, drawing his attention back to me. Knowing Alison wouldn't listen to anything I had to say, he was the only path to reason. "If Estelle meant to do this, wouldn't she have done it without Alison knowing she'd done it? Why execute it so obviously?"

With a surprised lift of his eyebrows, he caught on to what I was doing and agreed. "As much as I hate to admit it, Alison, the Weatherford is right. When was the last time you could actually tell a Weatherford was the one to blame?"

That was when I realized it. Jameson didn't put as much stock as his family did in blaming us for unexplainable problems arising. At some point, he'd concluded it wasn't feasible or reasonable. And that was his way. He was logical. It was that very trait that allowed him to look beyond the past and see me as more than an enemy. Now he was attempting to do the same with his family.

It seemed like Alison was listening, starting to waver in her belief that Estelle had preplanned the spill down her shirt, her hesitation seeming almost palpable...and then she spoke.

"I really don't care if it was intentional or not." She'd made up her mind. And with that she opened her mouth and said, "Incant-"

In that moment, several things happened at once. Jameson seized Alison by the mouth and hauled her backwards. I stepped in front of Estelle to form a wall between them. My cousins stepped forward forming a wall behind me. And the crowd around us went wild, screaming and clapping at the event playing out in front of them.

I watched as Jameson struggled to contain his sister, shoving backwards through the horde until they'd been swallowed up by it, the guys around them bent over in laughter, the girls leaned together in gossip.

Ignoring the crowd, I spun around. "Estelle, are you all right?"

Her expression said it all. She was astonished. If there had ever been any question as to whether the Caldwells had the gumption to cast in public, it was now erased. Estelle, nor the rest of us, would ever refute that again.

"She's fine," said Oscar after a quick assessment and then he addressed the crowd. "Get to class everyone. You're late. Show's over."

While a few boos rose up, they did disperse and I headed for second period. Jameson was delayed by another minute and received just as harsh a glare from Ms. Wizner as I did.

When he took a seat, he didn't address me. Instead, he ducked his head, pulled out his laptop and began typing. Peeking in his direction, I wondered if somehow the incident in the hall had come between us, that he was mad at me. When he didn't acknowledge my sly look, and I knew he'd seen it, I settled on the conclusion that he could believe what he wanted.

Let him be angry, I thought. What he saw wasn't my fault. I didn't start it. I was trying to-

Then, with no one watching, his arm rose and he settled his hand over mine. It was warm, firm, and comforting.

His voice came through clearly, at the same slow cadence and easy going tone he typically used. Only this time, I heard it in my head.

"Good," he said, jolting me. He waited for my muscles to relax again, to unwind from the shock of hearing him in my head, before he spoke. "You're not hurt, are you?"

I shook my head, still keeping my eyes straight forward, on Ms. Wizner; although at that point, I wouldn't have cared if she saw Jameson holding my hand or not. What was going on in my head was enough to handle.

"That's all I wanted to know," he said and started to pull his hand away.

I rushed to place my free hand on top of his. And then I said without moving my lips, "You're channeling, aren't you?"

For no good reason, I was surprised when he answered because it meant he'd heard me.

"Yes."

"You said you channel other's abilities," I said, inferring he'd never mentioned that he could channel thoughts.

I heard his laughter clearly in my head. "You speak, right? That's what I'm channeling; your ability to speak."

"And can you do it any time?"

"Only when I'm touching you," he allayed my fears.

Still, I thought back through all the times we'd connected and wondered if I'd ever been thinking about how I felt when he was around.

"No," came his voice. "But the secret's out now..." Then I heard him chuckle.

Reflex made me draw in a quick breath, offended at his teasing, causing Janice Beltro in front of us to glance over her shoulder. But Jameson swiftly dropped his hand before her head made it all the way around.

Ms. Wizner didn't notice and continued on with her lecture, which we listened to for a few minutes. But I couldn't resist for too long and soon held my hand out, dropping it down beside my desk in a gesture that asked Jameson to take it.

As his fingers brushed against my palm and slipped between mine, intertwining, I struggled to inhale steadily.

"Yes?" he asked and I could hear the smile in his voice without looking at him.

"This was how you knew what I was like in Olivia's shop the first time we met - when the things began flying off the shelves. You channeled me then, didn't you?"

He didn't immediately respond and I got the sense that I was correct and he was embarrassed by it.

"Didn't you?" I persisted, unwilling to let him off the hook.

"Yes, sorry…"

"And the candle you gave me that same day - which you sent my birthday gift through. That was you channeling your message through the smoke, wasn't it?"

"Yes."

"And when I'm healing others - and you're holding my hand - you're reading my thoughts then too?"

"No," he stated so quickly that I believed him. "I only feel your ability then. I think it overpowers whatever is going through your mind."

"So what have you figured out about me during the times you have channeled my thoughts?" I asked, knowing the anger came through in my tone even without speaking the words.

I'd been looking for confirmation on what I'd said but he didn't offer it. Instead, he returned the favor I'd given him on the first day I'd found out that he was a Caldwell. He assessed me as I'd done him.

"You surprised me. You aren't what I expected a Weatherford to be. You're kind and you have a strength and courage that you tap when dealing with others. You don't take on others' beliefs as your own but choose to make the decision yourself. And you don't like authority. You don't like to be told what to do. And you're irresistibly gorgeous."

Despite my best efforts, my heart warmed to him again and my anger melted away. Then he ruined all that built-up collateral.

"But you lack patience, Jocelyn, and you don't trust easily; which, granted, may or may not be such a bad thing."

He heard, or saw, my responding sigh of irritation.

"I probably shouldn't have mentioned that," he said, his tone guilty.

"The skepticism is something that I've been taught," I replied, thinking of my mother and her insistence that I question everything.

"And being a Weatherford, I don't blame you."

"Speaking of trust, there's something I need to tell you," I said, again feeling my muscles stiffen.

"What?" he asked, nervously, sensing my reaction.

"Alison needs to be warned, your whole family does, they can't cast against me or anyone else in my family again."

"I've been working on that-"

"Tell them the Vires visited Ms. Veilleux. Maybe that will help."

He didn't reply for what felt like a very long time. I tried to sense, to capture whatever it was he was thinking but, unlike him, I didn't have the ability to read someone else's mind. He had to channel his thoughts and he wasn't doing it now.

Finally, he sighed, something I would have noticed even if we hadn't been holding hands. Then his head dropped and he closed his eyes briefly clearing his thoughts.

"They didn't visit her for the reasons you're thinking. The Vires were here because of us, because we cured the village and they've never seen anything like that before."

"I don't understand…"

When he spoke he didn't try to hide his despair. "They found out, somehow…probably through their emissaries…that an entire village was healed overnight. That's unheard of in our world…in anyone's world for that matter. And it means that someone got around their cast, that someone was able to help those they punished." Jameson sighed and his jaw clenched down in anger. "I'm so sorry, Jocelyn. I think…" He drew in struggled breath. "I think I've put you in danger."

For the first time since our conversation began, Jameson looked at me, his eyes filled with remorse. And I wanted so desperately to reach across the aisle and comfort him.

Still holding my hand, he sensed this, or saw my thoughts in his mind. And in reaction he blinked, distracted from the guilt running through him and replacing it with inhibited shock. Then a hesitant grin rose up.

He knew I wanted to kiss him. That much I was certain of.

Given our surroundings, I settled for a much less satisfying squeeze of his hand and a message that I hoped would pacify him. "It's not your fault. I chose to go. And before you make the argument that I didn't know it would be dangerous, you need to know that I thought we were visiting convicts - which is never safe. I went in to danger with my eyes open."

He laughed under his breath and then shook his head. "That doesn't surprise me."

"Next time, we'll just make sure to pace ourselves so not everyone is healed at once. Maybe take the worst patients first…" I suggested and his eyes widened in frustration.

"You don't think I'd agree with you going again?" he asked in disbelief.

"You can't stop me, Jameson. I already know where to find them and if they need my help I'm going."

His jaw shifted in disapproval as he returned his attention to Ms. Wizner, or so it seemed. By continuing to hold my hand, our connection to each other, he told me that he wasn't ending our conversation but calming his anger before continuing.

Or maybe he was waiting for me to back down. If so, he'd be waiting a while. I'd coursed through my life until this point, teasing those who had authority over me, denying my gift, never truly considering anyone else's needs, sneaking out to look for trouble and if I didn't find it then starting it. Those were the actions of a little girl, an immature and insignificant child. But I was no longer that child. The night in the backyard when I'd accepted my fate, my heritage, I'd accepted something else - I had a responsibility now. For the first time in my life, I had a reason for being, a goal, a hunger that didn't seem capable of being fulfilled. I was now here to help others and I would do it to the best of my ability.

Satisfied, I drew in a deep breath and found Ms. Wizner discussing 18th century novelists, the same lecture Professor Clements had been giving the day my life had suddenly and drastically changed. So much had happened since then...I mused. And whatever kind of danger I might be in now, I was happy with my new, altered life's direction.

Then Jameson's voice ran through my mind again. "Umm, I heard all that..." he admitted sheepishly.

"Everything?"

He tilted his head to the side and gave me a look that meant...yes. "Thought you should know. I wasn't trying to violate your private dialogue, I just...I couldn't avoid it. Your voice gets louder when you're...determined."

"Well, I meant what I said...thought," I corrected myself. "I'm not backing down."

He didn't agree with my decision, which was clear by the expression in his face. Figuring there was no possible way he would win this argument, he changed the subject. "In case you don't have enough danger in your life...there's something I've wanted to ask you." He paused and looked directly at me, his hand flinching as the nervousness coursed through him. "Will you go out with me this Saturday?"

My obstinacy fell away and I was overtaken by flattery.

"What did you have in mind? Planning to pick me up at my house?" I asked playfully.

"Not sure I'd make it passed the driveway," he said through a laugh. "No, I had something else in mind."

Then he laid out his plan and by the end of it I was having trouble containing the excitement surging through me.

With a content grin, he released my hand and I sat in a surreal state, realizing we'd just held an entire conversation, had agreed to a secret date, all without anyone hearing us or the need to open our mouths.

It dawned on me that since I'd met Jameson we'd managed to keep the true nature of our relationship a secret, limited to platonic, even if contested, interactions in evening classes once a week. No one knew of our private conversations or secret rendezvous' and it made me feel as if we were getting away with something.

I had no idea, no premonition at all, that everything was about to change.

14. DATE

Halloween was treated entirely different in New Orleans than it was at Wentworth Preparatory Academy in New York. There, we were given juice and an extra cookie for dessert while treated to an obligatory talent contest in order to satisfy the need for costumes. New Orleans, on the other hand, exploded into a visual parade of colors and disguises. Houses hosted sophisticated galas and Frenchmen Street prepared for thousands of people to descend on it during its annual, elaborate parade of frighteningly detailed floats. Local bars boasted contests while stores throughout The Quarter sold costumes ranging from fancy to startling. It felt as if electricity buzzed in the air as the city transformed itself.

Then, of course, there were the clandestine preparations made within our world to which few were privy. Specialty candles and exotic scents were bought in mass quantity from stores hidden to the regular public. Decorations of a different kind were taken down from the rafters. Rather than witches with broomsticks there were wreaths of dried herbs hanging at the door. Instead of ghosts and tombstones propped in the front yard, there were books of messages and family keepsakes left for dead relatives in case they decided to stop by.

As signs of Halloween crept up around New Orleans, Jameson and I continued meeting at the back of the gym after school for our unusual tryst to find people to heal. Wednesday was included because Ms. Veilleux's school needed it to prepare for their own Samhain celebration, giving Jameson and me an extra day together. Against his preference, I accompanied him to the village and helped deliver supplies. There and on the way back, our hands found each other across the car's console and remained entwined for the duration we were driving. There were no more instances of La Terreur so we saw Isadora briefly, where she again wrapped my family stone in a red cloth.

The rest of my free time that week was spent preparing for Saturday, either deciding on a costume for myself or helping my cousins select theirs.

Then Saturday arrived and all I could think about was my date with Jameson.

"Can you help me?" was the first time I really heard anyone speak that day. It came from Estelle sometime around five o'clock in the evening when the sun was just about to drop below the horizon.

"Sure," I said, glancing up from a book I'd found in Aunt Lizzy's library on medicinal herbs. While it captured my attention for the first five minutes, the last two hours had been spent gazing impassively at the words on the page and wondering how tonight would evolve with Jameson.

"I just need you to thip me up." Estelle had chosen to be a fairy with fangs, which made it difficult for her to speak.

I stifled a giggle at her expense and secured the back of her deep purple layered chiffon dress. She looked exquisite.

"We leafff in thirty minutes," she said with a clap of her hands. "Do you need helf getting ready?"

"No, Miss Mabelle found something for me to wear."

I didn't mention how oddly appropriate her selection was either. Part of Jameson's plan to escape the prying eyes of our relatives was to dress in masquerade and the outfit Miss Mabelle left in my closet without my having to ask, fit the occasion perfectly.

Taken directly out of a fairy tale, the dress was entirely white, sleeveless and narrowed at the waist to flare out until reaching my feet. It came with a white chocker and a mask that looked as if it had been dipped in diamonds. And, what stood out the most was that it seemed to be custom-tailored to my tall height. With my hair coiled and loosely pinned up, the ensemble fit me perfectly.

I heard gasps as I came down the stairs, confirming it.

Having no interest in being the center of my cousins' doting attention, when they looked stunning themselves, I asked before anyone could comment, "Ready?"

"Abtholutely!" exclaimed Estelle.

Then we left, with me trailing behind Oscar as a mobster, Nolan as a barbarian, Spencer as a mad scientist, Estelle in her wicked fairy outfit, and Vinnia as a traditional witch. Each of their costumes fit them perfectly in size and personality and I knew before they mentioned it that they'd found the outfit hung in their closet by Miss Mabelle, too.

The rest of the students showed no shortage of creativity. With ten-foot tall wings, a Pinocchio nose two feet long, and Pippi Longstocking braids extending out arms length on both sides it was intriguing to walk into the courtyard.

Our evening school had been transformed, too. Ms. Veilleux and her staff made the most of their spare days to set up tarot card stations, palm reading stations, food stations with dishes like edible fingers and spider popcorn, drink stations with cauldrons of steaming brews, and a place for leaving private messages for the dead. If there was music, however, it couldn't be heard over the squeals of laughter as we assessed one another's costumes.

No one seemed to notice when the Caldwells arrived, me included even though my attention was on that sole purpose since entering the courtyard.

"Tarot cards?" he whispered, referring to the fact I was standing beside Miranda having her cards read. "And I thought you didn't believe in this hocus pocus…"

My lips turning up in a smile, I rotated at the waist to find him standing beside me. Dressed in a black tuxedo, his sturdy build showed the outline of his muscles through the fabric, and the diagonal white face mask revealed only his cheek, half of his seductively contoured lips, and the remnants of the scar above his lip. I was momentarily distracted.

Apparently, he was too, because his grin fell and he swallowed back the passion so evident in his eyes. "You're stunning," he whispered passed an unmistakable lump in his throat.

"Thank you," I said demurely though not intending it.

We stood awkwardly in silence, drinking in the sight of each other, and then another voice broke through our focus.

It was more of a gasp actually.

Jameson and I turned in unison to find Miranda was no longer at the table but tarot cards were, nonetheless, laid across it. The woman, dressed in a colorful silk wrap, spoke limited English with a thick Spanish accent as she placed a painted nail on top of one card.

"Enemies," she stated.

Her finger moved to the card next to it.

"Lovers…"

Her face contorted into confusion then.

"Enemies…but lovers?"

Jameson briefly placed a hand on her shoulder while he explained through a chuckle as best he could. "It stumps us, too."

Then Jameson's hand was on my back, guiding me through the crowd. He directed me toward the stairs running up the side of both ends of the courtyard to the second floor where the voices from below became more muffled. This level was vacant and dimmer, without the gas lamps lit like those on the bottom floor. We took a third flight of stairs, curving around the edge of the building until the courtyard was behind us and the city lights extended out ahead.

It took me a second to realize we were on the roof. In fact, only when I finished surveying where we'd ended up did I find what Jameson had done.

To our right, on the flattest part, he'd brought up a canvas bag similar to the ones used on deliveries to the village. It leaned against one side of the layered rooftop, unidentifiable items protruding through the top. Other than that, the roof was empty.

"We're not supposed to be up here but I wanted to show you..." he said while removing his mask.

I took my mask off too and glanced around before teasing, "You shouldn't have..."

"Wait," he chuckled. "Just a second..."

He moved quickly then and I got the impression it was because he didn't want me to lose hope he'd put any effort into his first date with me. Pulling a lantern from the bag and lighting it, he stooped down in the front of the horizontal wall.

"Here," he urged.

Curious, I stepped forward, although I did it cautiously. The building we were standing on was old enough to send us through the ceiling at any given moment. But once at his side, the age of the structure became unpredictably heartwarming.

In the lantern's glow, Jameson pointed to carvings made in the wall - a list of names. They were cut into the wood with various techniques and angles so I deduced each one was made by their respective owner.

"Remember when Ms. Veilleux disciplined us that night in the courtyard? She mentioned that this school had created some of the most gifted of our kind? These are their names…"

"Huh, think we should add ours?" I asked mischievous but joking with him.

He smiled and then insisted, "Look at the names, Jocelyn."

I did take a closer look and then I couldn't take my eyes off them, not only because of their significance, but because of the surnames. Ms. Veilleux was noted among them along with ten others, but it was two names in particular that made my lungs freeze for a few seconds. One was Louis Caldwell, Jameson's relative I figured, and the other one I lingered on much longer. It was Isabella Weatherford…my mother's name.

I drew in a breath, finally, and then absentmindedly reached out to touch it, instantly missing her, trying to reach across to her through the carving.

"She was a student here…" I sighed. "I never…I never even considered that to be possible."

"So was my dad," said Jameson and I knew he was referring to the name Louis, the one above my mother's.

"If these are in order, they went to school here close to the same time," I pointed out.

Jameson nodded. "Or during the very same time."

The comparison was striking. Jameson and I. His father and my mother. I wondered if they had a volatile relationship like the rest of our relatives had throughout history.

"I…I'm sorry about your father," he said with sincere empathy. "Do you know if he went to school here?"

I shrugged. "I don't know much of anything. My mother never talks about my family."

"Ever?" That seemed to shock him but with the Caldwell's being so close knit I understood why.

"No, I didn't have a clue about my family here in New Orleans until I met them a few weeks ago."

"Nothing at all?" he said but didn't wait for an answer. He already knew what it would be. "What do you talk about with your mother? Wait...maybe I don't want to know..."

"Not girl stuff," I alleviated his fears.

"Oh...all right."

I laughed with him for a second before explaining. "When she picked me up for the holidays, she mostly spent the time quizzing me."

"On what?" he asked, deeply intrigued.

"Herbs, stones, Latin. Although I didn't pay as much attention to the language part and now I wish I would have."

He laughed to himself. "I know the feeling. Those seem like...if you don't mind me saying...like odd things to talk about with your mother."

"I think she's been preparing me for this world, our world, for a long time. She just never specifically mentioned it." I shrugged. "But it's what we do. We travel, she teaches, I learn."

"Travel?" He lifted his eyebrows curiously. "Where do you go?"

"Everywhere. My mother introduced me to her friends in every major city. London, Rome, Amsterdam, Munich. Name it and I've probably been there."

His forehead creased as he analyzed something he'd picked up on. "Hmm, that's interesting..."

"What is?" I asked trying to understand whatever it was I'd missed.

"It's probably just coincidence but those are the cities where our world has major provinces."

That was stunning and for a moment I was speechless. Then, without much else to say, I replied, "Well...if there's one thing that's certain about my mother it's that she's mysterious."

I looked up when he paused to find him openly evaluating me, a content smile hovering below the surface. "I heard your mother is breathtaking...You must have gotten her looks."

Before I could even respond, he'd stood and walked to the canvas bag. From it, he pulled a blanket and pillows to lay them out against the back wall.

"That's..." I started and then contemplated whether I should finish my sentence.

"Hmm?" he said over his shoulder as he finished setting up and then sat down with his back against the wall. "That's...what?"

Still hesitant, I stated, "That's not exactly the kind of description I'd expect about my mother coming from the Caldwells."

His eyebrows rose. "We're not as bad as you probably assume. Actually, we're pretty fair when describing you Weatherfords."

I believed him. Everything I'd seen so far from both families had involved childish behavior, but they'd always respected their adversaries nonetheless. There just wasn't any trust between them.

"I'd have to say the same for my family," I said, moving to sit down beside him. Not so close that we touched but close enough that I felt the tension arise between us.

"Is that right?" he replied stiffly, reacting to my presence so close. And then he relaxed a little. "What do they say about us?"

I described his family like Oscar had during lunch on the first day of school and when I was done his gaze drifted to the city landscape, contemplating, an amused expression lifting his lips.

"I'll have to tell them," he said finally. "Maybe it'll stop the haranguing I regularly get for choosing you as a partner during our Wednesday classes."

"Might take a little more than that," I warned and we laughed together knowing the truth behind my statement.

"Your family still doesn't know, do they?"

I shook my head. "I figured those in our class aren't the gossiping type."

He snickered through his nose. "I have another theory."

"Which is?"

"Sometimes it's more frightening to be the messenger of bad news than it is to simply avoid delivering the message at all."

"Fear is a strong motivator," I agreed.

"And so is courage," he stated before reaching for my hand. I felt his fingers gently touch mine in the dark, curling around mine, sending a current of pleasure through me.

"Is this all right?" he asked tenderly.

"Yes," I breathed, still trying to control the emotions coursing through me.

"I could tell it made you nervous to hold my hand in the beginning," he confessed. "You're getting better at it."

I scoffed and then realized he was conveying that he wasn't picking up as many erratic thoughts.

"I'm taking that as a good sign. Should I?" he asked anxiously.

"Yes," I said meaning to soothe him. "Is that why you hesitated in kissing me on the edge of the water after we got back from the village?"

"You've been wondering about that?"

"Mmmhmm…"

He didn't answer my question right away and I was certain he was evaluating how straightforward he should be. Then, he resolved his internal issue and confirmed, "I don't want to move so fast that I scare you away. I figured you've been fed a steady diet of fear of us Caldwells so breaking down that barrier will take time. But I'm willing to wait. You're worth it, Jocelyn."

His honesty was staggering, catching me off guard. "Thank you," I replied in a whisper, unable to coax my voice any higher.

He had stunned me, which didn't happen often.

Before he could witness my reaction to him, I rapidly thought of something to say, to carry on the conversation so that I could overcome his affect on me. "There's something else I've been curious to know. That scar over your lip. How did you get it?"

I felt a subconscious squeeze of his hand and wondered if I'd treaded into territory I shouldn't have, and then he began to tell a story so riveting I couldn't bring myself to stop encouraging it.

"Well, the public version is that I was testing my channeling when I first figured out that I had it, around the time I was four, which is about a year earlier than most. I channeled Alison's ability to levitate and sent a sharp object across the room where it nicked me."

"But that's the official story, not the real one?" I asked, sensing there was that explanation too.

"Right. The real one is not so politically correct." He paused, seeming to prepare himself for his next statement. "I was almost abducted when I was born."

I gasped, although probably not for the reason he assumed. While I did feel genuine concern for him, it was the fact that once again another similarity between us had crept up.

"The kidnapping failed but I was left with the scar when my family fought back."

I tightened my hold on his hand, an unexpected protectiveness creeping over me.

"Did they ever…Was the kidnapper ever apprehended?"

"Nah, got away," he said clearly relieved. "Got away and never came back."

I slowly nodded my head, taking in everything he'd said. "What are the odds that attempted kidnappings are made on newborns from the two most volatile feuding families in the same year, the same timeframe?"

He looked at me perplexed. "What are you saying? There was an attempted kidnapping on you, too?"

Very slowly, I nodded my head, allowing him time for that fact to sink in. I knew it had when he released his breath in a rush and then he was blinking to clear the notions of the truth running through his mind.

"You don't think…" he said before his voice trailed off.

"No," I replied, already having deduced what he was thinking. "There's no evidence to point at either family being involved, right?"

"Nothing but the assumption of it," he said flatly, while still pondering it.

"Then let's not play in to that assumption," I suggested.

"You know…" he said, perplexed. "The affect that news has on me isn't what is expected of me. I still feel frustrated by the lack of facts, and angry that anyone would attempt to steal a baby, but mostly…I feel protective of you. Whether my family is involved or not, I don't want you hurt."

"Funny…" I said. "I feel the same way about you…"

Slowly, I felt his hand tighten, firm but gentle, around mine. His breathing quickened as our eyes locked. He leaned toward me, bending to the side. Our shoulders touched first, the feeling of his muscles there exploding through me. Then our lips found each other, soft and exploring, fitting perfectly to my contours. Moving to a rhythm all our own, they pressed tighter, growing more intense. His hand lifted to rest on my cheek, cupping it gently, guiding me closer to him. And his scent was all around me, tantalizing, seductive. My hands were in his hair suddenly, drawing him to me, curling through their softness.

And then he pulled away, his arms dropping, his body straightening, distancing himself.

In a daze, I looked at him and found he was no longer focused on me.

He knew they were there before I did.

Now his attention was on Ms. Veilleux and our class standing behind her.

15. DIVISION

"I'm so very sorry…" Miranda stood with her chin down, bashful, overwhelmed with guilt, and barely able to look at us. It was clear her apology was meant for Jameson and me. But it wasn't immediately apparent to the rest of the group, including the Caldwells and Weatherfords, until she added, "I didn't know it was you two."

Charlotte's head snapped in her direction. "And had you known, you would have kept it a secret?"

"I…I…" Miranda, feeling the full onslaught of Charlotte's rage, cowered away.

"Don't yell at her, Charlotte," said Jameson calmly.

He was the first of us to stand up and then he offered me a hand. This, I thought, was incredibly bold in light of what we were facing. I wondered if he understood the magnitude of it. He had just been caught kissing a Weatherford, his family's mortal enemy, and now he was going to help her up.

I took his hand, nonetheless, and then stood at his side in an exhibition of solidarity.

Without having to look for confirmation, I knew my cousins watched every movement. What I didn't know for certain was what expressions they wore, although I could guess. Pain. Anger. Offense. Shock. All of which would be warranted by my betrayal. I couldn't seem to bring myself to raise my eyes and confirm it though.

"What were you thinking?" demanded Alison to her brother, a question I'm sure he would be required to answer whether here or at home.

"Students, I asked you to stay down-" Ms. Veilleux began to reprimand but another voice began speaking over her.

It was Jameson, who still held on to my hand and was using it to channel his thoughts.

"I'm sorry, I think our date is over," he said as an obvious understatement and I had to restrain myself from laughing.

"I had a great time, Jameson."

He didn't respond right away but when he did the sincerity in his tone made his hesitation worthwhile. "It was the best night of my life, Jocelyn." There was another pause and then his tone came through my head deeper, more reserved. "They're going to try to separate us. They'll tell us stories, try to remind us that we should be enemies. My family's been doing this all along but I haven't listened to them - and I won't start now."

By this point, the students had cleared off the roof, our families being the last to leave, but they eventually did. It was just Ms. Veilleux now and she was walking toward us.

Stopping directly in front, she tilted her head at our hands. "Do you mind?" she said, conveying she knew we were channeling.

Reluctantly, we released our hold on each other and she replied graciously. "Thank you. Now, while I am pleased to find a Caldwell and a Weatherford getting along well, it does cause some consternation among others. Not simply your family, mind you. The students here, the faculty, we have quietly accepted the blossoming of your relationship.

We have done so with discretion so as to avoid possible conflicts between your two families. Not to mention, none of us sought to be the deliverer of that news."

So, I thought, Jameson had been correct.

"However," Ms. Veilleux went on, "we do not…cannot allow your relationship to ignite a battle, of which I am quite certain would be cataclysmic in magnitude. Thus, I would ask that any future meetings between the two of you be in public view where your behavior cannot be called in to question or conduct them in an absolutely and completely private and secure setting. In other words…do not get caught." She tugged at the ends of her sleeves indignantly and finished with, "I'll leave the remaining details of your trysts up to you."

"So…" I said before I could catch myself.

"Yes?" She stopped halfway around since she'd already been turning to leave.

"So you don't mind if we see each other?" I asked, not trying to hide my amazement.

"Child, it warms my heart to know you two have the maturity and awareness to look beyond hearsay and unconfirmed scandals. Maybe, just maybe, when your families are ready, your love will warm the ice around their hearts."

With that, she spun around and walked across the roof. However, rather than taking the stairs, she stepped off the edge of the building. Floating there, she raised both her arms outward and suddenly Jameson and I were lifted, too, and carried alongside her, down and around to the courtyard.

By then, it was cleared of everyone but our two families. They were standing on opposite ends, glaring at each other until they saw us coming. Then their anger was redirected to us.

Ms. Villeiux had the forethought to land Jameson and me on the sides of our respective families and then she paused beneath the eaves to address us one last time.

"You will remember what I relayed the last time we were all in this courtyard together." It was a warning, one that much more potent knowing the true risk came from The Sevens threat to send in "peace-keeping" Vires.

Leaving us to our own willpower, she disappeared inside her office and the courtyard fell silent.

"Weatherfords," Oscar commanded and we left in a group toward the exit. He'd done this quickly because there was a distinct sense that a conflict was brewing.

Despite the guilt building over what I'd done and the miserable impression of again being an outsider in my own family, I looked back to find Jameson.

He stood square-shouldered, head held high, and with an air of defiance as he faced his family.

My heart literally pulled toward him, pressing against my chest, desperate to avoid separation. Then I was in the tunnel heading for the street and he was drawn out of my view by Burke's massive hand.

Not a single word was spoken on the walk to our cars or on the drive back to the house. And I didn't blame them. Restraining anger in this situation would have been a challenge for me, too. But then the silent treatment continued on throughout the next day. I made several attempts to explain but every one of them responded the same way…a raised hand motioning me to stop as they left the room, sadness embedded in their faces.

With Aunt Lizzy gone on an extended meeting and Miss Mabelle's usual sparse presence, the house was disturbingly quiet, a complete departure from the constant hum of conversation between my cousins. It reminded me of a cemetery with the only difference being that the dead were actually walking.

Not until Sunday dinner did I actually hear a voice again.

"So, are we going to talk about this or what?" Estelle asked in a huff, setting her fork down before staring at the rest of us. "I'm ready," she added flatly.

"What's the use?" asked Vinnia complacently. "She won't stop seeing him." Again, she surprised me with her accuracy when assessing someone else's emotions. In this case...mine.

"Well how do you know?" argued Spencer. "You haven't asked her."

At that point, I found all heads turned toward me.

The room fell silent again as they waited for my answer, which didn't come quickly. I had little interest in rushing to it, already knowing they weren't going to approve of it.

"He's not what you think," I said avoiding a direct denial to their request. They saw around it anyway.

"See?" said Vinnia, throwing up her hands.

"Let her speak," Oscar demanded.

I gave him a smile, which he didn't return. Knowing I was walking a fine line, I used the time given to disprove what they'd grown up believing.

"His secret trips each week are to deliver supplies to the needy. He's agreed to, and followed through on, helping me find and heal the sick and injured almost every day after school. He's protected and defended me whenever his own family has tried to cast against me. He tried protecting you, too, but the hexes have been too strong." I stopped and stared at them before delivering my final argument. "Are those the actions of an evil person?"

Estelle gawked at me before saying, "You really have no idea who you are dealing with, do you?"

My shoulders fell then, knowing she hadn't listened to anything I just said.

"Should we tell her?" asked Estelle to the rest of the table.

Immediately, their eyes fell, surveying their half-eaten jambalaya. No one replied.

"Tell me what?" I asked hesitantly.

Oscar groaned and then explained, "Two years ago, a distant uncle of ours died, his body found to be burnt so badly he wasn't recognizable other than from his teeth. The year before that, a distant aunt was found drowned. Two years before that, two of our cousins died in a freak hailstorm in which no other people were hit. Every few years, a Weatherford dies." His eyes seemed to take on a shadow before summing it up for me. "All of these, Jocelyn, can be traced back to the Caldwells."

Estelle sighed loudly then. Having lost her patience, she demanded, "Should…we…tell…her?"

Apparently, whatever it was Estelle was insisting be brought up had been excluded in Oscar's explanation.

"No," said Spencer. "We promised we wouldn't. Mother wants to break the news."

"The news about what?" I pressed.

Nolan pushed back his chair, screeching it along the hardwood floors without care of the damage it could do. After dropping his plate in the sink, he left the room without commenting. The others soon followed leaving only Oscar and me.

"You're always the peacekeeper, aren't you?" I asked.

"They're not mad at you. They're worried for you."

"Tell them not to be. If Jameson wanted to hurt me, he's had plenty of chances to do it. And obviously I'm still here, unharmed."

That didn't seem to assuage him much.

"Look, I just want all of you to know that I'm not giving away family secrets. When we have talked about each other's families it has always been complimentary."

Oscar raised an eyebrow in disbelief.

"He's never said a negative word about any of you. I expected him to, but he hasn't, not once. It's been the opposite. You won't believe me when I say this but Jameson respects you, all of you. I think…I think they're just as scared of you as you are of them. There's so much built up distrust between the families."

I was waiting for Oscar to roll his eyes, pierce his lips together, show any sign of skepticism, but he didn't. He simply dropped his gaze to the table and digested what I'd relayed. Then he stood up, deposited his plate in the sink, and stopped at the door, rotating at the waist toward me.

"That distrust has been built up for a reason, Jocelyn. Keep that in mind."

After the door closed behind him and all throughout the night and into the next morning, his warning stayed with me. It was a clear sign that it would take my family as much time to convince as Jameson's. Then, I saw Jameson in the parking lot when I pulled in for school and the butterflies in my stomach helped to ebb the memory of it.

He was waiting for me, his hands casually slipped into the pockets of his dark jeans, his book bag slung over his brawny shoulder. His mouth was turned down in a telling way, conveying that he was excited to see me but didn't want to make it so obvious.

"You survived your family's haranguing," I pointed out after he'd crossed the lot to meet me.

"Again…" he stated and the smile he'd been hiding broke through.

It was breathtaking.

We stood in silence for a moment, allowing the thrill of seeing each other to pass over us, and then he held out his hand.

"Ready?"

I replied by slipping my fingers through his.

Without having to discuss it, we'd both come to the same conclusion. Our families knew about our relationship, now we were about to announce it to the world.

The hallway was busy as usual with students and teachers huddled in groups or making their way through the crowd to their classroom.

Then the slamming lockers stopped and the chatter fell away and all eyes were on the Caldwell and Weatherford walking together down the hall holding hands. Even Mrs. Temple tugged at Ms. Brack's sweater before turning to gawk with the rest of the students.

"This will get the gossipers going," Jameson channeled into my head and I didn't bother to bury my laughter.

He walked all the way to my classroom door where his other hand then moved to cup my cheek as he stared into my eyes. The energy that pulsed between us stunned me and I unconsciously leaned closer to it. Our lips were inches away, the heat from them, the strain of having them so close yet so untouchable left me aching.

"I'd like to kiss you," he whispered, unable to deny the yearning.

"I'm waiting," I replied, doing my best to entice him.

Then very tenderly his lips pressed briefly against mine, the touch of them sending an instant wave of pleasure through me.

And then gasps erupted around us.

When he stepped back and the crowd became visible to us again, all I saw were dropped jaws and wide eyes.

As he left me to head for his first period, he squeezed my fingers once, gently, and then he was gone, moving through the gawking throng of students.

In class it took no longer than a minute before several frenzied girls asked me if I was dating Jameson Caldwell. The rest of the girls and every guy in the room were staring too, waiting for my answer.

"Yes," I said with a firm nod, putting my attention in to pulling out my laptop.

Again, they gawked.

"But…But, I thought you hated each other," one of the girls insisted.

"There's a fine line between love and hate…" I replied just before Mr. Gonzales started his lecture.

A few astounded chuckles rang out around the room before Mr. Gonzales shushed them and then I was left alone for the remainder of the hour, only having to deal with quick, curious glances.

I found Jameson at my classroom door when class was over and we again strolled hand-in-hand to our second period, the stares being no less intense, the number of onlookers actually increasing. It seemed as if more of the student body had to witness for themselves the spectacle we were making and specifically sought us out in the hallways. The only ones we didn't spot were our relatives and I had the feeling they were intentionally veering away.

In our second class, after we'd sat down, Jameson spun his legs around and faced me as he typically did. The exception this time was that he didn't bother turning away when other students entered.

It seemed that even Ms. Wizner had heard because she didn't attempt to separate us or wear her usual frown of concern when looking in our direction.

At lunch, we agreed that sitting with either family would be pushing the level of decorum so we chose a corner of the library to eat our lunch. Surrounded by books and sandwich paper wrappings, our hands touched as we talked in hushed voices about how it felt to channel another's energy and what it felt like to be able to levitate an object.

When the day was over, he walked me to my car, the magnetism between us so powerful that we prolonged our goodbye. As we leaned against the side of my car, his fingers curled around mine, playing softly with the palm of my hand. Then his crystal green eyes drew me in until our chests touched and our heads tilted back.

The kiss was slow and gentle, placing his lips on mine without a word. My arms came around his expansive shoulders dragging him against me as he pulled my waist closer to him. His lips moved tenderly across mine, riveting me so deeply that I was only vaguely aware of his fingers gripping the sides of my shirt. As the intensity rose between us, our lips pressed harder, unable to satisfy our craving for each other.

Only the honk next to us had the power to pull us apart. It came from Charlotte who, it seemed, had intentionally parked next to me. After jolting us from our embrace, she giggled, lifted her shoulders in a shrug, and sped off.

Jameson's glare faded as he turned back to me, his eyes brightening as they locked with mine.

"We're going to need to leave now or I'm going to keep you here all night. That kiss was…" his voice trailed off as he searched for an accurate description.

"Was what?" I pressed, curiously.

A grin came across his handsome face and he chuckled. "Bewitching…"

"Well that's appropriate."

We shared a laugh as I slid into the driver's seat and he circled the car for the passenger's seat, where we headed out for the day's healing errands.

The week passed the very same way, with Jameson and me spending every possible minute together. Students and teachers continued to gawk. Jameson's brothers and sisters did their best to intervene whenever possible. My cousins and I, however, never crossed paths. I never saw them in the halls and always returned home too late for dinner. But I found a plate each night on my nightstand, wrapped to stay warm, and I knew it was Miss Mabelle who'd made the effort to leave it. After trying twice to knock on her door to thank her and getting no answer, I gave up. But I did appreciate the fact she took care of me, everyone in the household for that matter.

Then Friday came and the first Weatherford I saw that week wasn't my cousins at all. Aunt Lizzy returned from her trip and was waiting for me when I came in the door.

The others had gone to sleep or were studying by themselves in their rooms so the house was, once again, silent…and to be honest a little depressing. When Aunt Lizzy called my name from the kitchen I actually jumped.

"Come here, my dear. We need to talk," she said and I immediately knew what the topic would be.

I disdained going into a conversation about whom I was dating so much that I had to remind myself it would be rude to tell her that she has no authority over me. Only my mother could deny me the right to see someone. And I'm not so certain I would listen to her. With these thoughts running through my mind, every muscle in my body had to be coaxed to move toward the kitchen door.

She was still in her business suit, I noticed while taking a seat at the table. Her usual chaotic energy was different now, more subdued, dispirited. She wasn't focused on me so much as whatever it was she had cupped her hands over on the edge of the table.

"You're home early," I commented.

"Oscar called me."

I didn't bother asking why. I already knew the answer.

"There's something I should have told you when we first met," she said quietly. "And I almost did while on the plane. It's what your cousins wanted to tell you a few nights ago."

I remembered that brief interaction when they had argued but finally decided Aunt Lizzy had wanted to relay the news. Apparently, this was the conversation in which she'd deliver it.

Goose bumps grew on my arms then, the same kind one gets when instinct tells you something bad is going to happen.

"Jameson Caldwell," she stated. "You are…" she paused to clear her throat, "seeing him, correct?"

I lifted my head a little higher. "Yes I am."

That was when she loosened her fingers and revealed what she'd been keeping hidden. Its rust-red surface gleamed in the light above the kitchen table like a beacon, or a warning. Even before she slid it across to me, I recognized it as the agate Caldwell family stone.

"How did you get this?" I asked, stunned, knowing there was no way anyone of them would give it to her.

Her eyebrows met as she struggled to form the words. "It…It was in your father's hand at the time of his death."

I blinked and jerked my head up. "What? No. No…" Then I was denying it vehemently, already knowing where she was headed with this accusation. Jameson had warned me that I'd be told stories designed to keep us apart. He wasn't going to listen to them and neither would I.

"The facts speak for themselves, Jocelyn," said Aunt Lizzy patiently.

My head was starting to spin and I felt something in the pit of my stomach, a feeling others had described just before being sick.

"You don't expect me to…" I started but couldn't seem to finish.

"The stone was left with your father as a message," she said cautiously, persistently, like a gentle force chipping away at the wall before her.

"To say what?" My voice was stiff, coming across angry to me. But I wasn't just angry. There was a maelstrom of emotions running through me, none of which were good.

"To declare that a Caldwell had been there at the time of his death."

I felt my teeth grinding and my breathing quicken, but I had to quell the blending of thoughts in my head before I could deal with my physical reaction.

Then I was on my feet, looking down at her peaceful countenance. It took me several long seconds before I could utter my next words. "You're saying…that a Caldwell killed my father."

"I'm giving you the facts. You can deduce from them as you wish, as we have all done."

She stood then, slowly, and without another word she left the room.

No…no. It was the only thought I was able to form in my mind. No…

That couldn't be the truth. It couldn't - Because if it were then the Caldwells were responsible for taking my father's life. And why would this be such a surprise? They'd taken the lives of so many Weatherfords. Why would my father be the exception? He wasn't. The fact they possessed the Caldwell family stone proved it.

But there was another truth tapping at my subconscious. My father had died protecting me. And he'd died protecting me from a Caldwell. And I was dating a Caldwell.

As this realization settled over me, I had to hold back the scream building in my throat.

Finally, I was able to wrap this new reality into one cohesive, disturbing thought: My father had lost his life to protect me from the very family I had become involved in.

There could be no greater betrayal.

And in those brief moments, Aunt Lizzy had accomplished what everyone had been striving for since Jameson and I met.

She divided us.

16. BREAKUP

With the Caldwell family stone clenched in my fist, I didn't bother with a car or my feet. Levitation would be the quickest means of transportation.

The air was cool tonight. Given that it was October that seemed reasonable. Still, I didn't pay much attention to the biting chill against my skin as I made my way over the houses. I was on a mission and I wouldn't be turning back for a simple sweater.

The Caldwell house had a few windows lit so I knew someone was awake. I wasn't sure what I'd do if they denied me the chance to see Jameson. I wasn't even certain if it would be safe. But by this point none of that mattered. I would not be deterred.

Landing on the doorstep, I took a quick look around and then wished I hadn't. They appeared so normal. Muddy tennis shoes had been left outside the house. A mat was set outside the door that played off their secret culture with the message "Welcome! Come in and sit for a spell!" Through the windows I saw pictures of the family placed across their mantle.

Pictures of the family that had killed my father...

Ringing the doorbell this late at night actually gave me comfort.

Then I prepared myself for the door to open. If it was Charlotte or Alison, there would be trouble, undoubtedly. If it was any of the other Caldwells, they'd be unlikely to allow me to see Jameson either. If it was Jameson, well...I wasn't looking forward to that either. Any way I looked at it, this unannounced visit would not be easy.

From inside, footsteps pattered toward the door and a shadow moved in front of the stained glass window embedded in the door. But when it opened, the person standing on the inside was none of those I'd planned.

She was short, no higher than my shoulders, with swarthy skin and curious, patient eyes. Large gold hoop earrings dangled through her black braided loops and the dress she wore had a pattern that reminded me of one I'd seen in Africa. She looked like a smaller version of Miss Mabelle, although with much less girth.

Then, for a moment, the sick, disturbed feeling that had found a home in my stomach since Aunt Lizzy delivered her news ebbed just slightly and I blurted, "Miss Celia?" Then I snapped my mouth shut realizing I'd just admitted that she'd been the topic of a conversation.

She didn't appear to mind, being too concentrated on evaluating me.

"Been lookin' forward ta meetin' ya," she replied, her voice soft and kind.

"Thank you," I said hesitantly, figuring Jameson had mentioned me to her. "I've...I've heard good things said about you."

She grinned, reflecting a row of beautiful white teeth, and then stated with humorous sass, "They ain't nothin' but good things ta say 'bout me."

Her reply was so unexpected that despite the pain in my gut I actually felt a smile surface. It was weak but it was there.

"May I see Jameson, ma'am?" I asked before she could make me start to rethink why I'd come.

She nodded, her eyes closing regally, as she replied, "Surely." Before she turned away, her hand reached out and took hold of mine, the one still clutching the Caldwell family stone. "Things…" she said. "They ain't always what they seem."

I couldn't be certain but it appeared as if she knew why I was there.

With that, she hobbled up the stairs and disappeared for a few minutes. She must have delivered the news that I was waiting downstairs quietly because I didn't hear doors slamming, raised voices, or pounding footsteps headed for the gun cabinet. Instead, Jameson appeared at the top of the stairs without a sound and silently descended. He maneuvered them as if he were avoiding the ones that creaked, I noticed.

The sight of him caused a stabbing pain in my abdomen, my muscles clenching, fighting against what I was planning to do. He was thrilled to see me, his eager eyes and lips curved into a smile confirmed it. I, however, was torn in seeing him. The reality that after the next few minutes passed I would no longer be able to laugh with him, learn from him, or touch him gripped my insides and made them churn.

When Jameson reached me, he didn't say a word but pulled me along with him to the swing on the front porch, his eyes wide and incredulous. Without releasing my hand, he channeled, "Do you know how risky it is for you to be here?"

Without answering him, I opened my other palm where the Caldwell family stone was cradled. I almost hesitated, not wanting this to end, this love affair I'd willingly entered. How could someone so generous, so altruistic be part of a family who had killed my father, so many of my relatives? He'd grown up around and been raised by these people and yet there was no sign of their crimes in him. And, here I was, about to punish him for something he didn't do and had no hand in creating. In the next few minutes I would bring our blissful relationship to a crushing halt because of the simple, pure bottom line: I couldn't bring myself to betray my father's dying wish…to keep me safe.

"What's that?" he asked, innocently, peering closer in the dim light. Then he blinked and his head jerked slightly as he identified it.

"I thought you should have it back," I said, sending the message without speaking.

"What…How did you get that?"

"My aunt," I replied stiffly.

He lifted his head, confused. "How did she get it?" His tone was not only suspicious but apprehensive, as if he wasn't certain he wanted to know. He determined as quickly as I had that a Weatherford owning a Caldwell family stone was not encouraging.

"They found it in my father's hand."

His forehead creased, still perplexed.

"On the night he died."

Then his eyes were on me, intense, alarmed.

"You think…your family thinks that one…" He stopped and swallowed, hard. "One of my relatives tried to kidnap you?"

As always, his first reaction was for my well being, I noticed, and again the stabbing pain of guilt and disappointment shook my insides.

Then he named the other disturbing insinuation, the one that held far more importance. "You think my family killed your father," he stated, finally understanding the depth of the situation.

My answer wasn't in words but it was just as clear. I pulled my fingers away from the grip that he was using to channel our thoughts and gave him back his family stone.

"Jocelyn…" he said, his voice hitting my ears loudly in the silence of the night. Then he stopped, knowing there was nothing more to say. His prevailing trait – logic - was helping him grasp what I'd already concluded. There was no evidence he could offer to refute the claim. This wasn't something you could simply apologize for and move on from. This news was life-altering.

I stood and ended the discussion by speaking my thought aloud. "When I ignore you in class, it's only to make it easier on us."

Then I was walking down the steps, feeling his eyes on my back, fighting the urge to turn and run back to his arms. It was more challenging than anything I'd ever done, testing me to the core of my being.

That night, I didn't sleep. I kept my face in my pillow, hiding my sobs from those who might hear me through the thin walls of the old house. I could actually feel my heart breaking, ripping through the muscle as it pulsed on, the pain being so deep I didn't think I could recover. Then I found the sun filtering into my room and I vaguely understood that it was daylight. Later, voices came underneath my door and a knock rattled it, I think. Day moved into night and the sobs stopped. I'd run out of hydration but I still didn't move. The next day, the door shook more frequently and with harder intensity, the voices outside it were more feverish.

"I'm going in," someone declared. I thought it was Estelle but couldn't have cared less who said it.

"No, she might not be ready." That one was Vinnia. I was certain of it.

"She's wasting away in there." That was Nolan. His deep voice couldn't be mistaken.

"Let's knock again." Oscar - Always the peacekeeper.

"Forget that." Estelle. She followed it with a scoff.

As the argument continued, I lifted my body until my feet hit the floor. It wasn't as chilly against the hardwood as I'd expected and only then did I find I still had my shoes on. They scuffed the floor as I made my way across the room.

"I'm getting Miss Mab-" Spencer was saying as I pulled the door open. He stopped in midsentence to stare at me, along with the rest of my cousins.

From their faces, it was clear I was a mess.

"See?" demanded Estelle, her bright purple shirt being the only element standing out to me in this surreal state. Then she lowered her voice to a whisper even though I was less than a foot away. "We should have gone in sooner."

I shuffled by them and headed down the stairs. From the sounds behind me, I figured they were following. As I entered the kitchen, Estelle called out supportively, "Good idea! Food!" Then to her brothers and sister she pronounced, "She needs that."

When I passed through the kitchen, barely aware of Miss Mabelle sleeping on her stool in the corner, and out to the backyard without stopping for bite I heard Estelle grunt and knew someone had nudged her, insisting that she realize she was wrong.

Outside, I collapsed on the first step, barely bracing myself against the fall. Gasps came from behind me but they were too far away to have helped balance me anyways.

"Get Miss Mabelle," said Vinnia. "Hurry."

It wouldn't matter. Not much did.

I found what I'd come for, a plant set in a beautiful blue pot. It was well fed, watered, giving the proper sunlight and it showed. Still, I reached out and placed my hand on it.

Fighting the tears that still threatened to spill over, I centered in on that energy inside me. I pushed it, pulled it, did everything I could to coax it to life, to tell me that I was still alive, that separating from Jameson wouldn't end me.

Then I saw the first blossom open…and then the second, unraveling their tiny petals to the light, showing themselves to the world.

There it was…that energy in me, surging through my torso and down my arm and through my fingers, passing the vacancy left in my chest as if it didn't even notice it was there.

The wooden step vibrated then and I found Miss Mabelle had plunked down beside me, her cane stretched out down the rest of the stairs.

"Told ya not ta touch my plants, didn't I?" she said, her lips turned down in a frown.

"Yes," I whispered. While normally I wouldn't have cared if she were mad about it, I didn't have the life in me to fight the guilt.

Miss Mabelle wasn't angry. That was just her way.

"So ya lost a little bitta life in ya n' decided to give some of it back? That it?"

I shrugged, having no interested in explaining.

"Then what ya doin' hea, chil'?"

Finally, I lifted my head to her.

My lip trembled as I said, "I can still heal others. Why can't I heal the pain in my heart?"

Then the tears won, swelling over and coursing down my cheeks. Her arms came around me and pulled me close, enveloping me. I leaned against her for an immeasurable amount of time, shuttering into her fleshy embrace, appreciating the comfort it gave.

She didn't offer any consoling words other than one sentence and it made me pause because I'd heard it before, recently.

"Just rememba…Things ain't always what they seem," she whispered into my ear.

I pulled away then and wiped the tears off, stunned. Miss Celia had said the very same thing.

She didn't give me the chance to respond because her legs were already heaving her body to a standing position. Then, as I watched her go, she hobbled into the house, where my cousins waited in an awkward cluster just inside the door.

No one said a word to me at dinner, allowing me to mend myself on my own. I tried some of the fried catfish but could only bring myself to chew a few biscuit crumbs.

I was thankful for a few families who stopped by to request a healing session. It kept my mind off Jameson, as much as was possible anyway, and it gave me the chance help those in my world. With my almost daily trips to the hospitals and clinics, they'd been neglected and I felt a little guilty about it.

Because of them, when the next morning came, I had the energy to dress for school. Still, I received concerned glances from my cousins as I struggled to take in a few bites of food as I headed out the door.

It was drizzling rain, which was fine because it matched my mood. When I reached school my cousins were back to walking me down the hall so when someone dared to say, "What? No Caldwell today?" Oscar had to stop Nolan from trouncing the guy.

The sting of that question hurt worse than I thought it would. The fact was people were curious. The entire week before, Jameson and I had been side-by-side, unabashedly displaying affection. His absence and the return of my cousins surrounding me made it good enough for another round of gossip.

None of that mattered much to me. I was mainly concentrating on what would happen in second period when Jameson and I would see each other again. As it turned out, it was worse than I'd expected.

He was already there, his head bowed, his arms crossed over the front of his desk.

When I saw him, my heart stopped and then started again at a quicker pace. He looked miserable. His hair was tousled, his clothes were wrinkled and unkempt, his skin was pale, and he slouched, something I'd never seen him do. Then he looked up and I saw the red in his eyes and knew he'd slept about the same number of hours as I had.

As our eyes met, there was no denying the despair and hopelessness we both felt. It was a message that didn't need to be channeled because it was already obvious.

His gaze followed me until I was a few desks away, and then they fell aside, unable to retain that connection at such a close range. When I sat down, it was unusually loud and clunky because the room was absolutely silent now. Awkwardly, I fumbled with my laptop while pulling it from the bag, nearly dropping it twice because my attention wasn't on it.

I was following, without looking, every action, or inaction, Jameson was making. His hands had tightened around the edge of the desk when I'd sat down, just before he slid them across the surface and dropped them to his lap. His head remained motionless, dipped slightly, as if he didn't trust himself to move it because he knew which direction it would go. His legs, which were normally stretched out in a relaxed state, were bent at the knee with both feet placed firmly in the floor.

When Ms. Wizner entered the room, she didn't bother to acknowledge us because she no longer feared a spat between Jameson and me. But the rest of the class did. They paid curious attention to us but were smart, or prudent, enough not to mention it.

Jameson and I didn't take a single note during Ms. Wizner's lecture; our laptops remained open and untouched. Instead, our attention remained on each other. I knew this when my foot scuffed back toward my chair and that slight motion caused Jameson to inhale. It was quiet but I'd heard it.

When class ended, he stayed in place as he usually did while I slipped my laptop into my bag and headed for the door. I didn't think it was possible but my heart broke even more when I left the room, knowing his eyes were following me out.

The next day was no better. And the day after was the same as the two before. Evening class arrived and we behaved the same there as we did in normal school, doing our best to ignore each other and failing horribly at it. His family kept him close with a wary eye on me, although they had no reason to. The separation caused more harm to Jameson and me than any hex ever could.

Neither of us cared or had the energy to make ourselves presentable for the rest of society any longer so we showed up disheveled, exhausted, and depressed. The toll was even greater on our bodies, drawing in our eyes, withering away our limbs and torsos from lack of food. I felt like a ghost and I knew Jameson did, too.

My only sense of life came when I healed others on my after-school errands, which I now took alone, or when those in the witch world stopped by the house for a quick healing session. At least that force was still in me. I felt sorry - and worried - for Jameson who had no motive to use the energy inside him. There was no one knocking on his door asking for help, inspiring him to conjure that force that told him that there was still life in him.

I wasn't the only one to see this happening in him either. Charlotte made that clear one rainy afternoon in the hallway outside my first period classroom.

"What did you do to my brother?"

The ever-present stupor kept me from immediately grasping the fact that someone was talking to me.

"Weatherford!"

That brought my feet to a halt, along with several others around me. I couldn't be certain but I thought someone uttered, "Uh oh. Here we go again…"

Turning, I found Charlotte standing, hands on hips, eyes narrowed at me as usual. Her sandy blonde hair had fallen over her eyes so she briskly flicked it away. If her tone didn't tell me what kind of mood she was in her gesture sure did.

"What? No freezing cast today?" I asked, not caring if this made no sense to anyone but the two of us. Caring even less if it did.

She ignored me and stated, "I asked you what you did to Jameson."

The sound of his name made the despair well up in me again and I dropped my head in reaction.

"Tell me what you did to him," she demanded, taking a step toward me.

I knew what she was really asking. She needed to know how to end the pain he was in. I didn't doubt she and the rest of the Caldwells had tried every blocking cast possible, pulled every spell book out, reviewed every note from class, asked every caster they knew. Now, as a last resort, she was turning to the person who had cast the hex. I was certain of it because behind the anger in her eyes was desperation.

"Tell me," she fumed under her breath.

The problem was that no blocking cast, no repeal of any cast could help Jameson because the despair he felt didn't stem from mystical properties. It was a natural reaction to losing someone he cared for.

She took another step and the crowd around us grew.

"I did nothing," I whispered. "And everything…"

"Don't play games with me."

"I wouldn't do that."

She scoffed. "Weatherfords cannot be trusted. I don't care what my brother says."

I jolted at the admission that Jameson had talked to his family about us.

"We aren't fooled, Jocelyn. We know you're just as bad as your mother."

An emotion stirred in me…irritation. The first reaction I've had to anything in days. "Don't act like you're familiar with my mother," I retorted. "I doubt you've ever met her."

"Where she works tells me all I need to know," said Charlotte flatly.

There was no contesting it. She did work for the ministry and what I'd learned about them wasn't complimentary. Regardless, the conversation was headed in a direction I didn't want it to take so I changed its course.

"I don't know how to help Jameson," I admitted. "If I did I would have found a way to tell you already. I…" My voice cracked forcing me to clear my throat. "I don't want him to suffer either."

"I don't believe you," she said and the intent look in her eyes confirmed it.

Then a voice came from behind me and the very sound of it shook me to my core.

"What's this about, Charlotte?" asked Jameson. His voice was croaky, like mine, as if he hadn't used it in a while, which I figured was the case.

My body froze, my heart wanting to turn around but my muscles refusing to comply with its command because my head told them not to. Then I heard footsteps and saw a body stop beside me. The fact he didn't come between Charlotte and me was telling. It meant he'd intervened not for Charlotte's sake but for mine. Again, after all I'd done, he was defending me.

Charlotte concluded this, too, but didn't seem surprised by it. "Jameson, aren't you going to be late for your next class?" she hinted, clearly trying to motivate him to leave.

It did no good.

He crossed his arms against his chest and replied, "You're right. I don't have time for this. But I'm not leaving until you do, Charlotte."

There were audible gasps from the gathering crowd.

Charlotte, furious now, marched up to him and hissed, "She's the reason you're like this."

"She's not the one to blame," he stated, telling me without saying the words that he held someone else, a person from his own family, at fault. "She did what she had to do. We all live by that rule, don't we?"

Charlotte sneered.

He lowered his voice then so fewer people surrounding us could overhear. "I appreciate that you're trying to help. I would do the same if our roles were reversed. But what you're doing directly counters what you are trying to accomplish because, Charlotte, it's not making my life any easier."

Her face twitched lightly but she remained silent.

"If you really want to help me, than all you need to do is leave Jocelyn alone." His next statement was more of a frustrated demand. "Leave them all alone."

No one had to tell me who "them" was. I knew he meant the rest of my family. This was a colossal request to Charlotte, who hadn't stopped her attempts once since I'd met her.

He was about to speak again when she cut him off. "For you. Only for you." She turned then and directed a glare at me before spinning around and walking off.

Then it was just the two of us in the center of a circle of gawking students.

Jameson's patience gave out at that point and he barked, "What?"

That got the crowd moving and they dispersed rapidly.

I didn't think he was going to address me at all, and if he did I wasn't sure what to expect from him given that I'd just seen his usually easy-going personality verbally assail onlookers. So when he rotated to face me, I was taken aback by what I saw.

Devastated sadness.

It changed then to reticent cordiality. "I broke our no-interaction rule," he said slowly making me think he didn't want to leave my side.

"That's all right," I replied, not particularly liking how demure my voice sounded.

Neither one of us moved. We simply stared into each other, our eyes locked, unable to break apart. The emotions swelling in my chest must have been comparable to his because his breathing was staggered.

I miss you, I wanted to say. I can't function without you. There's a void where the feeling of being alive used to be and the only things that can shake it are your laugh, the unique way you think, the sound of your voice, the sight of you.

I could have said these things. The hallway was empty now. But I remained silent, staring at him, soaking him up.

It looked as if he were making similar statements in his own mind, battling with telling me the truth to how our separation was destroying him. But he elected to do the same as me and avoided opening himself up to the potential for further harm. Instead, he focused on something else and when he did all thoughts of my own needs were discarded.

"La Terreur is back...They need your help. They're dying at an alarming rate."

17. LA TERREUR

"Marie Dupart…the little girl…has passed away."

That news sent a sharp pain through my chest.

"More of them are passing each day," Jameson continued. "It's spread to villages in other provinces."

"Why didn't anyone come for me?" I asked already heading for the exit, Jameson in step with me.

"Isadora is my main contact…" he replied.

My head snapped in his direction, knowing what he was implying. "She's sick, too?"

He nodded. "I didn't find out until last night when I made the deliveries."

I released a moan, wondering how many we could have saved if the news had only reached us.

He stepped forward to push the main entrance door open for us. "I was there all night and came straight to get you," he admitted, acknowledging that he'd intended to break our no-interaction rule anyway.

None of that mattered at the moment. I didn't care I was leaving school without permission or that I was doing it with a Caldwell. My only goal was to reach the village as quickly as possible.

We halted directly outside the door, staring first at the parking lot jammed with cars and then overhead, both thinking the same thing.

"Think we can risk it?" he asked.

"It doesn't sound like we have a choice." I drew in a deep breath, preparing to break our world's most stringent law.

"Good thing it's raining," he reasoned.

"Right." I nodded, surveying the sky. "Cloud coverage."

I reached out my hand, the one with the family stone.

He hesitated for only a second and then took it, the warmth of his palm wrapping around my chilly fingers. "Have you ever levitated anyone…?"

Before he could finish, we were in the air, his voice easing into a shocked chuckle. It actually gave me some satisfaction to throw him off a bit.

It took me only until we broke through the clouds to the warm, radiant sunshine on the other side for me to realize I was going much faster than ever before, and I was doing it with another person. While I didn't levitate myself often I knew it had taken me a few minutes to reach the height we were at. This time it took seconds. Oddly enough, our clothes weren't rustled as much as they should have been and I didn't feel the usual sting of the rushing air. Confused, I looked down at Jameson, curious if he was noticing the same thing. It was then that I understood. He was channeling, amplifying my power while subduing the energy around us.

Jameson was already watching me, respect evident in his expression. He gave me a tentative grin and I knew my face reflected the same.

Every so often we needed to dip below the cloud line to evaluate the geography and make sure we were on course but we still made it to the village in record time. We landed on Isadora's dock just as another bout of rain began to fall. Jameson opened the door without knocking, telling me that she was in serious condition, which caused my heart to beat double time.

Inside, candles illuminated the room just enough to show Isadora curled in a ball on her bed, shuddering, her arm limply held out to us, beckoning for us. The door left open during our urgency, we ran across the room toward her, our hands clasped together and then taking each of hers to form a circle.

Jameson and I had worked together for weeks, healing the sick and injured, but we'd never used this method before. It was instinctual, natural, and clearly needed.

Without hesitation, I began my incantation, conjuring the force inside me while Jameson magnified it. Isadora jolted, the surge of us together being a force greater than anything her frail body was ready to accept.

I backed off and Jameson knew it. "Keep going," he urged.

"We might be hurting-"

"Don't stop," he said, his voice taking on the hint of a French accent.

I glanced at him, puzzled, and found him staring at her. "She's telling you…" he said through gritting teeth, straining against the power rushing through us, "that she can take it."

Accepting this as truth, realizing there were nuances to channeling I couldn't begin to grasp, I refocused and allowed the force inside me to fully release.

Her eyes opened and found me then. They spoke to me without channeling, without words, and they said they believed in me. She had seen my ability and it was powerful. Then her lids closed and her thin, parched lips released.

"Isadora," Jameson called out, the urgency in his voice conveying just how much he cared for her.

"Don't shout," she whispered weakly. "I'm right here."

Jameson began chuckling through his nose.

I sat back, exhausted but feeling the reward of accomplishing something I was beginning to think was impossible.

"What…" I said, catching my breath. "What…just happened? I…heard her voice through you."

Jameson, his energy spent enough to make him bent at the waist and prop his hands on his knees, looked up at me. "As I channeled your power into her, she channeled her voice back through me. It happens…just not often."

"Channelers have that aptitude," said Isadora, her skin tone already returning to its natural color. She hadn't sat up yet, still biding her time until her recovery was entirely complete. "Not all of them use it. It can be intimidating…accessing our abilities to their capacity." As she spoke, she focused in on me and I knew she was referring to my backing away just a moment ago. "When we realize our gifts are there for a purpose, a means to an end, it alleviates inhibitions."

This was the most I'd ever heard Isadora say and I understood why. She was trying to counsel me to unleash my power, to trust my judgment and use it when it is needed.

It turned out to be good advice because after we helped Isadora to her feet and, at her insistence, allowed her to accompany us to the remaining shacks I witnessed just how ill the rest of the village had become. Her boat, being much quieter than Jameson's, gave us a well-rounded picture of it.

Whereas before, the swamp had a peaceful silence to it, now screams echoed across the water every few minutes, a sign of another person falling ill. These were the sounds of La Terreur and they mixed with the patter of rain against the water's surface and the shacks' wooden roofs, making a once mysterious and intriguing place feel gloomy, repressed. The windows of more and more houses darkened as those inside became too sick to light another candle when the others extinguished. There was no more laughter and the music had been silenced.

We worked as fast as we could, healing entire households at times. But I had no idea how deep into the swamp the village ran. There were so many more to go. Even as night came and we headed farther in, I began to wonder if Jameson and I would ever see the end.

Each stop tested my will power as I felt the strain of using my energy in such a concentrated amount so continuously. Around midnight, Jameson recognized it in me, too.

I found him assessing me, an apprehensive frown visible in the dim light of the swamp as we made our way to the next shack. He placed a hand on my knee, which should have tested my resolve to keep our distance. It didn't. I allowed him to keep it there, wanted it, really. It was intimate and despite what I'd learned about my father and his family there was no denying the feeling in my heart.

"You look…tired," he said.

"Thanks," I muttered.

"I mean it, Jocelyn. Maybe we should take a break."

"No," I replied flatly. "There's no time for one." I thought of all the people we'd seen tonight, which numbered over a hundred, and wished I'd arrived sooner. Each of them looked on the verge of death, the memory of their drawn faces and feeble bodies like a stamp in the back of my mind. No, I would not rest. Something in my response told Jameson not to persist. He didn't but he didn't back down either.

A few seconds later, I felt my lungs expand deeper and my back straighten farther. The grogginess behind my eyelids dissipated and my muscles throughout my body flexed vigorously. A surge of energy had suddenly entered my body but there was no explanation for it until my gaze landed on Jameson's hand. He was channeling again.

I met his eyes and he shrugged. "Thought it would help."

"It did," I replied and he started to remove his hand. By pure impulse, I dropped my hand over his, ending his attempt.

The move shocked me as much as it did him. But having no objective in mind, I simply stared ahead, again fully aware of his attentiveness to me. Without having to be told, I knew he was smiling, content, accepting what he could for the moment because neither of us knew what might happen tomorrow.

Jameson's additional energy helped me last through the rest of the night and into the next day. At that point, hours began blurring together. What might have distinguished one shack from the rest no longer penetrated the haziness in my mind and my limbs began to feel awkward, like cooked noodles hanging from my torso. Jameson didn't look much better so that, ironically, our glimpses at each other conveyed that we were both now more concerned for the other than for ourselves.

Isadora, having been revived when our energies were at their highest and thus made a full recovery, was now the one at the boat's helm. It had turned night again when her faint French accent penetrated my surreal state.

"Last one."

My eyes drew open to find the largest dwelling yet. It appeared to be ten structures connected to walkways between them.

This is going to take the last of my energy, I thought.

Still, I was able, with Jameson's assistance, to pull myself up.

"How many live here?"

"This is an outpost," explained Jameson. "It's not a home. Those in the village stay here while taking turns acting as watch guards for the perimeters."

"Guarding them from what?"

"The ministry."

I didn't ask any more questions after that but I did make certain the red cloth was still wrapped around the bracelet carrying my family stone.

The outpost was designed to be utilitarian. Bins of supplies and the lack of comfortable furniture easily conveyed it. Floor rugs served as beds and crates became chairs and tables. This was a place without frills.

Conventional weapons also hung from the walls, sad tools that I now knew would be ineffective if used against more mystical defenses.

Apparently, they selected only the stockiest men to be watch guards because all ten of the men still at the outpost were a foot taller than me. And with my height, that's saying something.

Only one of them had been stricken with La Terreur. He laid on his side, curled into a ball, his skin the same sickening green hue, and perspiring despite the chill in the air.

Isadora stepped inside first and named each of the men for us, although I couldn't commit most to memory. Then she addressed them. "We've brought the healer."

"Jocelyn," said Jameson. "Her name is Jocelyn."

"Thank you for coming," said one of the men, sitting legs apart on a crate facing the man who was ill. It looked like he'd been there a while.

"How long has he been sick?" I asked, already squatting at the man's side.

"A day," said Alexander, the man Isadora stood beside. His voice was gruff, and with his massive body, he reminded me of a titan.

"His name is Aurelius?" I asked, placing my hand on the man's arm.

I was surprised when one of the men confirmed it, not believing I had the attentiveness still in me. This was a good sign. It meant there was still energy left to heal the man.

"Aurelius," I whispered into his ear. "You're going to feel a jolt." I had learned several attempts back that giving them fair warning calmed us both.

Jameson, who had been at my side since we'd entered, was preparing to drop to his knees where he would help channel his energy. But he never got the chance.

Aurelius began thrashing.

His limbs flailed, his eyes rolled back, his body arched, writhing maniacally.

Suddenly, bodies were surrounding us, holding Aurelius down, taking the strength of every one of the men to do it. I did my best to help, settling my hands on him and pressing the weight of my body down. Still, his arms swung in all directions, his fingers clawing against the pain.

Gradually, over the period of several seconds, the violent shudder seized and, finally, Aurelius went limp.

I took in a breath and let it out with a relieved laugh.

That was when I noticed no one else was reacting. Only me because I hadn't seen it yet.

Every eye was now on my wrist, the one where I wore my mother's bracelet. The red cloth I'd used to hide it was gone, clutched between Aurelius's fingers.

During his thrashing, he'd revealed what we'd kept so well hidden from every other prisoner in the village.

"You've allowed a Weatherford here?" Alexander's voice boomed inside the narrow walls, shaking the wooden structure with its force. His eyes were wide, incensed, as they moved between Isadora and Jameson.

Looking around, I saw the irate faces of ten strangers and I knew what was coming.

Jameson saw it before me and was prepared when the fists began to fly.

Ducking and finding cover would have been a wise choice but logic was Jameson's trait, which I was sure he used to deduce that winning a brawl with ten stout men was going to leave him bloodied. This dawned on me too, even as I saw Jameson deftly maneuver around flying fists to take down three of the men. By the time I was able to conjure the last of my energy inside me, a fourth had collapsed in a pile on the floor. Then, just as the rest surrounded him, their feet left the ground.

Their arms and legs swung with precision but found nothing to land on as I levitated them a foot above the ground. Jameson, stunned, stepped back, his fists falling to his sides.

I still had my hands on Aurelius but could feel the energy in me slipping away.

I was running out of time.

Summoning the last of my energy, splitting it between keeping the men in the air and healing Aurelius, I opened my mouth and released a scream that rattled my eardrums.

Then I was falling back, my body crumpling like a rag doll against the hard wooden floor.

The sharp screech of my family stone as it slammed down and dragged along the planks...Aurelius's eyes fluttering open...Jameson's determined expression hovering above me...The blurred outline of the men as they advanced behind him.

These were the last things I saw before I disappeared into exhaustion.

18. MISLED

Something was on fire.

The pungent aroma of burning wood and the flicker of light beyond my eyelids told me so.

I was about to dart up when Jameson's voice reached my ears. It was calm, thoughtful. Not the kind I would expect when defending us against ten mammoth men.

"Her family should know where she is."

"In time, they will learn," said Isadora unconcerned.

For a moment, I wondered where exactly I was. The ground my body now lay on was not the hard, rutted planks making up the floor of the village shacks. It was soft and bumpy and when my fingers moved against it I felt the distinct, crisp surface of cotton. Outside, rain softly pattered the roof above and dripped down the storm drain in a quiet, steady stream. These sounds, along with the crackling fire and the groan of the floorboards, made me think that we were back at Isadora's home.

I'd been preparing to sit up when her next statement caught me off guard. In fact, I froze listening to it.

"She'll need to recover fully now that her secret is out."
I read between the lines and knew she was suggesting I
was at risk.

"You mean now that others know she's The
Relicuum?" Jameson mused. His voice grew more distinct
so I thought he might have turned to look at me, check on
me.

"The one who can pick up other's residue..." Isadora
reflected. "Generations have waited for her."

"I remember reading about her when I was a kid."

"We all do," said Isadora wistfully. There was a
shuffling and she changed the course of the conversation
to something I wasn't expecting. "That kind of power
invites its own brand of danger. Not here, but...out there."
And I knew she meant beyond the village.

"You're right. Before it was only you, me, and, I would
bet, her family who knew."

"And now the men at the outpost know," Isadora
mentioned.

"That's right. And that's one too many people."
Jameson sighed warily.

"It's only a matter of time before the rest of our world
discovers who she is," warned Isadora.

He agreed with her. "I think that time has already
come." I listened as he drew in a deep, concerned breath.

After a long silence Jameson made a declaration that
sent tickling warmth through my chest. "I'm going to keep
her safe, Isadora. Whatever it takes."

She chuckled lightly and then asked with bemused
curiosity, "Well now...When did a Caldwell start to care
for the needs of a Weatherford?"

Jameson laughed quietly through his nose.

"You fought hard to protect her," Isadora pointed out.
"I've never seen one man handle ten guards on his
own...not even a Vire."

"Well, it's a good thing they understand now she's not a risk to them. It'll keep her safe when she visits here at least."

"Don't change the subject," Isadora said in a maternal way and I knew then that was exactly what she was to Jameson. A surrogate mother. And just as a mother would, she didn't allow the conversation to end until she was finished. Persisting, she asked, "Does Jocelyn know?"

"Know what?" asked Jameson tightly. "That she's a Weatherford and they don't associate with Caldwells?"

"That's not what I'm referring to."

He went on as if he hadn't heard her. "That no one wants us to be together? That there are those, our families specifically, who will do anything to keep us apart?" His voice turned bitter then. "Yes, she understands all that."

"I meant-"

"I know what you're referring to," he stated, irritated.

"Then answer my question."

When he didn't, she demanded, "Does she know how much you care for her?"

"What does it matter? She's stubborn, Isadora. She makes up her mind and then commits to it."

I should have been insulted but coming from Jameson I knew that should be taken as a compliment.

"Hmm," mused Isadora.

"What?"

"I know someone else with that very same trait." She chuckled under her breath. "It's no wonder you've found each other. You've been looking for one another all along. No one else would do."

When I didn't hear him deny her observation my heart skipped a beat.

"Is she worth the danger?" asked Isadora, not in warning but to test him.

"Isadora…" he drew in a deep, troubled breath. My heart leapt at Jameson's next statement, meant only for

Isadora's ears. "I'm in love with her. Everything is worth it."

I'm in love with her echoed in my thoughts. Jameson is in love with me. Then happiness on a level I never knew possible overwhelmed me. Tickling warmth was sent through my chest and my body felt so light I had to move my hand against the sheet to make certain I wasn't levitating. Beneath the sheets, I felt my lips curve in to a smile, unable to contain it.

"Have you told her?" Isadora asked gently.

"No," he said plainly. "There's no reason to. It won't change her mind."

"Why?" she retorted.

"She'll never see passed our history."

"What history?"

His feet scuffed across the floor before he answered. Then, as if he were at a last resort to convince Isadora she were wrong, he pronounced, "My family killed her father."

Isadora didn't immediately respond and I wanted so desperately to open my eyes, to watch this conversation playing out, to confirm I wasn't in the middle of some surreal dream. Only as the conversation went on did I know for certain I was not in a dream state. This was reality - because it made me sick to my stomach.

"Maybe it would help if the two of you were to learn the truth…" suggested Isadora.

"About what?"

"Her father's death."

There was a pause and during that time I imagined Jameson's eyes widening and the contour of his jaw tightening. The very subject was a tense one and from the sounds of it Jameson didn't know the entirety of it.

"Do you recall me once telling you the ministry punished me, all of us here, in fact, for the very same reason?"

He answered suspiciously, "Because you were all guilty of the same thing. You have information that The Sevens want to hide."

My muscles stiffened at that news. These people, the ones sent here by my mother's employer, the ones Jameson and I have been helping were committed for crimes of knowledge. They were imprisoned while Vires were free to commit crimes against those they were there to protect. The idea of it left me enflamed. Then Isadora admitted to something and the opposite affect took place. I went cold.

"My transgression," said Isadora patiently, "was witnessing her father's death."

"You were there?" Jameson asked, his voice rising uneasily. "How could you have been there?" Clearly, the idea that she may have crossed paths with my parents had never occurred to him before.

"I was their friend…"

Those words stunned me, making me wish I could move and plug my ears. Every bit of information I was learning about my mother was negative, devastating. I wanted to sit up and tell them that this was not the person I know. She's kind and caring, a bit strict…but with loving intentions. I couldn't. My muscles wouldn't move.

"Her mother was your friend and she sent you here?" Jameson said disgusted, voicing the same issue I had.

"She didn't work for the ministry then," said Isadora offhandedly. "Her mother and father - They were young, innocent. They knew nothing about the evils of our world even though they'd both grown up in it. Both were sheltered. They learned, in a very difficult way, who not to trust. That night, as a typical family taking their usual stroll around our streets, they came for her. The abduction was planned but not well enough. Jocelyn's father, Nicolas, picked her up, defending against them as her mother, Isabella, ran for my house. When we reached them, the attackers had fled and Nicolas, still clutching Jocelyn, was taking his last breath. With it, he told us who they'd been - 'Vires'."

"Vires?" breathed Jameson, as shocked and guarded as I was.

"His hand fell open, the neighbors saw the Caldwell family stone the Vires had placed in his palm, and no one believed otherwise from then on. Not Isabella. She couldn't prove it but she knew the truth. We both did. I made the mistake of telling someone that I didn't think the Caldwells were involved and they came for me the following morning. Because they knew what I'd done. I'd witnessed a crime the Vires wanted covered up."

"And Jocelyn's mother sent her to New York..." Jameson summed it up.

In the serenity of her home, just above the rainfall, she whispered, "His death haunts me."

Their voices stopped, and in the silence my now rapidly pounding heart beat was magnified against my ear drums.

"But why?" Jameson implored. "Why abduct her? Did they already know she was The Relicuum? Is that why?"

"No, that couldn't have been the reason," she cogitated. "But it is my belief that whatever caused them to take such extreme measures... it relates directly to you."

"Me?" he said astounded.

"Yes, because when they failed to abduct Jocelyn, they went after you."

Stunned silence followed and then Jameson deliberated casually, "So they were the ones..."

I had a different reaction. Several thoughts swam around in my consciousness, none of them staying still long enough for me to grasp them in full.

...My family has been misled...

...Jameson's family was not to blame...

...My father hadn't been trying to protect me from the Caldwells...

...The Caldwells are at risk as much as I was...as much as I am...as much as I've always been...

...and I'm not the only one...

...Jameson...

"You need to tell her," said Isadora, and I knew she was referring to me.

"I will."

"Soon," she insisted.

Only a brief pause later, she asked, patient but firm. "Does that shed light on why no one can know she was here?"

"Isadora," said Jameson cautiously, as if he knew she wouldn't like hearing what he had to say. "No one is safe here. Look at the evidence. La Terreur hasn't hit anywhere but in our world. And it's spreading but only to other villages. The villages are hundreds of miles apart. How did it spread?" He gave her the chance to answer but continued when she didn't. "There's only one reasonable solution. Someone placed it there. But why? Who has the motive? Who has the most to gain by eliminating you?"

A chair scrapped lightly across the floor and footsteps took the person from the table.

When Jameson spoke again, it was farther away. His voice was flat, speculative, but his message sent chills down my spine. "The Vires are becoming more bold."

"At the request of those who control them...The Sevens."

"La Terreur is their way of making sure that information never gets out, isn't it?" asked Jameson. "By purging their enemies..."

"Yes," said Isadora, her French accent accentuating as her anger surfaced.

A heaviness surrounded us then, choking off words, stirring up our nerves until it was hard to breath.

I'd heard enough depressing news for one day so, needing it to end, I slid my legs over the edge of the bed and lifted the sheets off me.

Jameson, who was at the window, turned and gave me a smile of relief. I returned one of my own, not bothering to hide the comfort in seeing him. It looked like he wanted to approach me but hesitated near the window. He still didn't know I'd overheard him.

"How long was I out for?" I asked my voice scratchy from lack of use.

"Long enough to worry me," he said gently, his face telling me that he was trying to hide just how excited he was to be talking to me.

"That long?" I asked, startled.

They chuckled at me.

"What you did was unheard of," explained Jameson. "Healing over a hundred people, one after the other. It's amazing you didn't take longer to recuperate. How do you feel?"

"Like a champ," I muttered.

Both he and Isadora laughed and seemed to relax a little. She stood and hobbled to the stove where she poured me a bowl of soup. Jameson saved her from a good scalding by carrying it to me though, and when he handed it to me I knew he was assessing me for the truth.

I was fine, a bit disoriented, but that may have been more because of the news I'd just overheard as opposed to three days on my back. Or maybe it was a little of both.

When he'd finished his evaluation, he didn't leave my side but instead sat down next to me. His thigh landed against mine, sending a shock wave through me, but neither of us bothered to move apart. Instead, our legs steadily pressed closer together, teasing both of us.

It took halfway through my bowl of soup before I realized he was giving me another dose of energy, channeling his own into me.

"You need to stop that," I reprimanded him. "Save your strength."

He frowned. "I didn't think you'd accept it outright...and I was right."

He did break our contact but did it while exchanging a look with Isadora that made me think this hadn't been the only time he'd given me a spike. I would have placed a bet that he'd been doing it regularly over the last three days.

The truth was, I wanted him to touch me but not just for that reason. I wanted it to be more than medical. Unfortunately, that wasn't where the medical part ended. They made me lift everything in the room, together. When that didn't prove I was fit enough to leave, I noticed Jameson's bruise, a remnant from when he'd protected me at the outpost, and healed it. That seemed to convince them.

While I'd recovered enough to levitate Jameson and me back the same way we'd come and even though it was night again we wouldn't have faced as much risk in getting caught, I just wasn't sure how far my energy would take us. So we said goodbye to Isadora and then took the boat she lent us, and the car keys to an old pickup truck she kept so we could reach New Orleans. A nice offshoot to this way of transportation was that he and I had more time together. What I didn't realize was that it would be spent in awkward silence.

Seeing things from his perspective made me realize that the last time we'd had a conversation of any real length was on his front porch, where I'd accused his family of killing my father and then told him that I wouldn't be speaking to him again. Neither of those proved to be true.

When we reached the city, the constant rattle of the pickup truck's cab was disrupted, thankfully, by Jameson's voice. It was restricted and insistent.

"You need to get rid of the rope," he stressed. "The Rope of The Sevens."

I blinked, taken by surprise. How could he know?

As if reading my thoughts, he said, "I figured it out the day you got it. And I thought it was an interesting artifact that might come in handy some day. But the risk of keeping it is too much…far greater than the possibility it could be helpful. You need to get rid of it. Don't destroy it. Just move it out of the house."

"You knew I stored it in the house?" I muttered, still overcoming my surprise. He could read me better than I thought. "And you never said anything about it to anyone else?"

He shook his head solemnly, his eyes frozen on the road in front of us.

"Even after you found out I was a Weatherford…?" I reflected on how much damage he could have done if he'd wanted to.

"No, Jocelyn," he replied tenderly.

I was dumbfounded. "Why did you keep it a secret?"

He shrugged and I noticed he was turning onto my street, preparing to drop me off in front of my house. I was temporarily speechless at his courage.

"Just do me a favor?" he sighed. "Get rid of the rope?"

He pulled to a stop next to the curb but kept the truck running, just in case a Weatherford stepped out.

In the dim light of the surrounding houses, I could see the handsome, rugged contours of his face. What saddened me was that they were downcast.

"Since we met," I mumbled. "Since the moment we met you've had feelings for me. My family's past didn't matter to you."

"Go inside," he instructed softly. "Your family is worried about you."

I didn't listen. "And here I am condemning you for your family's past…and it wasn't even true."

Wallowing in my self-criticism, I barely noticed his head jerk back.

"What?" he said. "How did…?"

I saw the awareness in his eyes, awakening them.

"How long were you awake?"

Before I even answered, the memory of the entire conversation came back to him.

"How long were you listening to us, Jocelyn?" he asked nervously.

"I heard it all," I admitted trying to deliver the news as gently as possible.

Still, his head dropped to his chest and he laughed. I knew how he felt. Completely exposed.

He'd been through so much my heart sank for him and I opened my mouth to tell him that he's not alone, that there's hope. I wanted to tell him that I loved him too.

But the words never came out.

Instead, he lifted his head and looked at me. And then his face fell because he'd seen something over my shoulder. His jaw clenched and his nostrils flared just before he stated urgently, "Whatever you tell her, it can't involve the swamp."

This sudden change in his behavior and the course of the conversation threw me a bit. "Ha?"

"Don't tell her that you were in the swamp these last three days." These words rushed passed his lips as if he were fighting against time to release them.

I couldn't understand why he'd start talking about the swamp or the fact that he didn't want me to mention I'd been there or who he was referring to by "her". Then the car door to my right swung open and I rotated my head toward the person, ready to demand they close it. But my mouth clamped shut.

Because I was suddenly staring in to my mother's eyes.

19. MISSING

"Are you all right?"

It was the second time my mother asked the question before I gained enough control to ask, "What are you doing here?"

She heaved a sigh of relief. "That's good. Attitude. It means you're all right."

Only slightly offended, I retorted, "Yes, I'm fine." And then followed it with, "Mom, what are you doing here?"

In turn, she gawked at me. "I should be asking you the same question."

My first thought was that she'd noticed who I was sitting with, a Caldwell, but that wasn't what she was referring to.

"You've been missing for three days."

"Two," I corrected her.

"Three," she stated. "You left school on Monday. It is now Wednesday. I was called back because they couldn't find you."

"You left the ministry?"

"Where have you been?" she repeated, avoiding my question.

She still had one hand on the open door and the other propped against the cab's frame, leaning forward toward me. She looked very imposing.

"Where?" she demanded.

"I went to heal others outside the city," I explained. "I'm sorry. I didn't think anyone would notice."

Her eyes widened. "Notice? We've contacted almost everyone in the province. We hired channelers to give us a hint as to where you were." She stopped, shaking her head, her mouth hanging open, speechless. Then she found her voice again and I wished she hadn't. "What have I always taught you? Safety first. You have to think, Jocelyn. You can't go running off on a whim."

"I was safe," I declared.

She stared at me briefly and then asked, "And do I have you to thank for it?"

My mother was now leaning to the side in order to peer around me at Jameson.

When I turned to look at him, I found him staring back at her with intensity, almost sternly.

"It helps if you speak," she said. "I don't channel."

In any other world, outside our society, this would have been funny. But my mother actually meant it.

"Yes," he replied tightly. "You can thank me for it."

Her eyes fell to his neck then and instantly it was me who was tense. She'd caught sight of his chain, from which his family stone hung.

"Which Caldwell are you?" she asked firmly.

"Jameson."

"All right," she said, without a hint of opposition. She did take a few seconds to assess him, looking him up and down as any parent concerned for their child's welfare would. But this was no simple comparison. He was a Caldwell. She should have been yanking me out of the truck by this point, terrified, angry, and screaming demands not to come around me again. She did none of

250

these things. In fact, she did the exact opposite. "Thank you, Jameson, for bring her home safely."

He blinked several times, as stunned as I was. There was no inhibition, no surprise, no incredulity in her reaction. It was as if Jameson were a Smith.

"You're…welcome," he replied uncertainly.

"If you wish to see her again, you'll need to ask me beforehand. Understood?"

His forehead folded in astonishment and I knew he was trying to determine if she was playing some sort of perverse practical joke on him.

"Do you understand?" she prompted in her typical straight forward manner, the kind that always intimidated me.

It was a colossal testament that he didn't waver. "Yes," he replied.

"Do you have our phone number here at the house?"

"No."

She glanced around the cab. "Then I'll need a piece of paper and a pen."

"I'll remember it."

Finally, she showed some measure of surprise but it was in relation to his excellent memorization skills. Not what I expected. Then she prattled off the number. "Repeat it back to me please," she demanded, verifying that he'd, in fact, remembered it.

He did and she seemed impressed. Then she launched in to a set of instructions that left me thoroughly confused, and I was certain Jameson felt the same way.

"Now when you do see Jocelyn again she will need to be home, nightly, before the eleven o'clock hour. She will not be pulled out of classes again, day or evening. She will not go beyond the city limits. Further rules may apply but you seem like an intelligent young man. Use your best judgment and we shouldn't have a problem. However, if any of these rules are broken you will suffer the consequences. And you, being a Caldwell, know full well that I, being a Weatherford, am prepared to deliver on that threat."

"You're allowing me to see your daughter, Ms. Weatherford?" asked Jameson, thoroughly confused at this point.

"Only if you follow the rules. Any rules are broken and…" she let her voice trail off.

When he didn't respond, she hinted, "And…?"

"I'll suffer the consequences," he answered slowly.

"Good," she stated. "You should do fine." She finally turned back to me, drawing a breath, preparing to tell me to get out of the car when he cut her off.

"Ms. Weatherford," he said. "Do you know anything about me?" Given the conversation so far, I didn't blame him for asking.

Then my mother chattered off his profile, one she'd clearly researched. "You maintain a 3.9 GPA. You drive a silver Range Rover. You're headed for an Ivy League college…if you don't screw it up. Your favorite food is shrimp po'boys and you like a wide range of music. You channel…and though it is not widely known, you are one of the best at it. Casting is difficult for you because your other gift absorbs the abundance of your energy. That doesn't sum you up but it is a good start."

Though he didn't admit it, I'd say my mother actually taught him something about himself. I wasn't surprised. She was always prepared.

"I meant…about my family?" he specified.

She stared at him and then replied flatly, "Your family and I have a lot of talking to do." Without mentioning it, she confirmed that she understood the history between the Caldwells and Weatherfords and yet she was still all right with two of us seeing each other.

Jameson and I were stumped, but we weren't able to reel in it for long. She stepped to the side and said, "I need your help, Jocelyn. Your cousins have gone missing, too."

I gave Jameson a quick, baffled look, which he returned, and then I stepped out of the truck.

"Remember what we discussed, Jameson," she warned through the window after slamming the door.

"I won't, Ms. Weatherford," he said and then his eyes drifted to me. They changed from confusion to longing, telling me that he didn't want to leave. I understood because I felt the same way.

"Jocelyn," my mother called from the walkway leading to the porch but I didn't turn until Jameson pulled away from the curb. Then I saw her and my breath caught.

Standing there in her grey business suit, her dark black hair curling down around her shoulders, she looked like someone who'd just come home from work and was about to prepare a healthy, balanced dinner. It was the image, the hope I'd carried with me the first few years at the academy in New York now actualized right before my eyes. It had defined my dreams of living a normal home life with a normal family. But I realized right then and there that I…we would never be normal. We were witches. We lived a secret existence. We moved things without touching them, cured others without pills or surgery, controlled the elements, channeled energy from one source to another. Just as significant, our world was far more treacherous than the one I'd dreamt of as a little girl. I knew that my cousins' disappearance was not something to be taken lightly. So by the time I'd reached the walkway my focus was on them.

"They weren't in school today," my mother said when we'd entered the foyer and the door was closed behind us. "Their casting supplies, all of them, are gone."

"That's odd. Practicals - meaning exams - are a few weeks away," I said, contemplating.

"Yes, I remember practicals," she replied and I thought about her name etched into the wall on the roof of our school.

I followed her into the library hearing her muttering about one down, five more to go and where they might be. "Lizzy is checking their friends' houses and the shops they frequent. I've been on the phone with…others." She didn't offer any more details. After dropping into Lizzy's desk chair, she tilted back, staring at the ceiling. "Let me think."

That always meant leave her alone. So I took a seat too. Minutes passed but she didn't speak again so I strolled around the room. It was only the second time I'd been in it and never knew it had so much information to offer. After perusing books on spells, hexes, and the casting of different cultures, Miss Mabelle appeared in the door.

"Any word?" she asked, tensely.

My mother, absorbed in her thoughts, didn't answer.

"Nothing yet," I replied.

"Hmmm," she muttered and turned to walk away, not bothering to offer dinner because it was the last thing on her mind. What struck me was the concern she showed. It was the first time I'd ever seen Miss Mabelle afraid for anyone. This didn't sit well with me because it meant that their disappearance had even broken through her tough exterior.

The clock ticked on and with it being the only sound in the house it was loud and unsettling, as if each second going by were another clue that my cousins weren't coming home any time soon. Eventually, the hands approached the hour when my evening class was supposed to start so I stood, found a piece of paper and pen on Aunt Lizzy's desk, and scratched a note on it.

"Where are you going?"

The sound of my mother's voice caught me off guard so that I'd ended my name with a jagged line across the paper.

"To class. They might show up there."

She nodded. "I'll drive."

We took my car since it was the only one in the driveway, my cousins and Aunt Lizzy having all taken theirs to wherever they were now. When we pulled out the vacancy in front of the house was unnerving.

Our drive was silent as I searched for their vehicles on the road. It was even more disturbing when I found my mother doing the same thing. Then she let me in on what was going through her mind and I became even more apprehensive.

"Kids leaving school without permission…that does happen. But all siblings leaving at once and not returning home. That's telling. And it tells me that somewhere…someone is in trouble." The side of her mouth dropped in a frown as she pulled up to the curb across from my school and turned off the engine.

Then I gasped.

"They're here," I stated, my chest swelling with relief.

"How do you know?"

"Their cars…" I waved my hand toward the row of them parked on the opposite side of the street.

My heart leapt at the sight of another vehicle - a silver Range Rover - parked a few places behind theirs.

Jameson had come, too.

My mother's frown hadn't changed yet, which told me that she was still unsure. She confirmed it when saying, "I'm coming in."

So together we walked down the tunnel and into the courtyard where the last of the students were filtering into their designated rooms. I marched toward my cousins' classroom and glanced through the door. Similar in style to mine, there were no chairs so it took a few seconds to search the collected groups.

"I don't see them," said my mother's voice over my shoulder.

"No," I replied uneasily. "They're not here."

Spinning around, I headed directly for Ms. Veilleux's office, with my mother at my side.

The door was ajar so we pushed it aside without knocking. It was just as old and weathered as the other rooms but her furniture was plush and comfortable. Lamps and candles gave the room a soft glow, barely illuminating the artifacts given by Mr. Thibodeaux to Ms. Boudreaux for showing in class. Set on a bookshelf, they were casting odd shadows up the walls.

We found Ms. Veilleux at her desk, casually scribbling her signature on a stack of documents. When she glanced up, her expression changed from indifference to apprehension.

"Isabella…" she said, stunned.

"Helene," said my mother, breaking into a smile for the first time since I'd seen her back.

Clearly, they remembered each other. Ms. Veilleux came around the desk then, stumbling in shock as she made her way to my mother, opening her arms for an embrace.

"I didn't receive word," she muttered.

When they pulled away, my mother explained, "I didn't know I'd be coming either. It was an emergency."

Ms. Veilleux's eyes, I noticed, didn't widen with concern. They became more concentrated, aware.

To alleviate her fears, my mother hurried to explain, "Jocelyn went missing but, as you can see, she's back." She paused to frown again. "Now I'm looking for her cousins."

Ms. Veilleux blinked. "All of them?"

My mother's lips pinched closed and she nodded once firmly.

"They're not in class?" she said, seeming to already know the answer. Without waiting for one, Ms. Veilleux sighed and dropped her gaze to the floor in contemplation.

"Jocelyn," said my mother. "Why don't you join your class? I'll be here when it ends." Then she turned back to Ms. Veilleux. "Let's work together and see if we might be able to figure out where they've gone."

That was my cue to leave so I did and headed for Ms. Boudreaux's room. When I entered, the class fell quiet but only briefly and then went back to listening to the lecture Ms. Boudreaux was giving on best practices with voodoo dolls. Only Jameson kept his eyes on me as I circled the room to stand next to him. They were intense and alert, making me wonder why until I began weaving through the students.

Then I realized what Jameson had been disturbed by.

The Caldwells were missing, too.

As I came to stand next to him, he purposefully shifted his arm so that it came in contact with mine. The bulge of his muscles caused a distraction until I heard his voice in my head.

"Have you seen your cousins?"

"No," I replied back telepathically. "And I saw that your brothers and sisters aren't in class either…"

"They weren't home when I got there so I don't know what they're up to." The uncertainty in his tone was tainted worse by his nervousness. "They have to be close by though," he added. "Their cars are here…"

"You don't have any idea where they could be?" I asked, meaning both families.

"No…I wish I did," he said pensively.

"Jameson…I have an uncomfortable feeling about this…"

I heard him sigh out loud and then respond by channeling, "Me, too."

Then the worst possibility came to me. "You don't think they're together?"

He didn't respond right away, seeming to decide whether to admit what was truly bothering him. "That is exactly what I'm worried about."

We didn't speak the remainder of the class but I was absolutely certain that Ms. Boudreaux could have been speaking an alien language and we wouldn't have noticed.

I felt, and I was sure Jameson did too, like a trapped animal. Unable to move, waiting for the worst to come.

When the class did end, we exited out into the courtyard with the rest of the students where they disappeared down the tunnel toward the street. Ms. Boudreaux asked us if we needed anything after seeing us loiter but I mentioned that we were waiting for our relatives, which was actually true. She took this at face value and left for her vehicle, too.

Finally, Jameson and I were alone.

I could see the light was off in Ms. Veilleux's office, which meant she and my mother likely went offsite to find my cousins. It also meant I would need to wait for her to return. In the interim, I took a seat on the nearest brick planter next to Jameson, stretching our legs out in front of us and using our hands to prop our arms along the sides of our bodies.

The awareness of Jameson so close to me was both thrilling and intimidating. I wanted to reach out to him and feel the touch of his skin again. I wanted to break down the wall I'd built up with my accusations. And I thought he might want it to, his body staying so firmly erect, unwilling to relax into any form of natural slouch, hinting at it. He seemed to be just as passionate and awkward around me as I was around him. But neither of us moved because there was a conversation that still needed to be finished.

"When we were in the truck - and my mom interrupted us - I never got a chance to-"

He motioned with his hand. "It's all right, Jocelyn."

"No, it's not. You need to…I have to explain, to clarify…"

"It's really not a problem," he said in his typical easygoing way.

I sighed in frustration, refusing to yield.

In response, he chuckled lightly and conceded, "Fine. If it'll make you feel better."

"It will," I said so resolutely I had to soften my tone when I spoke again. "I'm sorry for accusing your family. I was wrong. It was the only information I had, that any of us had. It just…It seems that there is so much misinformation between our families that it's hard to know what's true and what's false. But the real truth is that none of that should matter. I know you. And you're kind, generous, charming. You fight to protect others, not to hurt them. You…"

"Jocelyn…" he tilted his lips up in a sideways smile, his beautiful scar curving with it. "I get it. I know how you feel about me."

The fact that he delivered this news while smiling was a good sign. It meant he at least knew it was positive.

My eyebrows creased as I tried to figure out exactly what he thought he knew. "Which is?" I asked.

"You're in love with me," he replied simply.

I opened my mouth, closed it, and then opened it again, searching for words. "When did you…? How did you…?"

"I feel it." He paused to take my hand, the touch of him, the very fact he had the motivation to hold just that small part of my body was such a relief I had to contain my enthusiasm.

Then he opened the channel and we began reading each other's minds. We were alone. There was little risk of someone overhearing so the reason wasn't to keep what we said private. It was to create an intimate space where only the two of us were allowed.

"It's in the way you look at me, Jocelyn. It's in the reaction I get when we're sitting together, the way you kiss me, the way you try to heal me, protect me, while I'm trying to protect you." He chuckled out loud at the irony of it. "It's in everything you do. You never needed to say the words. I already knew, Jocelyn. Have known, for a while…"

"That long, ha?"

He nodded. "That's why it was so hard for me after…"

"After I accused your family," I said, feeling guilty all over again but he, realizing it, assuaged me.

"After you told me that we were through." The pain was still evident in his voice. "Being apart when it's so clear we both want to be together…It was…"

"Ridiculous," I offered.

He had a different description. "Destructive."

The feelings of only a few days ago flooded back to me. Images of how he'd looked and how I'd forgone caring for myself flashed across my mind - haggard, worn impersonations of ourselves. His depiction couldn't have been more accurate.

"All right," he said gently. "My turn."

"You're turn?" I said, wondering what he could possibly have to apologize for.

But he had something different in mind.

"I got the rare chance to know you before learning who you were. That made all the difference. If you hadn't walked into Olivia's shop when you did and if I hadn't been there at the same time, we would never have gotten to know each other like we do now. I would have discovered you were a Weatherford from one of my family members and avoided you, like I do with the rest of your family. You would have probably done the same with me. But we did meet and I did get to know you. So by the time I saw that bracelet of yours…"

"The one with my family stone," I filled in.

"Yes," he grinned. "That one. I'd already fallen for you." He paused and then hastened to clarify. "Not in love. That came later." Even the hint of Jameson falling in love with me tickled my insides. "I knew I was taking a chance. You could have turned out to be someone deserving of a Weatherford reputation. But you kept proving that to be wrong. It didn't define you. Contrary to what my family and friends think - you want to help others. You try to prevent conflicts with us, not escalate them. You're funny, sensitive…You're innocent. Not weak," he clarified when seeing my mouth fall open in offense. "Just unaware. You didn't know anything about us, about what my family is capable of doing, and had no idea how to protect yourself. And they can be vicious. So I wanted to protect you. And that protection grew into something more. When I finally acknowledged it, I didn't care about stopping it, even when I told my family."

"You told them?" I asked, astounded. "They couldn't have taken that well…"

He laughed sarcastically under his breath. "It was the night you said you didn't want to see me anymore."

I sucked in a breath and held it. "Bad timing…" I thought spontaneously and wondered if he'd heard it.

He had. "Oh, yeah. I'd agree with that. What that did to me - our separation - how that felt…I've never experienced anything remotely close to it in my life. It was…"

I knew exactly what he was trying to say because I'd felt it, too. "Agony."

"Yes, that's exactly what it was."

We fell silent for a moment and then I said, "Let's make sure it doesn't happen again."

He turned to find my eyes, to hold them as he declared, "That is my intention." He drew in a breath, shuffled his feet and fell silent. After a long pause, he changed the subject. "It's why I'm a little nervous our families haven't shown up yet."

Impulsively, we glanced toward the tunnel leading to the street but it was empty. They wouldn't have come down it together, obviously. Still, seeing any one of them enter the courtyard would have been comforting.

As it turned out, we didn't see them. We heard them.

A wooden board above us creaked, a sound that was clearly not the settling of an old building but by the weight of a foot. It came from the overhang, telling us that we weren't alone and that the person was on the second floor, directly overhead.

Seconds later, a giggle rang out into the night.

"We've been waiting for you…" someone hissed and I recognized it as Alison.

"Funny," said Estelle, casual, confident, and from somewhere in the darkness. "We've been doing the same."

20. FEUD

It was late, past eleven o'clock now. The noise from Bourbon Street was escalating so that voices, shouts, and a mingling of jazz, blues, and rock music rose over the rooftops. The temperature had dipped so that we could now see faded white puffs as we breathed. Light was sparse. Other than the gas lamps hanging beside each door, only the half moon offered any clarity to our surroundings. With Ms. Veilleux's office light still off, it looked like the courtyard was vacant.

It wasn't.

Gradually, indeterminate figures stepped toward the railing on the second floor, heads ducked, arms at their sides, five on one side of the courtyard and four on the other. There were five children in the Caldwell family and with one of them sitting beside me it was easy to conclude that the four above Jameson and me, standing to our left, were the Caldwells.

"Did you really think we wouldn't retaliate?" Burke's voice called across the courtyard.

It was eerie being unable to place where exactly it originated.

Jameson had a different reaction to it. His shoulders fell and he shook his head, realizing their aim was to fight...again. Slowly, he stood up and, still holding my hand, he channeled to me, "Stay here. This might get ugly."

Not being in the habit of listening to instructions, I readied myself to enter and separate the fighters, if they came together.

At the same time, the battle of words raged above us.

"Hand him over and there won't be any bloodshed," someone warned. It was a voice I hadn't heard before, higher-pitched, and one I deemed came from Dillon.

Estelle retorted, quickly and fierce. "Hand her over and we'll let you live."

This was rapidly spiraling out of reason.

"You've gone too far Caldwells," shouted Nolan. "Hand over Jocelyn!"

I was then on my feet. They were talking about me.

Jameson, who heard it too, took a misstep. He glanced back and I knew he was thinking the same thing: Our absence over the last several days convinced them that the Caldwells had done something to me and they were now demanding I be returned.

"You hand over Jameson!" Charlotte snapped back.

Then the full reality dawned on me. Both families thought the other had taken their relative.

I took a step and heard something slam against the wall above us. Shards of wood fluttered on top of me as I instinctively ducked and covered my head.

"Are you all right?" Jameson was suddenly crouched at my side.

"Yes," I said, already standing. "We need to stop this."

Our voices alone might have done it, ended the fight before it really got started because they would have known that the both of us were fine, but our words were never heard. They hadn't heard us before because we were channeling and they didn't hear us now because they were in the midst of a full-blown conflict.

The object that hit the wall a moment ago turned out to be Charlotte. I knew this after I heard her grunt while trying to stand back up. Someone had levitated her and the only one with that ability was Vinnia. Charlotte apparently knew this because I looked up just in time to find her bent over the railing, arm stretched out, palm facing the opposite side of the courtyard. As soon as the arm reached its full extension Charlotte uttered her incantation and Vinnia was lifted into the air and shoved backwards by the force.

By that point, Estelle had pursed her lips and blown, picking up the gas flame from the lamp below and circling it through the air until it snaked under the railing at Alison. Her intended victim side stepped the flame but not before the damage was done. It left a scalding mark on her thigh and ignited the railing. Dillon responded with a burst of flame across the courtyard toward Estelle, which set the railing on fire in front of them.

Smoke began to fill the courtyard as the fragile wood went up, obscuring the bodies moving swiftly on both sides. Oscar used this to his benefit, capturing the drifts with bouts of air and swirling them around the Caldwells. Dillon fought it, dispelling and sending the smoke across the courtyard and back to Estelle and Oscar.

Spencer and Nolan, both gifted in channeling, had their eyes pinned on Burke, their lips moving frantically as they cast. Burke responded with a roar and then tilted his head in their direction and began moving his lips at the same blurred pace as theirs. Without having to be told, I knew they were trying to get into each other's heads.

All of this happened in a matter of seconds.

Then Jameson stepped into the open and roared, "STOP!" He had his chin up and his hands in fists, showing the frustration he felt. But a second later, they no longer seemed to be under his command.

I watched in horror as he was lifted into the air, his limbs being frozen in place. He couldn't even rotate his head to find who it was levitating him.

"NO!" I shouted and ran toward him, halting a foot away as if an invisible wall had been dropped in front of me.

"Get back," I heard Jameson shout and I thought it might be directed at me but it was too late.

My feet left the ground and my extremities became cement blocks, unwilling to move. My eyes darted around, looking for the source and I found Charlotte, her lip curled up to one side in a snarl, entirely focused on levitating me.

In the midst of chaos, flashes of flames through a smoke-filled courtyard, shouts and cries of pain, disintegrating balconies, they didn't realize that their respective relative was no longer missing. Charlotte knew I was here and Vinnia knew Jameson was here but neither family knew it about their respective relative.

We were now in a war zone where everything was distorted.

Through clearings in the smoke, I searched for any eyes, any face with reason or sound mind. All I saw were faces contorting in pain or mouths open to release incantations, which had risen from murmurs to piercing shrieks.

Oscar's arms were now lifted, his fingers spread making it look like he was grasping for something. He was. It turned out to be rain collected in the spouts, which he threw into a whirlwind, twisting it toward various Caldwells. Dillon responded with flames, wrapping them around the spouts when he could catch them.

Vinnia had taken to splitting her focus between suspending Jameson and using broken pieces of wood, turning them horizontally and shooting them like arrows across the courtyard. In turn, she dodged the shards of glass Charlotte sent in her direction.

Estelle was collecting fire in the shape of basketballs near her feet, sending them across one at a time, while attempting to miss the ones Alison was sending back with her ability to levitate.

Spencer and Nolan now had their hands on parts of the railing that still existed, gripping hard and sending their energy outward toward Burke. He in turn had started to shake his head as if a hornet were buzzing around inside it, a clear attempt at trying to keep Spencer and Nolan from infiltrating.

Jameson and I were the only ones left untouched as the battle raged overhead. In the midst of it, I focused on him, preparing myself for what I was about to do. Vinnia didn't know it yet but I was going up against her, my own cousin. I would have to tear through her levitation, just as I'd torn through the ministry's hex on the outcasts. Only then could I lower Jameson to the ground where he'd be safe.

Shutting out the chilling sights and sounds around me, I made the potent force inside my focal point. From the depth of my torso, it awakened and I felt it rise up like a sleeping animal clawing toward the surface and then across the conduit between Jameson and me. I worked on intensifying it, dedicated to breaking through Vinnia's concentration.

Gradually, his arms fell and his head turned back, peering over his shoulder at me.

I nodded, answering the inquisitive look he gave. That's me.

His lips turned up in a confident smile and he tilted his head once toward me, acknowledging that he understood.

I didn't hear Vinnia scream in anger as Jameson landed on the ground but I deduced it was because she couldn't see where he was. With the smoke so thick in the courtyard now only gaps and swirls allowed anyone to see what was happening throughout it.

Then Jameson was sprinting toward me, reaching for my legs, but I was yanked upward, well outside his reach.

I knew immediately what had happened.

Charlotte had seen.

His head swiveled from side to side, searching for something to reach me, something he could drag out to stand on, something he could climb. But there was nothing. I was in the very center, well away from anyone or anything that could help. I was Charlotte's tool now.

Jameson recognized it too and released a tormented roar and I shook at his fury. I was in the middle of a coughing fit as the smoke overwhelmed me I began to inhale the heady, thick air.

There was only one thing that might be able to help now.

"The...talisman," I shouted down to him between coughs. He glanced up, puzzled, his eyebrows furrowing. "The Tristan Talisman...from class. It's in Ms. Veilleux's office."

He lifted up his shoulders in a confused shrug.

"It incapacitates others," I reminded him.

Blinking a few times, he tried to recall and then his eyes widened and, without confirming he'd understood, his feet were suddenly sprinting across the courtyard.

Only then did I relax. Just a few minutes longer and this would all be over. We'd debilitate our families, the fires eating away the balconies would be doused, the air would clear, and we'd help them see that Jameson and I were here, and that there was no need to fight.

As I contemplated this, the smoke cleared and what I saw caused a scream to rattle up through my throat and echo against the buildings.

"NOOOOOOOO!"

Jameson lay face down, sprawled across the cobblestones, the smoke curling around his arms and legs as if it were trying to pick him up, help him get moving again.

Watching this, an emotion I'd never had reason to experience before filled me, blanketed me, caused my fingers to curl into fists and my chest to swell to capacity.

Fury.

Without entirely realizing it, I churned that emotion, blended it with my own ability to levitate, and countered Charlotte's energy.

The next thing I knew, I was on the ground, a throb moving up my palms and forearms, pain radiating from my knees as my limbs took the brunt of the impact.

Without time on my side, I shoved aside the affects of my fall to the ground and picked myself up. Fireballs and slivers of wood shot passed me and I wondered if any of these were what hit Jameson.

I was at his side in seconds, rolling him toward me.

His face had already started to swell. A gash around his left eye seeped blood and his skin was singed across his forehead.

"Jameson?" I called out. "Jameson!"

His eyes remained closed.

"Jameson!" I shouted again but he gave no response.

With my focus on the open wound I didn't immediately notice the changes happening elsewhere on his face.

Steadily, the skin across his forehead smoothed over and the blackened discoloration faded away. The bulge around his chin sunk back until the inflammation disappeared completely. Finally, the stream of blood down his temple and into his hair tapered away and I watched as the skin around the gap merged together, sealing the wound.

"Jameson," I said, my voice calmer, recognizing that my touch was healing him. "Jameson."

"Almost there, sweetheart. Just give me a second."

At least he had his wits back.

Then his eyes opened and he gave me a weak smile. "Careful. You'll heal the last of that scar over my mouth you love so much."

I laughed lightly and countered, "And how do you know I love it?"

"Admit it," he moaned, pushing himself up. "It's one of the reasons you can't take your eyes off me."

I wasn't about to succumb to his conceit, even if he'd just been knocked out. Instead, I helped him to his feet.

"Can you make it?" I asked referring to Ms. Veilleux's office.

"Race you," he muttered playfully.

We did race, although not against each other. It was against our families. From the sounds above, their aggression was growing.

Inside Ms. Veilleux's office, Jameson tried to find the light switch but there was none and resorted to lighting a candle. I swung around the edge of the desk, making my way toward Mr. Thibodeaux's talisman stored on the bookshelf.

The noise outside was muffled but thumps through the ceiling told us that the fight had made its way inside the walls of our school.

"Got it," I said, spinning around with the talisman in hand.

"Just in time too," he said. "They're going to destroy this place."

"Along with themselves," I added.

With those words still hanging in the air, we sprinted back to the courtyard, through the hazy smoke and flashing fireballs, and into the center of the battle.

Inopportune time or not, my mind drifted back to the first time Jameson and I had worked together in class. Even though we'd only been attempting to cure the rash given to him by my cousins, together, we'd ended up healing everyone in the room. We had no idea back then that only a few weeks later we'd be tapping that same channeling of energy to prevent our families from killing one another. And here we were, in the middle of their fight, risking our own lives.

I held up the talisman, still wrapped in its cloth, and asked, "Think we can do this?"

"We'll know in a minute," he said, uncertain himself. "Just don't let go of me, Jocelyn. That's the last thing you'll want to do."

I wouldn't. I couldn't if this was going to work. And it was chancy as it was. Assumedly, if Jameson could channel the energy from the talisman to our families, it would disable them. But I would need to be holding Jameson to heal him from the affects of the mystical artifact as well. The only element of surprise, the one unsure thing was whether the talisman would disable my abilities too.

Doubt clear on his face, Jameson pulled at the overlapped corners of the cloth, revealing the artifact inside. His hand slipped into mine. The other came up, fingers extended, ready to take hold…

The explosion came down directly between us, throwing our bodies backwards, our legs sweeping up from underneath us as we were carried across the ground.

I landed with my back against something hard, knocking the wind from me, pain searing across my shoulder blades. The world outside suddenly reflected a churning washing machine with images and sounds tumbling around indistinctly. My hands were at my sides, resting in the gravel of something that had been blown apart during the battle. The talisman was gone.

I've been hit. I heard the words more as a voice than a thought. Then it occurred to me that Jameson had been, too.

From then on, I attempted to stand. Moving forward, bending at the waist, I drew in a hoarse, staggered breath only to cough it out, carrying dust, smoke, and flecks of unidentifiable material. Although they were weakened, I slid my arms alongside my body and braced myself. I then shifted my weight to the left, hoping for the momentum to roll over on to all fours. From there I could use whatever I'd landed against to crawl upwards.

But that didn't happen.

I buckled beneath my own weight, my legs spreading outward, bearing the brunt of my failed attempt.

Trying again, I pushed my torso off the ground only to collapse again. From there, I simply rolled to my back and realized I'd landed beneath the smoldering remains of the balcony.

"Jameson," my voice called out, too gruff to be distinguishable. It didn't matter. I wasn't calling for him. I needed to hear the sound of his name, knowing it would motivate me passed the pain and weakness pulsing through me.

It worked. I pushed myself up and over until I was propped on my hands and knees.

Tilting my head up, I found the thing that had split us apart.

A balcony pillar had come down, directly where we'd been standing, splitting in two from the impact. And somewhere on the other side was Jameson.

Unable to stand, I crawled over broken glass, burning shards of wood, and charred plants toward him. Only vaguely, I noticed the tearing of my skin, the layers of my palms peeling away and the flaps of skin scraping along the ground as my knees dragged me forward.

"Jameson," I shouted only to hear it come out a whisper.

Reaching the pillar, I heaved for air, summoning the strength to speak it louder. He had to be there - on the other side. He had to be breathing. He had to be alive. He had to be. He was too strong. Too resilient. And we'd gone through too much to get to this point. Against all the odds, despite our family's wishes, we were together and our love had survived. But he didn't know it. Because I'd never told him. That I love him. I never said the actual words. I only hinted and right now, right here that wasn't enough. He deserved better. He deserved to know.

"Jameson!" I screamed, this time his name carrying past the edge of my lips.

Then he was there.

His arms swung over the pillar, pulling himself up, his face crusty and blackened, his forearms bleeding from wounds down both sides.

"Jocelyn," he breathed, relieved.

"Jameson," I chocked. "I thought...I thought..."

He slid down and wrapped me in an embrace, locking me in an iron embrace that said he wouldn't allow us to separate again.

"I know, I thought I lost you, too," he sighed into my hair. And then he was kissing me, his hands on my cheeks, his lips passionate and tender.

I returned it with the same vigor, my body trembling against his.

Then I pulled my lips away and, with my hands on his face, told him what I should have said a long time ago. "I love you, Jameson."

He swallowed, his nose flaring with a deep inhale as he reacted to hearing me finally say the words. "I wondered how long it would take you..."

I laughed, my head rolling back, despite the pain it caused. As it fell forward, I gently rested my forehead on his, captivated by the weight of his hands on my hips and the feel of his arms resting against mine.

Only then did I realize that the courtyard was calm. Just the crackling of the embers could be heard.

"Jameson?" I asked, looking up, wondering where the screams, incantations, and sizzling fireballs had gone.

We straightened but didn't pull away, surveying the area around us. More than one pillar had fallen and they lay burning across the courtyard. Beneath them were the remnants of the balconies and railings, no more than shreds of wood now. Broken glass, pieces of what had once been classroom windows, gleamed in the flames. Branches and leaves from healthy, lush plants were now burnt and littering the ground. Everything seemed to smolder. The air, however, had cleared. There were no more fireballs or makeshift arrows. The smoke had lifted, giving way to the true damage. The courtyard and the building's façade around it were entirely destroyed.

It was eerily silent but we weren't alone. The faces of our families peered over the edges of what had been the balcony. They were motionless, captivated by what they were witnessing.

"What are they looking at?" I whispered to Jameson, apprehensive that any louder voice might disrupt the peace.

He caught my eyes and smiled.

"Us."

21. THE TRUTH

For a brief second, I thought my cousins and the Caldwells had stopped themselves by their own free will, that they'd come to their senses, and realized there was no need to fight. But that was too much to hope for.

The destruction would have continued and someone would have been seriously injured if my mother and Ms. Veilleux hadn't returned. They stood at the opening of the tunnel, not shocked so much as disappointed.

I felt like a child being admonished without words. And I'd been trying to stop the fight. I couldn't imagine what my cousins and Jameson's brothers and sisters felt like.

Cautiously, they stepped forward, through the devastation.

"This…" said Ms. Veilleux "is more than I ever imagined."

My mother simply shook her head.

"We didn't realize-" Estelle began to say but my mother languidly swept a hand through the air in her direction and Estelle's mouth clamped down. Whether my mother had cast against her or not, I couldn't tell but she'd done the job. Estelle remained quiet.

None of those on the upper level had moved and I began to question why until Ms. Veilleux motioned above her head and they began to drift down over the edge to land on the ground floor. She had stopped the fight, levitating and restricting them enough to prevent any further damage from taking place. Only Jameson and I were free to move about and that was probably because we weren't causing the ruins...we were part of them.

Still, it was easy to see from the disbelief in their expressions that they had heard Jameson and me pronounce our love for each other. They never removed their gaze from us as we stood together, hand in hand.

"You're going to have to accept it," Jameson said to everyone listening, including my mother and Ms. Veilleux. "I love her. Nothing's changing that. Not my last name and not hers."

"It's not just a last name," Alison said exasperated, referring to the years of animosity, treachery, and deceit between our two families.

When Jameson didn't answer, Burke suggested defiantly, "Maybe we should have let you go missing. Maybe we shouldn't have tried to get you back. It might have helped you remember where you come from." That was designed to provoke Jameson, to get him to think about what he was doing, but it didn't work.

"If this is the result...yes." Jameson pinched his lips in irritation. "I understand that you want to keep me safe. I appreciate that because there might be a time when I actually need it. With Jocelyn, I don't."

"Where were you the last few days?" Burke countered, insisting that Jameson remember that he'd just disappeared because of a Weatherford.

"Outside the city, healing others."

I noticed Jameson gave the same explanation I'd given to my mother, which was good because she and Ms. Veilleux were patiently listening to their exchange.

The Caldwells fell silent, awkwardly glancing at each other. They'd thought it was so much worse that it took them a while to absorb the truth.

"It's as simple as this…" said Charlotte, attempting to step forward but unable to pick up her foot. She sighed in aggravation at Ms. Veilleux for keeping her movements restrained but still wouldn't be deterred. "The confession of your love just now was touching…I'll give you that. But the fact is it endangers all of us if you stay together. We'll need to watch what we say around you, keep things we do a secret. Because it's just not safe for us…for anyone if you two stay together."

It was the most lucid argument I'd heard yet and I wasn't the only one impressed by it, albeit for a different reason.

"Wow," muttered Estelle. "We actually agree on something."

Charlotte wasn't able to respond as my family started up.

"Jocelyn," said Vinnia, "you are a Weatherford. Being one comes with certain responsibilities. One of those is not falling in love with the enemy."

"Or even consorting with one," added Spencer.

"Or even looking at one…" said Nolan, and then corrected himself, "Unless you're casting."

"But I did," I stopped them gently. "And sooner or later, both families are going to realize that the other isn't the enemy." Scoffs rose up from both sides of the courtyard. "The reality is that the Weatherfords and the Caldwells have a lot more in common than you think." Actual laughter followed my implausible statement. "Both families are tight knit. You would do anything for your brothers and sisters - including destroy your school in defense of them." Although no one would concede and move their heads, their eyes did a quick scan of the destruction around them. "You both grew up with prickly housekeepers as guidance counselors because your parents were elsewhere. Those on both sides have dangerously effective casting skills. No one on either side is evil - manipulative and destructive - maybe but not evil. All of you are just trying to defend yourselves from the other. And you all dislike the idea of Jameson and me together."

While I didn't see any nods of agreement, their expressions told me what I needed to see.

They were recognizing, probably for the first time, that their enemies weren't all that different. I wondered if it would matter to them, if it would help change their perspective and then Estelle gave me the answer.

"Jocelyn," she said, dumbfounded. "Your mother hid you in New York to protect you from these people, because she knew what they've done to us and what they can do to you."

My heart sank. I was running out of ways to help them see the truth. Part of me wanted to scream it and the other wanted to give in, walk away with Jameson and handle what may come.

Then I felt a hand on my shoulder and my mother's voice in my ear. "I'll take it from here, Jocelyn."

She'd crossed the still smoldering courtyard and now continued on to the center where she was easily visible by both families.

"It's well known and documented the lengths to which both the Weatherfords and the Caldwells are assumed to have gone in their deceit toward one another."

"Assumed to have gone?" mumbled Oscar, confused. And I had a feeling he was speaking what everyone else was thinking.

My mother ignored his reference and continued. "What I have to say may fill in a few holes…misconceptions that still exist. Things are not always what they seem."

There was that statement again. I'd heard it from Miss Mabelle, Miss Celia, and now my mother.

"First, let me clarify that my decision to bring Jocelyn to the academy in New York was not to protect her from the Caldwells. They were…and still are…the least of my worries."

This drew looks from both families, which only grew tenser as she went on.

"The Caldwells are victims as much as we are."

"Victims?" Spencer scoffed.

"Allow me to finish," my mother said and it was not posed as a question. "My rationale for hiding Jocelyn at the academy in New York…my rationale for working at the ministry…and my rationale for not coming forward earlier are each embedded in the same reasoning…We are all in grave danger."

Charlotte sighed loudly. "This has nothing to do with us."

My mother aimed her gaze at Charlotte. "We includes you," she replied stiffly. "The Caldwells, in fact, are in a greater position of risk because you are unaware of what is coming."

The furrowed eyebrows and apprehensive looks now aimed at my mother told me that even if they didn't believe her, they were listening.

"Working at the ministry has made me privy to certain information. The feud between the Caldwells and Weatherfords is well documented. It is known even in the most remote provinces that our two families have cast against each other for generations. What is not known, what I've only recently learned through friends with access at levels higher than mine, is that the most egregious acts…every murder…every attempted murder…every loss of fortune…every long-term illness…these were all manufactured."

"Manufactured?" asked Oscar, confused.

"They were fraudulent, designed to look as if the other family committed these crimes." She paused to assess the expressions of those around her. Only Ms. Veilleux didn't appear to be in shock. "We have been pitted against each other, deceived in to believing that the cause of our relatives' deaths or financial ruin or ill health had all been delivered at the hands of the other family. When, in fact, they have not."

Spencer shook his head slightly. "That doesn't make sense. Why would anyone do that?"

My mother paused to pivot her head and look at Jameson and me. I thought this was a little unusual and then she answered. "To keep these two separated."

"Us?" I slapped my free hand to my chest and then glanced at Jameson, who was equally as astounded.

"Everything they've done to our two families has been to prevent the two of you from ever meeting."

"Why us?" asked Jameson, still stunned.

Ms. Veilleux stepped forward then, stopping my mother from answering. "I think this news would be best understood coming from me."

My mother hesitated but I saw her working things through in her mind. And I knew that whatever they were about to tell us would be circumspect coming from my mother, a Weatherford.

"The Sevens have known since the first channelers that Jocelyn and Jameson would eventually be born and they've been told by those channelers that, together, Jocelyn and Jameson will be their downfall. So they've taken immeasurable steps to keep the two apart. Long before they were born, elaborate schemes were created to build mistrust and animosity between your families so there was no hope that any of you would willingly cross paths, so that no friendships could be built or even considered. They concocted ways to eliminate both families' money in attempts to force you to relocate. Then, as infants, an abduction attempt was made on both Jameson and Jocelyn. They failed and Jocelyn's mother secured her in upstate New York with a unit to watch over her while the Caldwells developed a unit of protection around Jameson here. The abduction was another attempt to keep Jocelyn and Jameson from ever meeting. When it was discovered that Jocelyn was no longer in the city, they suspended their efforts. But they're aware of her return because their emissaries are aware of it. And they are currently looking for a reason the rest of our world won't question that will legitimize the return of their forces here, where your lives will be in far greater danger than a boil hex." Her mouth turned down on one side and she finished by looking around the ruined courtyard. "And I think you've just given them the reason they've been waiting for."

We studied our surroundings, realizing for the first time that our conflict here didn't only destroy our school, it threatened our lives.

"Just a second...You keep saying 'they' or 'them'," Alison commented. "Who are you referring to? Who is doing all this? Only the Vires are capable of pulling those kinds of things off."

"The Vires act on behalf of The Sevens..." my mother pointed out. Then she allowed the rest of us to process what she'd said, to come to terms with exactly what it meant. Only after eyes widened and jaws went slack, did she speak again.

Very slowly, she nodded. "The Sevens are the reason for all of this..." She swept her hand around the courtyard. "This retaliation upon retaliation...It is exactly what The Sevens want."

And the words that came to mind were ones that I'd heard over these past few weeks, ones that simmered to the surface, having lingered beneath until there was reason for them to rise up.

Things aren't always what they seem.

Charlotte, however, wasn't immediately convinced. She scoffed quietly, contesting, "I have a hard time believing that story. I'm sorry, Ms. Veilleux, but this woman works for the ministry, which is commanded by The Sevens."

While Ms. Veilleux attempted to respond, a far greater confidante supported my mother and Ms. Veilleux's claims.

"She's right about my abduction," Jameson stated. "And if she's right about that..." He left the rest to be insinuated, placing his trust in my mother in the face of his guarded siblings.

His courage stunned me.

When Burke spoke up his tone was curious but not suspicious and it was a testament to how much he respected Jameson's integrity. "You knew who abducted you? How did you find out? And why didn't you tell us?"

"I learned about it yesterday, from someone who's proven to be trustworthy."

"Isadora," my mother concluded.

He was slightly thrown that she identified his source so quickly. That reaction alone confirmed the truth to my mother.

She nodded. "Isadora's the only other person who knew."

Fear crossed his face then, for reasons I couldn't quite grasp until my mother responded.

"Your secret is safe, Jameson. I've known about your supply route for some time now."

Of course she did. She always did her homework and had researched Jameson well, as demonstrated by her summary of him outside Aunt Lizzy's house. How could his confidential trips to the swamp be excluded from his profile?

"You knew and didn't turn him in?" asked Charlotte, suspiciously.

"We knew when your family started it. If I'd wanted to turn any of you in, I would have done it a long time ago." She looked at Jameson and gave him a nod of approval before encouraging, "Keep it up. We'll make sure The Sevens are looking the other way."

The Caldwells glanced at each other with a mixture of appreciation and revelation.

Jameson's forehead creased in contemplation then. He'd caught something I hadn't. "You said 'we'?" he prompted.

"I'm not alone in my insights about The Sevens. There are others of us and our numbers are growing."

"So…" ventured Burke, "you…and others…are working for the ministry to deceive them?"

"We work for them in order to be in a position to protect the interests of those who aren't capable of defending themselves," she corrected.

Then something amazing happened. The Caldwells began to smile and nod, a show of appreciation for a Weatherford that I didn't think was possible.

"Not what you expected?" my mother asked, grinning. "Thought I was ruthless and corrupt?"

Alison burst in to laughter while the rest of the Caldwells nodded vehemently.

My cousins were just as speechless as the Caldwells, I noticed.

"You never knew?" I asked Oscar, who stood the closest to me.

"I didn't tell anyone," my mother answered. "It was too risky for them - and for me. And it would destroy my chances at finding the truth and helping others."

The expressions of those around me changed rapidly. We'd all realized it at the same time but it was Jameson who put it into words. "You went into the enemy's nest, unaccompanied, without any other support only so that you could keep us safe?"

"It had to be done," she replied plainly.

He shook his head at her, deeply amazed, and he wasn't alone.

"You're worth it," she said to me and then repeated it to everyone else. "You're all worth it."

Charlotte, the most contentious of the Caldwells, the one who was the first to strike and ask questions later asked Ms. Veilleux to release her and then approached my mother. "If what you're saying is true…and I have the instinct it is-"

"And she has great instincts," added Dillon.

She sighed at being interrupted and then finished, "It's a pleasure to finally meet one of the Weatherfords." Then she extended her hand and my mother took it without reserve.

After a brief handshake Charlotte turned to me. "I'm sorry for all the trouble I've started. My brother…" she glanced at Jameson "seems to be right about you. I'm glad you two are together…" She paused to smirk, one that was for the first time not aimed at me. "If it aggravates The Sevens."

Vinnia laughed under her breath. "I'm with you on that…"

I laughed with Charlotte and Vinnia, as friends do in any other setting, something I enjoyed more than I imagined I would, and from that point Ms. Veilleux seemed to feel safe enough to release the rest of them. They moved unrestricted around the debris and as I watched them I noticed how they seemed more relaxed around each other, not quite friendly but on the same level of newly formed acquaintances. We were starting from scratch with a new perspective. And it gave me hope.

"Amazing what the truth can accomplish…" muttered Jameson.

I laughed softly, released his hand, and wrapped an arm around his sculpted waist, enjoying the feel of his muscles beneath my fingertips. "I was thinking the same thing."

He leaned over and kissed my temple, stirring excitement in me so that I rotated my head and met his kiss with my lips.

Charlotte groaned.

"Sorry," I said through a smile, pulling away as Jameson laughed without remorse.

Burke, standing a few feet away didn't notice. His attention was on something else as he kicked a singed piece of railing. "Ms. Veilleux, I'm sorry about this...about the school...about everything."

"We all are," said Estelle, humbled.

"What...What will you tell them?" Alison asked, openly dismayed.

Ms. Veilleux's lips tucked under briefly as she contemplated it. "The truth. That we had a fire we couldn't immediately contain." She winked then, in case we missed her analogy. "Unfortunately, they'll still use it as an excuse." That message wasn't lost either. We all knew what she meant. The Sevens had their reason to send in Vires, to surround us, to find some way to eliminate their threat.

"And they'll act quickly," cautioned my mother.

"Then so will we," I said, surprising myself at my resolute tone. It earned a smile of respect from my mother and nods of agreement from everyone else. "First things first..."

"Right, we start by spreading the news," Jameson said, following my line of thought. Then he grinned and said, "Jocelyn, I think it's about time you met my parents..."

22. THE PLAN

A layer of fog sat like a thick, white skin over the water's edge drifting toward the lowest branches of the cypress trees. The smell of moss and decay was strong tonight, lingering in the still air. In the distance, an owl made its presence known giving the swamp an eerie quality.

"I've heard of this place but…" Spencer whispered as if he were on sacred ground.

"But you never thought you'd see it?" I finished, not bothering to hide my voice.

"Never…"

Estelle laughed to herself. "When I was a little girl, I used to think I'd end up here."

"That's still possible," Oscar warned with a smile. He was teasing but a few others raised their eyebrows suspecting.

Aunt Lizzy, who had been chattering continuously since we'd left the house, was now tentative and speechless, telling me that this was her first trip here as well.

For once, I was introducing them to something new.

As we stood on the bank, my mother and Aunt Lizzy to the left and my cousins to the right, dense air began to swirl in the distance and the faint sound of a motorboat rose over the water. The fog broke and Jameson's boat glided toward us, around cypress stumps and shallow sand bars. By the time he'd docked and roped it, I was grinning excitedly. His frequent glances in my direction as he secured the boat were proof that he'd missed me too.

His sandy blonde hair was combed back to expose his bright, expectant green eyes. I was momentarily captured by them only to be drawn away by the crisp white button down curving in on his muscles underneath. He looked out of place, like someone stepping off a GQ cover.

It had been two days since the incident in the courtyard and although we'd spent those days together, he'd left me tonight to arrive earlier with his family. Because of that, it had been a very long evening for both of us.

When he pulled his eyes away, he finally addressed those standing around me. "All of you came," Jameson stated, nodding. "Good. It'll be helpful for everyone on both sides to meet."

Aunt Lizzy, who was now carefully stepping across the dock's rotting boards, her arms spread eagle for stability, said, "Thank you for the ride."

"Here," said Jameson hastily climbing out of the boat. "Let me help you."

"Oh…pish," she said in frustration and a second later her feet were lifted up over the bow of the boat to her seat.

Vinnia chuckled in awe before following Aunt Lizzy's example and simply levitating into the boat. She, Aunt Lizzy and I then lifted the rest of my cousins to their seats.

My mother and I, being the last ones on the dock, gave each other a fleeting glance before she asked, "You don't need my assistance, do you?"

"No," I replied, briefly stunned that she knew I had the ability to levitate. We'd kept that information hidden from

Aunt Lizzy and Miss Mabelle. I'd also been careful not to use it since my mother arrived. But she had her ways of learning details about others which she had no qualms about applying to me. "How long have you known?"

"A while," she replied coyly, gave me a wink, and levitated herself to her seat.

I could have levitated. Everyone knew this. But standing alone on the dock, I bent down and accepted Jameson's hand. Knowing our touch would be limited under the eyes of our families tonight, I was going to take advantage of every situation I could. And as his hand came around mine and our eyes met, the heat of exhilaration settled in my stomach and I was glad to have decided on it.

Then Estelle threatened my plan by suggesting, "Think we should just levitate everyone there?"

Jameson came to my rescue by mentioning, "I need to get the boat back anyways - for my family."

"Okay," she shrugged and settled back against the boat's edge, to my relief.

Jameson winked at me and then sat down. It was a calculated move so that he landed with our thighs pressed together. He must have known we would need to act with restraint too because he didn't move the entire trip.

As we passed smoothly through the village I noticed that it was back to normal. Lanterns were lit outside the stilted homes. From within, light and laughter flowed out. As I watched, the heat from my stomach rose and settled in my chest, warming my heart.

Behind me, it remained silent and I knew my mother, aunt and cousins were studying the village. Then we reached our destination where people I assumed to be Jameson's parents had congregated with Isadora at the end of her dock.

"And here we go..." Estelle chortled beneath her breath.

Mrs. Caldwell, a stout woman with shoulder-length blonde hair and a defined chin, was assessing us as we approached. She looked like someone who knew how to handle just about any situation, someone my mother could relate to. She was holding hands with Mr. Caldwell, a man with kind eyes, notably long legs, a stocky torso, and graying beard. He looked like Jameson might in fifty years if someone were to tell Jameson that his son had fallen in love with the enemy. In other words, he accepted it with poise and dignity.

Once we were tied to the dock and everyone had disembarked, Jameson ushered his parents forward and introduced us each by name.

Very carefully and with a great amount of hesitation, Mrs. Caldwell offered her hand. Only when my mother stepped up and took it did it seem like everyone breathed again. From there, the timidity lessened as hands crossed and genuine salutations were extended.

At the end of our introductions, Mrs. Caldwell hesitated just before admitting what was going through her mind. "I'll be honest with you, Isabella. My initial instinct was to reject this meeting. I was also inclined to refute what Jameson has said about you and your family. But I think you can appreciate our sense of prudence."

My mother smiled knowingly in response. "I'm glad you came."

"We can thank Jameson's persistence, the insistence of his brothers and sisters, and Ms. Veilleux for it."

"Ah," said my mother, realizing they'd made efforts to verify her story. "I would have met with her too."

"We needed to…feel comfortable," explained Mrs. Caldwell with a quick tilt of her head.

"Understandably. I imagine you've met with Isadora as well?"

"Yes."

"Excellent," sighed my mother. "I won't have to repeat myself then."

They laughed together and then fell into an awkward silence, each staring at each other, waiting for the other to make a move. Jameson and I stiffened, both wondering if we'd need to intervene and then Mrs. Caldwell spoke.

"And all this time we considered you to be the enemies," she said reflectively.

"You weren't alone in that perception," my mother replied.

"And this is the young woman who helped redefine that perception?" asked Mrs. Caldwell, turning toward me and assessing.

"Yes," my mother answered before I could. "You can always count on Jocelyn to disrupt the norm."

"Thanks," I replied, sarcastically.

While others laughed, Mrs. Caldwell took my hand in hers. "It's us who should be thanking you...you and your mother." It was genuine and receptive and not something I would ever have expected a few weeks ago.

I gave her an appreciative smile which she returned before spinning around before beginning introductions with Aunt Lizzy, who accepted her hand with some reticence. My aunt was an emotive person who would take a little more time to sway. And I was sure she wasn't the only one. Mrs. Caldwell appeared not to notice her reaction and casually suggested, "Shall we?" before strolling toward the door.

Jameson and I exchanged a look of relief then as we followed our families into Isadora's home, his fingers playfully entwining with mine, tickling my palm softly, enticing me.

Once we entered, he dropped his arm, knowing as we crossed the threshold that it would be time again for solemn discussion.

Isadora's small home had been converted into a meeting room with half as much space as was needed. Therefore, windows had been opened to relieve the stuffiness and floor space was scarce.

The Caldwells watched us file in and find a seat where we could. Charlotte watched everyone especially close. "You met outside already?" asked Charlotte, astutely, not bothering to hide her distress.

"Why?" asked Mr. Caldwell, taking a seat at the table along with the rest of the adults.

All eyes were now on Charlotte but she didn't seem to care. "Well I wanted to see how it would go over."

Jameson gave her a glare while their mother replied crossly, "It went over fine, Charlotte."

Charlotte opened her mouth to speak but, knowing this, Mr. Caldwell cut her off. "So The Sevens have perfected the art of keeping us apart. What do we do now that they've failed?"

Blank stares were passed around the room then we all began to speak at once. In the midst of it, I heard Jameson's voice in my head.

"Fresh air?" he asked.

I glanced down and noted that our knees were touching. Trying to hold back a smile, I replied without speaking, "Definitely."

"I'll go first," he said, already moving to stand.

He left without anyone becoming aware of it. The discussion had turned heated but for the first time the Caldwells weren't pitted against the Weatherfords. The dissenters were intermingled. So I left a few minutes later.

The voices from inside were unabated in their travels outside so the swamp was no longer peaceful tonight. As I stepped away from the door, I wondered if the farthest home could hear us.

"Jameson?" I called out in a hushed voice because he had disappeared into the dark. Even the lantern beneath

Isadora's rafters casting a glow across the dock did little good.

"Jameson?" I said again, a little louder.

When I came around the corner he was there at the end of the dock, gazing out across the swamp, his shoulders square, his legs standing slightly apart.

I moved down the dock toward him, stepping on a loose board and drawing his attention. He rotated at the waist and finding me there his eyes brightened.

"I didn't hear you come out."

"I guessed that," I replied teasing.

He strode the two steps to meet me and then taking my hand pulled me back to the edge of the dock.

"I was...thinking."

"About what to do?" I asked, nodding my head toward the shack.

"No, fate's already determined that."

"I know what you mean. Looks like they'll need to figure it out on their own." Because there was no way I would ever initiate the conclusion they would inevitably come to. I simply couldn't bring myself to do it.

He smiled sadly in response, understanding, and then changed the subject. "I was thinking about when I first came here...the smells, the sounds, the people, everything about it was like a foreign world to me...a refuge to me. The people here have built a home based on a common bond that The Sevens created."

"And if they can do it so can we," I replied, inferring his message.

"Right. The Sevens failed to truly punish these people. Because the villagers found a way around it. And now so have our families." His arms wrapped around me in a solid grip, amazement playing with his features. "It's the first time I've recognized the kink in their armor. And it's all because of you."

"Me?" I asked, jerking my head back.

"You challenge my logic, make me question theories, ideas, and things that I've never bothered to see before. You make me see the world in a different way. Because of you, I have awakened."

He dropped his lips to my forehead, kissing there gently and then left a trail of feather-light kisses down the edges of my temple to my ear. From there, he whispered, "Jocelyn Weatherford…"

"Mmmhmm?"

"Do you know how unwound I am around you?" he asked in awe.

I pulled back slightly, stunned. "Really?" I hoped but I wasn't certain.

"Really," he said soft but emphatic. Then his lips were on mine, a perfect match to the contours of my own, tenderly discovering me in ways no one else had.

A clearing of the throat gave us the hint that we weren't alone and we found Isadora at her door. Her expression was blithe but her actions, the point of a finger toward the inside, told us we shouldn't push our luck.

"Funny, I was just wondering how much more time we would have together." Without bothering to elaborate, we walked back inside, hand in hand.

Mrs. Caldwell was in the middle of asking my mother a question so she was the only one who seemed to be unaware that we were back in the room. "So you believe that Vires will begin to appear…"

"…Within a day or two," my mother confirmed.

"We'll need to warn others…" said Mrs. Caldwell.

My mother nodded in agreement. "That is under way. Dissemination has begun from neighbor to neighbor."

"That's good," said Mr. Caldwell. "It'll take time to reach the entire province."

"Yes," my mother agreed, "and very soon we will find Vires in every public area that those in our world frequent…including Ms. Veilleux's school."

"Once it's repaired," Burke commented.

"That is under way as well," my mother replied. "Should be complete in the next few weeks."

"And now…" Mrs. Caldwell said pivoting her body in her chair. Apparently, she'd just found a need to address Jameson and me. "There is the question of how to handle the two of you."

"Yes." My mother shifted to face us as if the two of them were sharing the same thought. "And they may not like what has been proposed."

From the looks on my cousin's faces and Jameson's siblings, I could tell that was an understatement. It wasn't until they spoke up did I know just how much they had seen of us proclaiming our love in the courtyard.

"Good luck with that…" Burke muttered under his breath.

"Yeah," agreed Vinnia. "What they have…you can't hide easily."

Charlotte, who'd been fiddling with a loose splinter in the floorboard, simply snickered as if she were about to watch an attempt at something fail miserably.

They received hard looks from their mothers while my mother delivered the news. Standing and strolling to a stop in front of Jameson and me, she said, "Given that Vires will be lurking around every corner, we think," she waited for Mrs. Caldwell's nod of support before continuing, "that it is best if you two were not to see each other for a while."

"We need to give them the impression that they've succeeded in keeping you separate," Mrs. Caldwell added hastily after seeing my face tighten.

Jameson and I glanced at each other, conveying in that brief second that neither of us was surprised by this change in course. We'd both faced the reality of our situation already. We knew it was coming.

He turned toward me, tenderly cupping my cheeks, his crystal green eyes gently evaluating me.

"Looks like fate has determined it," I whispered so only he could hear.

"We both knew it was coming, didn't we?" he replied, channeling his thoughts to keep them private. He waited for me to nod, which I did, dejectedly. "We can do this, Jocelyn." I nodded again but not before swallowing back tears. "We were told the first day we met…"

"Fated lovers," I channeled back to him.

"Yes," he replied feverishly, drawing my face toward his in a moment of passion. "We are meant to be together. I waited for you all these years, not really knowing it. And now that we found each other, something that was never supposed to happen, we aren't going to let it fail. I love you, Jocelyn. Forever. No amount of space or time will change it."

"No…" I said back, my lips remaining still, letting him feel the intensity of my response. "No, we won't let it. The Sevens will not win." He grinned at the flat refusal in my tone, which deepened when I stated, "I love you. Every part of you, including the part that makes you a Caldwell."

Only then did I notice our families watching but not trying to be noticeable.

With Jameson's gorgeous clear green eyes warm and yearning, he released me but not after a long hesitation.

Mr. Caldwell cleared his throat uneasily. It seemed we'd caught him off guard with our display of affection and he wanted to get back to business. "It's important that everyone behave as usual. Behave as if the status quo remains. No obvious camaraderie, no signs of cooperation."

"Oh, I think it might take more than that to convince others," Burke said while Oscar nodded agreement.

"In other words," said Alison, snickering, "let's not let our audience down."

"Which means more fights in the hallways," Estelle called out, gleefully.

"More dirty looks," Charlotte added, just as loud and with far too much exuberance to keep the adults comfortable.

"More snide remarks," said someone else.

Before long, the room was full of entertaining ways to act with vengeance against one another. While it was all done with humor eventually the adults in the room quieted us and responded in their own way. They all condoned our ideas but none were thrilled in giving the approval to act disobediently. It was better than the alternative which meant dealing with The Sevens' reprisal.

Jameson and I were the only ones who didn't participate. We stood back, watching, holding hands, knowing that the longer they talked the longer we could stay together. Jameson and I didn't leave each other's side for the duration of it as we listened to our families build a friendship we didn't think possible. The conversation did go on but eventually the moment came. And as everyone else said their goodbyes, Jameson and I waited, rebelling against time.

Being the most qualified to maneuver the boat Jameson would need to take us back to the bank where we'd left my car, which granted us just a few more minutes. It was tight but we managed to fit everyone in. Again Jameson and I sat with thighs pressed against each other, causing sparks of excitement to shoot through me. They competed with the sorrow I felt at inching closer to the dock. Soon Jameson and I would need to part completely and for an indeterminate length. My only consolation was that the motor ran slower from the sheer weight it carried. When I saw the sliver of wood in the distance I actually felt my heart sink deeper in my chest.

After Jameson pulled up, tied the boat, and our families stepped out, he and I made certain to be the last to leave.

Our legs carried us slowly down the dock and up the small embankment. Then Jameson's arms were around my hips, pulling me close to him, and our chests were touching.

Knowing that in some moment's words fail, we stood in silence, the intensity of our stare, the set of his jaw, and the struggle to contain my tremble conveyed everything we needed before our separation began.

Our families gave us time, a testament to their understanding of what this was going to do to us.

Then someone cleared their throat and we painfully pulled away. Our feet moved with the weight of cement blocks toward them, our hands releasing only at the very last possible moment. My heart wrenched with each step as they carried me away from Jameson, toward beginning the illusion that he and I were strangers.

Only then did I see the two figures standing hidden in the shadows below the trees.

I recognized them instantly.

The Vires had arrived.

*for more spellbinding romantic suspense
read the remainder of the Residue Series*

Birthright
Savior
Prophecy

ABOUT THE AUTHOR

Laury Falter is the bestselling author of the Guardian Trilogy (Fallen, Eternity, & Reckoning). When she isn't writing young adult paranormal romance and urban fantasy novels, she likes to take her two stray dogs for walks and enjoy date nights with her husband.

Find out more news and information about Laury and her novels on her website at lauryfalter.com

48306477R00184

Made in the USA
Lexington, KY
23 December 2015